# nine eyes

## C.J. Waller

Severed Press
Hobart Tasmania

# Nine Eyes

# prologue

The scream ripped the night apart. It lashed the small, drab stone houses of the village and whipped out over the hills, echoing over the waters of the loch. On it went, a feral howl that spoke of pain, of fear, and of a deep longing until it was as if it had always been there, a primal thing that had no name yet spoke to every living thing that heard it.

"Come on, girl. Push!"

Another groan started up from deep within her swollen belly. The pain was a crashing symphony, at once both deep and throbbing yet also sharp and tearing. It rolled down, boiling over until it rose into an animalistic yowl.

"Again! Come on, girl. I can see the head!"

By her side, a man stood. He watched through widened eyes, his heart singing in his throat, perfectly caught between elation and terror. They said birth was the most natural thing in the world, but how could it be? Blood and fluid flooded the rug, and he was sure no man could ever withstand the titanic forces that ripped through his wife as she fought to bring their child into the world. She lunged out, gripping his hand as the contraction took her. He winced, for a split second wondering if he could ask her to stop because she was grinding his bones together, but in the face of her bared teeth and bulging eyes, he decided not to. In this state, she looked more like a possessed monster that an imminent mother.

Her belly rippled again as the contraction peaked. It couldn't be much longer, could it? He raised his eyes to the ceiling and dared to mutter a little prayer: *Let it be a girl. Please let it be a girl.*

The old woman kneeling between his wife's knees gave a triumphant shout. "Yes! That's it... keep pushing. Keep it up. Don't stop now! It's coming... one more... You can do it..."

He felt his wife withdraw, folding in on herself as she sought out the last of her reserves to expel the child she had carried for so long. This time she didn't so much scream as growl, long and loud. No wonder ancient man had seen this and worshipped nature as a mother; in her small frame, she held more power than he could ever dream of. The power of life.

"Yes!" the old woman panted. "Yes... he is here! He is here!"

*He?*

The heat of the man's instinctive elation turned to ice.

The old woman cradled the squirming babe and smiled. She held it up to him, still covered in bloody mucus, its umbilical cord snaking out from in between his wife's legs.

"Yes," she beamed. "Look. A boy. A boy, John. You have a son!"

He took the child with leaden arms. His wife looked over and let out a keening wail that bore no resemblance to the cries of her birthing. This was borne of an anguish so deep, he thought he might drown.

*A boy.*

*The curse lived on.*

# chapter one

*Is it a mirror? A reflection? A memory, buried for so long that it feels more like something he'd dreamt? He doesn't know, not yet. It sits, just out of reach, waiting for the day when he finally plucks up the courage to take that leap of faith and grab it, turn it over in his hands and fathom it out once and for all. But until then, the speculation continues. Maybe forever. Maybe tomorrow. For who knows what tomorrow may bring?*

oOo

[.REC]

"Okay- is it on?"

*[The camera focuses on a tall woman standing stiffly to attention]*

"Yeah. Try to relax. Right... in three... two..."

"Hello, I'm Yolanda Ndiaye, and welcome to the Highlands of Scotland. In this episode, we are investigating the legend of the Bees... uh, Beiyust..."

"Bèist an t-Sluic."

*[The woman fidgets and works her mouth]*

"Okay. I'll start again, Right. Hello, I'm Yolanda Ndiaye, and welcome to the Highlands of Scotland. In this episode, we are investigating the legend of the *[she pauses, preparing herself to copy the cameraman's pronunciation]* Bayst an Tlooeek, also known as the Beast of the Hollow. Many people think the only loch worth mentioning in Scotland when it comes to lake monsters is the infamous Loch Ness, but they'd be wrong. Locals have long shared stories of a demon that is said to inhabit this lonely stretch of water, with tales of occult activity and even human sacrifice, but they never made the mainstream... until now, that is. We're here to uncover the truth behind the Beast and find out if there really is a monster haunting these waters. I'm Yolanda Ndaiye, and you're watching Hunting Monsters."

"Okay – cut."

Yolanda visibly relaxed. "How was that?"

From the sidelines, Paul gave her a nod. "Yeah, not bad for a first try. What do you think, Decker?"

The man behind the camera looked up and shrugged. "Camera seems to like her. Need to tighten the pronunciations. Plus, you said who you were twice."

Yolanda winced. "I know. I'm sorry. I realised when I said it. You want to go again?"

"Yeah, okay. Right. And... three... two..."

Paul grinned to himself and wandered away to find the other two members of his crew. It didn't take long.

One of them turned to him as he approached and smiled at him. "Wow. It's beautiful here." Mags inhaled deeply, her eyes closed. "Smell that clean air. You know, legend or not, it was worth coming here just to get London out of my lungs."

Paul couldn't help but agree with her. It might have be a pain in the neck to get here, but it had been worth it. The loch stretched out before them, a vast, glittering expanse of blue bordered by a green ribbon of pine trees. Behind them, hills dotted with heather rolled and beyond that rose ancient outcrops of dark, grey stone that pierced the clouds with jagged teeth. The scenery alone would bring in the punters, and once they'd factored in the local legends that had brought them there... Paul smiled to himself. Yeah. Things were going to be okay. He could feel it.

His crew – himself, Decker, Mags and Piers – had filmed the Great Lakes, been down to the Bayou, explored the icy wastes of Alaska. They'd only come home because their money ran out. Despondent, Paul had thought that was the end of their adventures and that this could very well be their last hurrah. He'd worried it might be somewhat anticlimactic after a year of chasing the legendary monsters that haunted the lakes of America. He'd fretted that outside of Nessie, the Highlands wouldn't have much to give, which just went to show what he knew. Turned out, Scotland did more than hold its own; it was a serious contender to the crown, which was typical, really. You went halfway around the world looking for something special when, in truth, it had been near enough on your front doorstep all along.

"So – where is it?" The question broke through Paul's musing. He bit back a retort. Typical Piers. Here they were, in one of the most gorgeous spots they'd visited yet, and he sounded bored.

"I don't know. Just wait. Decker won't be long."

They continued to admire the scenery until Decker and Yolanda finished filming. The question duly repeated, Decker pointed out over the water. "Look over there. From here it's a bit hard to spot, but it's there."

They all squinted, following his finger. Paul was the first to let out a low whistle. Mags looked stunned, mouthing another 'wow'. Even Piers looked impressed. After a few seconds, Yolanda shook her head and fished her glasses out of her pocket. He allowed the camera to linger on her, to see how she fared. She was the new girl, brought in more as a favour to a friend than anything else, and Paul still had his reservations about her presence. She said she wanted to be a news anchor (didn't they all?) and being allowed to host their little adventure vlog would look good on her CV. Thank God she wasn't expecting to get paid; the work experience alone was enough.

"My God, Decker. You weren't kidding, were you?" Mags said.

"Why? You think I was lying?" Decker said.

"No… just over exaggerating." She smiled. "Glad to see you weren't."

The angle of the late-afternoon sun made it difficult to pick out against the glittering backdrop of the water, but once you got your eye in, it stood out, as clear as day.

A church spire.

"No one knows the exact date the church was first built, but judging by its structure, they reckon it was around the fifteenth or early sixteenth century," Decker said, answering their unspoken question. "As far as I know, by the time the valley was earmarked for the reservoir, it was half-flooded already following an earlier landslide further up the valley. Still, it's pretty amazing, huh?"

"God, yeah," Mags said. "And we have permission to dive down there?"

"Of course we have," Paul said, a little too quickly. He tried not to wince as Mags' attention flickered from the spire and over to him. He contrived to look the picture of innocence, but Decker ratted him out with a single, incredulous glance. Mags frowned, and Yolanda's eyes widened.

"Excellent." Piers rubbed his hands together. Whether he was truly oblivious or chose to ignore the others silent reservation, Paul wasn't sure. "So, what's the plan, chief? Set up now, scope it out?"

"We're going up to the town first," said Paul. "I thought we might interview a few locals, get the whole legend down from their point of view. Deck says there's a guesthouse, so we can check in and make ourselves comfortable." His gaze slid towards Decker, who resolutely refused to meet it. Paul held in the desire to roll his eyes at him. Not this again. "Anyway," he continued, "we'll go there, savour the local colour, see what we can dig up. Then we can set up some cameras to see what we can see."

"So... you really think there's something in there?" Mags asked. "In the loch?"

Paul nudged Decker, who shrugged.

"I dunno," he said. "I mean, whether there's anything in it all. I grew up with tales of the loch... nothing too detailed, just that the church was haunted by something. Mam didn't like us talking about it and I haven't been here since I was a kid." He folded his arms over his chest and turned away, making it clear he didn't want to answer any more questions. Paul sighed inwardly. He hated it when he did this.

"That's why I figured it best to ask the locals," Paul said. "Get their versions. Plus, no one can call bullshit on us if it's townsfolk doing the telling."

That was the truth. It had taken a hell of a lot of defending their corner the last time they'd forgone the interviews. People liked local colour. Without local colour, people were quick to shout 'fix'. No point going to a lake or a reservoir or whatever and trying to pin some kind of legend on it – people wanted proof in the form of seventy year old town patriarchs declarin' that yup, this is the place where the monster lives, my grandpappy knew, he'd see'd it once, and that kid Billy got too close to the water and he weren't never seen again...

Well, they weren't going to make the same mistake twice. Revenue had fallen off a cliff after their last broadcast, and all talk of getting them their own cable series had dried up. This was their last chance to show that they were serious – and that they knew what they were doing.

Paul was a little ticked off that Decker hadn't told him about this place before things had become this desperate, but that didn't mean he didn't understand. He knew his father had died a long time ago and maybe he didn't want this particular circus to somehow sully that memory, but times were tough and audiences were fickle... Paul just hoped that sullying the memory of Decker's dearly departed Dad was going to be worth it in the end.

They all spent a little while longer admiring the scenery before they clambered up the track back to their vehicles: one beat-up Astra and a VW Camper in dire need of a tune-up that towed their small motor boat. The road up to Dùisg a' Pheacaich was winding and more pot holes than tarmac, and Paul was convinced it was only their collective will that kept both vehicles from crapping out on them completely.

Paul allowed Decker to drive in silence, sensing his trepidation. Of course he had known about Decker's childhood: that his father had died when he was a young boy and had subsequently been raised by his mother, but he'd never really offered any more detail – and Paul had never pushed him. After he'd told him about the Beast, though, he hadn't really had a choice. It had taken Decker a full day to summon the courage to tell him. Even then, he hadn't said much about it: his father had told him about Beast of the Hollow when he was a boy whilst they watched the water together, and it hadn't been so much as story as a warning, which is why he hadn't said anything.

Until now.

He said his father had told him never to swim in the loch on account of the Beast, which kind of sounded more like something a good father might tell his inquisitive son in an attempt at keeping him out of trouble, at least for a few years. But he insisted the legend was true, that it wasn't just his father's invention – everyone in the village knew about the Beast and despite, knew about the shadow in the water and the rumours of its taste for human flesh, and that despite their close proximity to a large body of water and potential to make money from fishing, no one in town owned a fishing rod, let alone a boat. Paul had pressed him, hoping for more details as a plan formed in his mind, but Decker said he couldn't remember anything else. As bad as it made him feel, Paul couldn't help but wonder if what he actually meant was 'wouldn't'.

Paul swiped his thumb across the screen of his mobile phone. It sparked to life, greeting him with pictures of happier times: of them smiling by the Grand Canyon, of them sipping cocktails together in Florida, of Decker kissing his cheek whilst he laughed in New Orleans. He sighed. Not that he was unhappy now... no... not that...never that, but... He let his attention slide again to Decker. His jaw was tight, his hands on the wheel, rigid.

Maybe they shouldn't do this. Maybe they should just cut their losses and leave. He couldn't stand what all of this was doing to Decker now, let alone once they actually arrived. But they were here, ready to go. This was their last chance. Giving this up meant giving up the dream, *their* dream, and surely that was worse than Decker potentially bumping into family members he hadn't seen in twenty-five years?

Damn. No reception. Paul cranked the window open in the vain hope it might coax a signal out of thin air. There was a tantalising moment when it looked like it might have picked up something resembling a WiFi connection, but it didn't hold. His mobile reverted back to an expensive plastic Filofax, stuffed full of memories Paul treasured more than anything else.

Well, nearly anything else.

"Brandon..."

Decker's eyes flickered towards him. Paul caught his look of concern and knew why. No one called him Brandon apart from his mother, and Paul knew this. It was his way of warning him the following conversation might be considered... difficult.

"Yeah?" he said.

"Are you sure you want to do this?"

Decker paused, his knuckles momentarily bleaching white as he tightened his grip on the steering wheel.

"Yeah. Of course I do. This is what it's all about, isn't it?"

"I don't know... I mean, usually, yes, but this is a big thing for you."

"Look, I wouldn't have told you if I didn't want us to look into it," Decker all but snapped. Paul recoiled a little, surprised. Decker never snapped. He was the laid back one, the nice one, the one everyone warmed to. He supposed that was what upset him the most about all of this. That it was doing this to him. That *he* was doing this to him. Before he could arrange a suitable response, Decker let out a long sigh and reached out with one hand to pat his knee, an endearing old-biddyish gesture that made Paul crack a smile.

"Seriously – I'm fine. It's sweet that you're bothered, but this is something I probably should have done a long time ago. Okay, so doing it with a camera crew in tow probably isn't the best way of going about it... but hey, beggars, choosers and all that jazz. Chances are, no one will remember me and we'll all just have a nice few days enjoying some good old fashioned Highland hospitality, get shitfaced on single malt and have fun scaring ourselves stupid with tales of boggins and beasties. If I'm honest, I wish I'd told you about this place before. Y'know, got it out of my system earlier. But Mam was always so..." He stopped and gave a little shake of his head. "Doesn't matter. Thing is, we're here now. I'm sorry I kept it from you. Whatever happens, the documentary and my family problems are two separate things. I won't let them affect the shoot. I promise."

A tight ball of shame clenched in Paul's stomach. Is that what Decker thought? That he was worried he was going to ruin everything? He stared out of the window and watched the trees rush by. He hadn't meant it that way. They could bail, even now. Okay, so they'd have to dig up something else, but the shoot wasn't everything...

His face flushed pink as treacherous memories winked in and out of existence, flashing back to arguments, to worries both shared and entirely his own, to selfish, bitter words exchanged that it was about the shoot, without the shoot they had nothing, without the shoot they were fucked...

"The new girl," Decker said. "You think she'll be okay?"

Paul looked back. He knew the game. Change the subject to avoid difficult things. For once, he was grateful for it and played along willingly.

"I think she'll be fine," he said. "She's a bit green, but her audition went well and she seemed comfortable enough up by the loch. Piers and Mags say she's very keen and she's easy on the eyes. She might be just what we need. Okay, so she may not be a believer-"

"But then, who is, right?" Decker grinned, and Paul couldn't help but grin back. This was far more comfortable territory.

"Hey, we might not have found anything yet, but that doesn't mean there's nothing out there."

"Oh man, you crack me up. How long are you going to keep searching, Paul? If the truth is out there, I don't see it banging on your door any time soon."

"Hey! You're one to talk. This is your recommendation, remember? If it's all made up bollocks, why are we here?"

As soon as the words were released, Paul regretted them. He wanted to steer clear of this and there he was, plunging headlong back into it all. Idiot.

Decker check his mirrors and snapped the indicator on. Ahead of them hung a sign – not the warped, battered mess he had been expecting, but a neatly painted banner that proclaimed: *Fàilte a Dùisg a' Pheacaich.*

Paul didn't have a clue what it meant, but guessed it was a welcome sign. Even with Decker's coaching, he still struggled to pronounce the name of the town – it sounded something like Dooshk uh fyechkeesch, but he wouldn't like to lay money on it – and so had asked him what it meant in English so he could talk about it without calling it 'the village' or 'that place'. Decker had looked uncomfortable, and for a split second Paul had feared he would shut him out again, which would then trigger another inevitable argument, but thankfully Decker had mumbled 'Sinner's Wake'.

Sinner's Wake. An odd name for a town, and a quick Google search hadn't dug up much, but it still played on his mind. Sinner's Wake. Who has sinned? And how? And what did it mean by 'wake'? Had sinners been awoken? Or did they go there to die? Was it all tied to the legend? And if so, how?

That thought sent a little shiver of traitorous excitement down his back.

"We're here because we need something special," Decker continued. Paul gave himself a little mental shake and focused back on his partner. "Do I believe there is something in the loch? I don't know. Chances are it is all just a load of old rubbish. But the legend is creepy, the people here believe in it, and that loch is beautiful in the most eerie, sinister way possible, especially after dark. And I figure that short of footage of Nessie herself, this is about as good as it gets for people in our trade. So that's why we're here, Paul. That reason, and no other."

Paul wished he could believe him.

# chapter Two

"Woah, Decker... you weren't kidding, were you?" Mags climbed down out of the camper and stretched. "This place is the real deal, isn't it? Backwater Central. Do they even have electricity here?"

She grinned as Decker aimed a fake punch at her, but it was a legitimate question. They spent a moment taking in their surroundings: no lights bordered the narrow cobbled streets, just small homes made of a drab grey stone capped with dark slate roofs whose chimneys dribbled soot and smoke. Only one other car was parked nearby, and judging by its numberplate, it had to be over thirty years old. The whole tableau gave the place a peculiar, lost-in-time quality, a feeling that was compounded by the thin mist that wreathed their feet and crept up the sides of the buildings. Mags shivered, her former ebullience forgotten. Paul knew how she felt. He didn't want to say anything that might offend Decker, but there was something off about this place – something creepy with a capital 'C'.

"One thing's for sure, their mobile reception is shot," Piers said, stabbing at his phone. "Not even a whisper of a connection. We'll be lucky to send texts, let alone get any teaser footage up as we work."

A curtain twitched in the window of a nearby house. So, there was life here after all. That should have made Paul feel better, but instead it only intensified the creepy vibe.

Someone was there, and they were watching them.

"That's okay," Paul said, trying to ignore the shudder that prickled its way down his spine. "We're not doing any teaser footage this time. That unedited crap is what kicked us in the teeth last time. This time, it's professional all the way. Our last chance with the TV suits. We've got to show them we can do this properly, or the deal is off the table."

"Heavy," Mags muttered, and everyone but Paul nodded.

"Heavy or not, that's what we've got to do," Paul said. "But first things first – we've got to find that guesthouse... what was it called, Decker?"

"Kelly's" Decker all but whispered. Mags' brow crinkled in question. Paul offered a short, sharp shake of his head in reply: *I know. And no, I don't know what's bothering him. Just leave it be.*

"Kelly's, yeah, that's right." He stuck his hands in his pockets and looked up and down the empty street. "Uh, which way is it?"

Decker sighed and pointed to his left. "It's up there. Last house." Without waiting to see if his friends were ready, he heaved his pack on his back and walked off.

"Shouldn't we take the car?" Paul asked his retreating form.

Decker didn't bother turning around. "No. No parking and the roads are narrow. I doubt we'd get it through. Best leave the vehicles where they are."

"A guesthouse with no parking?" Piers said. "Never heard of that."

Neither had Paul, but he decided to leave that one hanging. With nothing else to do, they gathered their possessions and followed Decker up the road.

"Is he always like this?" Yolanda whispered. Paul shook his head, but said nothing. Thankfully, Yolanda didn't press the issue.

"So, what's the plan, chief?" Mags said. Paul could tell by the way she watched Decker that she was as concerned as he was, but knew better than to say anything.

"I guess we'll unpack, freshen up and then hit the streets, see who might consent to an interview. We'll go back to the loch tomorrow and set up cameras there. We're going to do this properly, chaps. Like I said – professional. Any questions?"

At this, Mags burst out laughing, but it was an uneasy laugh borne out of a desire to lighten the mood rather than out of genuine humour.

"Come on, Paul – why so serious? Last time I checked, 'being professional' meant grabbing ourselves a beer and talking to people. Or as professional as you can be when you're talking to people about demons living in lakes."

oOo

Kelly's Guesthouse lived up to the promise of the rest of the town. A drab stone building, it reared up before them like something out of a Hammer horror movie, which only enhanced the feeling of stepping into a time warp.

"Doesn't look like many people stay here," Piers said. Paul could only agree. There was no sign, no star rating displayed and the curtains were drawn tight against the world. He'd never seen a more uninviting house in all his life.

"Are you sure this is it?" he asked Decker.

Decker nodded.

"Funny how there's a guesthouse here," Yolanda said. Everyone looked at her. As the new girl, she hadn't really said much, much less offer opinions.

"Why do you say that?" Paul said.

"Well... it's a pretty remote place and judging by the lack of tourist tat, I'm guessing they don't get much in the way of visitors... so why have a guesthouse at all?"

"She's got a point," Piers said. "Why bother?"

They all switched their attention to Decker, who just shrugged. "I don't know. It's just always been here, I suppose."

"You ever remember anyone staying?" Piers said.

Decker mumbled something that might have sounded like 'not really' and started climbing the steps to the front door. No one questioned him; instead, they all trudged up after him whilst he heaved the door open.

Entering the guesthouse was something different altogether. Chintz covered every surface, complete with flowery wallpaper and a pervading scent of lavender and rosewater. There was even a sweet, grey haired Granny-type who looked up from the front desk and greeted them with a smile that didn't quite reach her eyes.

"Hullo? Can I help you?" Her brogue was thick and melodious, full of heather and peat, but, like the town, there was something about her manner that didn't quite add up.

"Uh, yeah," Paul said. "We'd like some rooms, please... we would have rung ahead, but we couldn't find any details to do so. Sorry."

Mrs Kelly pursed her lips, but nodded all the same. "Aye. I see. Well, we aren't exactly on the beaten track. Don't have many visitors, you know."

"Right." Paul didn't know quite what else to say. If they didn't have visitors, then why have a guesthouse at all? Where did they get the money to run the place? The only conclusion her could draw was people were strange, and who was he to question? After all, he chased lake monsters for a living. Before he could say anything, Yolanda piped up.

"You don't have any visitors?" she asked. "Not even people looking for the monster in the loch?"

Paul froze, as did the others. Lesson #1 in dealing with the locals: get comfortable, ingratiate yourself and then ask questions.

Mrs Kelly stiffened.

"Oh. I see. You're out after that, are you? Well, I'm not here to stop you, but I would say you're wasting your time."

"We are?" Paul said, cutting across Yolanda before she could wedge her foot any deeper into her mouth.

"Aye."

He paused, inviting her to elaborate, but she didn't oblige.

"Well, we're also here because this is a beautiful place," he continued, hoping to warm the chill in her eyes. "Decker is from this part of the world – he was the one who told us about you, so, uh, if you don't mind... could we book some rooms? Please? We don't mind sharing..."

He trailed off. Mrs Kelly's face had hardened to something resembling granite.

"I see. So, what do we have? Two ladies, three gentlemen... I suppose I can do that. But you are going to have to share, mind"

"That's fine, Mrs Kelly – as I said, we don't mind sharing," Paul said, offering her his most winning smile. She narrowed her eyes just long enough for him to realise this tactic wasn't going to work and it was probably worth knocking it off before she threw them out.

"I suppose I've a nice suite for the ladies, and for you gentlemen, three adjoining rooms with a shared bathroom," she said brusquely. "Does that sound all right to you?"

"That sounds fine," And even if it wasn't, he wasn't going to say so. "Do you serve dinner?"

"Aye, well, I guess so. Nothing fancy, mind you. Just good, honest fare."

Paul rubbed his hands together. "Good honest fare sounds just what we're after, Mrs Kelly. Thank you."

If she heard him, she made no indication. "The tea rooms are along the hall and to your right. Frank here will help you with your bags, and I hope you have a lovely stay." By the way she spat that out, Paul doubted she meant it. *Note to self*, he thought. *Next time, ring ahead. Always ring ahead.*

A wheeze from behind them made them all turn around. There stood Frank, who looked like he'd been dug up and reanimated. When he went to pick up their luggage, they all waved and smiled politely, refusing any kind of help. Mrs Kelly's lips pursed again, but none of them were willing to watch Frank struggle, so they loaded everything up between them and instead followed him up the stairs to their rooms.

The first to be dropped off were Yolanda and Mags, whose rooms were as chintzy as the rest of the guesthouse. The rest of them then went up another flight of stairs to a narrow corridor with four doors: three bedrooms and one bathroom.

"Just like being back at Uni, eh Decker?" Paul remarked.

Decker didn't reply. Instead, he just stood there, looking distracted, biting the skin around his thumb. Paul shot him a concerned look, and Piers, who had been at university with them, took up the slack.

"Yeah," he said. "If our digs had been decorated and maintained by a pair of maiden aunts, maybe." He peered into the first room and let out a low whistle. "Jesus… it's like The Room That Taste Forgot. That bedspread alone should be taken in for crimes against humanity."

"Tell me about it, Paul said as Piers wandered off to the next room. "What's it like in there?"

"Wow!" Piers' voice floated in. "Whoever gets that room should count themselves lucky, 'cos whoever gets this room also gets the shelf full of those creepy china dolls."

# chapter three

They didn't so much unpack as dump all their stuff on the floor and dig out their research before meeting in the dining room. It took all of Paul's courage to ask Mrs Kelly if they could use it for a little meeting; she hadn't looked too happy at the prospect, but he was rapidly coming to the conclusion that Mrs Kelly never looked pleased about anything. In the end she relented as long as they promised to leave the room tidy. Oaths sworn and hearts crossed, he set the laptop up and they all huddled around the screen, only to discover that the problem with the wifi extended here as well. He thought of asking Mrs Kelly if she knew what was going on, but decided against it. He'd printed off the meagre research he'd managed to dig up so the laptop wasn't all that essential – and, of course, they had Decker, who'd grown up hearing nothing else.

This wasn't the first time they'd been through his research, but now they were actually here, it all took on a new significance. Or, rather, the lack of it did. Because that's what had surprised – and now excited – Paul the most... just how little there was to find. Usually, a town with any kind of monster legend attached to it quickly hyped it, marketed it and then sold it to as many tourists as it could. Not this place. Very little apart from the barest of details were available, with some people wondering if the whole thing was in fact tied up with nearby Loch Ness and was more likely a misidentification, or someone had filed some information in the wrong place. Others argued that near enough every body of water in Scotland had some kind of legend attached to it, be it Kelpies or Boggins or some other kind of Gaelic boogeyman, and so it wasn't all that unusual if you thought about it. In fact, the only thing that made it stand out from hundreds of other, similar tales was the church – and Decker's personal tales. If it hadn't been for those, Paul probably wouldn't have even considered this place.

"Well, now, what are you all doing?" Mrs Kelly's question cut through their musing. Paul looked up and laid his sheaf of papers down.

"Just swotting up, Mrs Kelly."

"So it is true? Like the girl said, you are looking into the legend?"

Paul glanced to Decker, who offered him a small shrug.

"Yes. We're here to make a documentary about the legend of the, um, Beast an ta Sloosh-" Beside him, Decker winced. "Uh, sorry, I mean the Beast of the Hollow." He leaned forward a little. It might be a long shot, but those who didn't ask, didn't get. "Do... do you know anything about it, Mrs Kelly?"

Mrs Kelly fixed him with a dead stare and set down the teapot she carried. A tiny drop tumbled from the spot and stained the pristine white cloth.

"Well, now, I don't know... it all depends on what you want to know, "she said in a clipped tone. "What I mean to say is, everyone knows of the legend – of course they do – but whether it's something to believe, well, that's another matter."

"Okay, that's fine," he said. "I understand that. So... what do you believe?"

"Me?" she seemed shocked, as if he'd asked her what kind of underwear she wore. "Oh, I don't know, I mean, it isn't something we really talk about in polite company, given everything-"

"Hang on – what?" Mags gave her an incredulous look. "It's a local legend, nothing more. Why don't you want to talk about it 'in polite company'?"

Mrs Kelly turned her laser stare on Mags. "Because, young lady, there are some of us around here who don't like to talk of such things."

"Things such as..." Mags said, undeterred.

"It's okay," Decker said, his tone placatory. He shot Mags a look. "I don't remember people being too keen to talk about it when I was a kid, so I don't see why that would had changed." He focused all of his attention on Mrs Kelly. "We're not here to spread any kind of malicious rumours or anything. My father was from Dùisg a' Pheacaich, and part of this is about me discovering more about my family. My name is Decker – Brandon Decker. I lived here until I was seven. My father was John Decker – my mother and I left when he died. I think my paternal grandmother might still be here, although she'd be about eighty or so now. You might know her. Her name's Sadie – Sadie Decker.

At the mention of Sadie Decker, Mrs Kelly's eyes widened for a fraction of a second, but she quickly schooled her face back to hard distaste.

"Do you… Do you know Sadie Decker, Mrs Kelly?" Decker continued. "Is she still alive? I haven't had any contact with her in twenty five years, and I'd love to-"

"No," said Mrs Kelly. "No. I don't know Sadie Decker. Never have. Now would you all like some tea? I have things to do."

"Yes, of course, tea would be great," Paul said before anyone could say anything else. He'd caught the look on Mrs Kelly's face when Decker mentioned his grandmother and knew a lie when he saw it. Quite why would she lie about something like that, though... "Look, I know it's intrusive, but could we interview you? My friend Decker here said there has been a guesthouse here for as long as he can remember, and so I wondered if you might have any tales to tell – anything you might be willing to share with our viewers and add some flavour to our search-"

Paul didn't think it was possible, but Mrs Kelly's demeanour turned even chillier. "I am not here to trade lies with you, young man. If you're looking for someone to do that, then Malcolm Allen is your man, may the Lord forgive his soul. He runs the Post Office and I have no doubt he'll be only too happy to spin you yarns and sell you postcards plastered with fake sightings of this so-called Beast. Other than that, leave people alone. There's nothing but good, honest people here, and that loch has dominated their lives for too long-" She stopped, and for a split second, her stony mask slipped and took on the air of something hunted.

"Mrs Kelly… we're not here to cause trouble," Yolanda said. Her voice was smooth, almost hypnotic, and Paul remembered all the reasons he'd agreed to let her join them. One day, whether she realised it or not, she was going to make an awful lot of money with that voice; he was just glad to get in at ground level. "We're here simply to take a few shots of the loch and ask about the legend. It's interesting. People like this sort of thing-"

"Oh, yes, people like this sort of thing," said Mrs Kelly. "They like this sort of thing a lot. What you folks who pander to them don't realise, is that we have to live with it! Coming here, dredging up the past, opening old wounds… Why can't you all leave it be? Find another town that wants this kind of attention – just leave us out of it!" She didn't sound as much angry as upset, which in turn made Paul feel ashamed. Judging the uneasy looks the others shared, they pretty much felt the same way.

"We're sorry, Mrs Kelly," Decker said. "We don't mean anything by it."

"No. Of course you don't. No one ever does."

"Does… does this mean other people have come here investigating the legend?" Paul said. "I only ask, because there's so little out there about it. If it wasn't for Decker, we would never have heard of it."

Mrs Kelly let out a little sigh that might have been a sob and picked up the teapot. "Look, you have to understand…" she stopped. Her hands shook, making the lid of the teapot rattle. As if to mask it, she set it back down again. "People don't come here much. In fact, they don't really come here at all.. We don't like it, don't like to see... don't..." She hid her mouth behind hand.

"Mrs Kelly...what are you so afraid of?" Paul hadn't meant to say this out loud, but still it fell unconsciously from his mouth.

"What?" she snapped. "I'm not afraid, young man!" But her hands betrayed her true feelings again. "Look - you don't live here," she continued in a low voice. "It doesn't matter what is true and what isn't – just living with the spectre of that story is enough to make any good, God-fearing soul shudder. That's why we like to keep it quiet. It may have been over a century past, but shame's still shame, and we don't like to talk about it to strangers. Now, if you wouldn't mind, I've chores to attend to." She straightened up, her demeanour stiff once again. "I hope you have a nice stay." *Just don't stay too long.* She didn't have to say it – every line in her body screamed it.

They watched her retreat to the sanctuary of her kitchen out of the corners of their eyes. By silent agreement, none of them spoke until the door swung shut, and even then, no one raised their voice above a whisper.

"Fuck," Mags said. "I wish we'd had a camera out to film that. She's scared shitless!"

"Eloquently put," Paul said. "But, yeah, I agree." He felt a shameful thrill of excitement. "Seems like there's more to this than meets the eye. I say we go and interview Malcolm Allen asap."

"What, today? It's already gone two… Why don't we wait until tomorrow?" Piers asked.

"Because if we wait until tomorrow, whatever has got the wind up Mrs Kelly's skirt may well have blown Malcolm Allen's way, despite what she said about his affection for spinning yarns. We need to get to him before anyone else does."

Everyone but Yolanda nodded. "Jeez," she said, looking a bit concerned. "Are you guys for real? Does this happen often? This is a little Highland village – you're talking as if the Mafia has rolled in with a truck-load of horses' heads. What are they going to do, threaten to kill his wife? If he wants to talk, he'll talk. Everyone just needs to chill out."

Although she spoke what, on the outside anyway, sounded like common sense, Paul's gut told him otherwise. The sheer, naked fear he had seen in Mrs Kelly's eyes was enough to tell him all he needed to know; that this town had a secret, and if he could drag it out of someone it could be the one thing that saved his dream from the curse of ignominy. This was his scoop, his Number One Chance, and he was going to grasp it with both hands, regardless of what anyone else said or thought.

"Drink up," he said. "Decks, grab your camera. Yolanda, as our new anchor-woman, you'll need to be there to ask the questions."

"Uh, what questions?"

"Don't worry – we'll sort them out on our way over there. Your main job is to keep him talking."

"What about me and Piers?" Mags asked.

"Shouldn't need you two. We don't want to spook him. Maybe you could dig around elsewhere – see if there's a local records office or something. Although I get the impression that anything of real interest won't be available for public perusal."

"Heh, you ain't jokin' there, bub," Mags said. "Ready to do some meddling, Piers me old mucker?" She slapped his knee and grinned.

Piers grinned back. "As ready as ever, Milady."

"Good," said Paul. "Since there's no mobile phone reception, we'll meet back here by, say, six? That way Mrs Kelly can't complain we're late for dinner." He raised his teacup in the parody of a toast. "Here's to uncovering unspeakable truths, people – this could be the big one, after all."

oOo

Mrs Kelly watched them leave from the comfort of her kitchen.

Why did he have to bring them? The time was nigh, she knew that much. They all did. They'd been waiting to find out who had been chosen, and many of them had begun to worry when no one stepped forward to accept the honour.

Then he'd shown up.

Given he had travelled from so far away meant he was definitely the one... but why bring friends? What had compelled him to tell them? Now it was only going to get harder.

She sighed. In the past, it had been easy. It had been kept very much in the family. That way, they all knew the purpose. No one questioned it, because there was nothing to question. One way or another, it had to be done. But outsiders? Outsiders didn't understand. Even when investigators were sent in, when they saw the truth of their ritual and how important it was they didn't get it. Outsiders only complicated things. She could only hope that Allen would give them enough of what they wanted so they would leave quickly. As insufferable as he was, Allen really was the best storyteller the village had.

But would they leave without him? She worried at a thread that dangled from her apron, inadvertently crafting it into a loop so it hung like a noose. Did he really know why he was here, what his true purpose was? Judging by how pale he looked, how confused he seemed, the chances were he didn't. Not the full extent of his obligation, anyway. In one way, that made this easier. He wouldn't tell, because he didn't know. But on the other hand...

Something in her mind clicked into place. Mrs Kelly scuttled over to the check-in desk and pulled out a battered address book. Her hands shook as she thumbed the pages over to 'D'. She dialled the number and waited with bated breath for someone to answer.

"Hullo?"

The voice was commanding, the voice of a woman used to being listened to and obeyed.

"Sadie? It's Audrey Kelly here. Sorry to bother you, but he's here..."

# chapter four

So this was the place. Not exactly the kind of tourist trap they were used to; there was a distinct lack of brightly coloured plastic buckets and tacky figurines declaring love for said trap. Plus, the ice cream selection was, quite frankly, appalling. Instead, there were everyday knick-knacks – cleaning products, batteries, ancient chocolate bars – piled high on shelves. In the corner, a prehistoric drinks cabinet wheezed.

The whole shop reeked of neglect, but then again, so did the whole village. There was nothing new to be found: no billboard advertisements, no evidence of anything even approaching modern technology, not even a new car. Everything was at least twenty-five years out of date, like the whole village had taken a look at the present and said 'nope' and scuttled back to the past. Even the magazines on the shelf dated back to 1987.

Behind the counter a sullen young man sat reading a faded copy of 'Smash Hits'. Wham grinned toothily from the cover. Paul frowned. Jesus, they really had turned being behind the times into some kind of art form here.

"Hello there." Paul strode over to the counter. The youth looked up which sent his flock-of-seagulls hairstyle bobbing, but said nothing. Paul stuck out a hand. The youth didn't take it. The smile Paul had plastered across his face faltered, and behind him came a spluttering as Yolanda tried not to giggle. Paul knew why: it was almost like that movie 'Deliverance' had come to life. If the boy picked up a banjo, he was getting the hell out of there.

"Uh, we're staying at Kelly's Guesthouse," Paul continued, undeterred. "We're researching the Beast of the Hollow. Uh, I mean the 'Bèist an t-Sluic'?" He looked self-consciously at Decker. "Did I say that right?"

Decker winced, but nodded.

"Whassat? Tha' a camera?" the youth asked, his attention on Decker. His accent was so thick it took them a minute to translate it into something they understood. "You from the television?"

"Uh, well, no – we've made a series of vlogs for the internet–"

"Vlogs?" He rolled the word around his mouth, as if to taste it. "Internet? Whassat?"

Paul's eyebrows shot up his head and gave Yolanda and Decker a 'what the hell?' look before turning back to the boy. "Uh, it's, er, it's... never mind. It's not important. We're here to speak to Malcolm Allen. Mrs Kelly said we would find him here. Is he in? We were told he might talk to us about the legend."

The youth carefully folded the corner of the page he had been perusing and nodded slowly.

"Uncle Malc is out the back. You wait here a moment." He shuffled off, through a doorway obscured by grubby-looking tendrils of coloured plastic.

"Wow," Paul said in a low voice. "And you come from here?"

"Hey, why do you think I wasn't about to shout it from the rooftops?" Decker muttered. "Mam vowed we'd never come back after my father died, and now I see why. What a dump."

Judging by the look of distaste he gave it, Paul knew he was referring to the shop, he couldn't help but wonder if that sentiment also extended to the town as a whole. Beyond its initial neat façade, there was an undeniable hint of decay, like rising damp hidden behind an old but respectable wardrobe. Everything here felt ancient, like the inhabitants thought they could hold back the tide of time by sheer will alone, and in many ways they'd succeeded... but at a cost. The town was stagnant. Yes, that was the word. Stagnant. Like a pond left to fester.

"Why, hello there!" The ebullience of the greeting catapulted Paul out of his thoughts. Malcolm Allen grinned at them, his hand held out expectantly. Paul paused. He had been expecting an old crank with mad hair and thick glasses; in reality, Malcolm Allen was a tall man of around sixty, athletically built but going a little to seed. He shook each of them by the hand enthusiastically, nodding when they each introduced themselves.

"Aye, aye, pleased to meet you. So... the boy says you're from the television and want to know about the legend?"

Paul nodded, looking guarded. Allen clapped his hands together and rubbed them in what could only be described as glee.

"Excellent. Excellent! My pet subject." He looked towards Decker. "Do you want to film me?"

"If that would be all right, sir," Decker said.

"Oh, now, none of that 'sir' nonsense – it's Malcolm, everyone knows that. Say, how's about we retire to the back room and I show you my collection? You'd like that. Good stuff for your interview. Come on – follow me. You want a cup of tea? Aye, of course you do. Now don't be shy – right here. I've got interesting stuff. You'll see!"

oOo

Mags and Piers walked side-by-side in a companionable silence. A little while ago this would have been awkward, and before that it would have been hand in hand. It had taken them a little while to get to this point, where they finally felt comfortable again. From friends to lovers to friends again – it wasn't something everyone could do, but they seemed to have managed it.

A few enquiries had directed them to the local pub, a tidy place that might have been fashionable around fifty years ago. The scarred wooden tables were old but clean, and a log fire crackled in the grate; after the dives they'd been used to frequenting, this place felt almost wholesome.

The barman regarded them with the same sense of suspicion as Mrs Kelly, but didn't voice his obvious concerns when they ordered a beer before sitting at a corner table. Their initial conversation was light, nothing more controversial than whether someone would finally spank Chelsea in the Premier League this year. Neither of them made any reference to why they were there and to a casual observer, they looked like nothing more than a young couple enjoying an evening out.

Usually, Mags liked to discuss what they were investigating. She might be just the electrician (yeah… 'just'. She'd like to see how they'd cope without her. As soon as a fuse blew or something needed recabling, she was all of a sudden numero uno in everybody's world), but she liked to listen to the stories locals spun about whatever legend they were looking in to. This one, though… this one was different. There was something odd about it, something she couldn't put her finger on. People often misjudged her, thinking her brash, but underneath it all she was a sensitive soul and even without talking to anyone, she knew there wasn't something quite right about this place.

She took a moment to sip at her pint and observe. There weren't many locals and those that were there didn't pay her or Piers much attention apart from the odd sullen glance, but that was enough for them to know they were not welcome here. It even shut Piers up, a feat in itself. They drained their drinks in silence, both of them mentally debating whether they should cut their losses and leave. Her mind made up, Mags defiantly picked up their empty glasses and headed back over to the bar, where the barman nodded and asked if they wanted the same again. Despite the ice in his eyes, she smiled and said yes, tapping her fingers on the bar whilst the beer flowed. No one was going to chase her out of a pub; not here, not anywhere.

"So… where you from?" The barman's question sounded more like an accusation. "We don't get many visitors here."

Mags was usually more than happy to indulge in small talk – it made a change from talking football with Piers if nothing else – but now she wished she had given in and left.

"We've come up from London," she said, feeling a little trapped.

"London? That's a long way to come to such a small town." The barman placed one full glass in front of her and started pulling the next. "What's got you up here, if you don't mind me asking?"

"'Course not," Mags said. She picked up her newly pulled pint and took a sip. "Now that hits the spot. Local brew?"

The barman eyed her for a moment and then nodded. "Aye. We don't bother much with the big breweries. Too industrialised, if you get my meaning." He passed over the second drink. "But I'm thinking you haven't come all this way just to taste my beer…"

He asked the question lightly, but the hairs on the back of Mags' neck stood to attention. She took another sip to mask her discomfiture.

"I don't think you could blame me if I did," she said. She offered him a grin. For some reason, she felt uneasy at the thought of sharing information with this guy. Normally she would have put his questions down to just being friendly, like bar staff desperate to keep drinkers happy and therefore spending money the world over, but the coldness in his eyes, similar to the that which lurked within Mrs Kelly's, gave her cause to pause. She chewed the inside of her cheek, conflicted. Should she say anything? She thought of the others interviewing that Allen bloke. Well, one way or another, he was going to hear about it soon enough, so was there any real harm in being truthful? "We're here to take a look at the Legend of the Hollow. You know, the Bèist an t-Sluic?"

"So... you're looking into the Beast, are you?" He softened his sharp tone with a quick smile. "Now who's got you on that goose-chase? Seems to me you get anything bigger than a puddle and everyone thinks it's going to be the next Loch Ness, know what I mean?"

"Yeah, I know what you mean," Mags didn't see any harm in agreeing with him. People often told you more that you (or, indeed, they) were expecting when they thought you agreed with them. "But the legend is there, and we're part of a small film crew – we make vlogs about things like this, and so – "

"Vlogs?" the barman interrupted her. "What's that? You mentioned a film crew? Are you with the television?"

"Well, no, not exactly, but we're hoping-"

The barkeep frowned as he picked up and glass and started polishing it. "So I take it you're those folks stopping with Audrey Kelly?"

Mags took a sip to mask her surprise. News obviously travelled fast round here.

"Yes, we are-"

"Oh. And so I guess you're intending on staying awhile, then?"

"Well, no, not too long, anyway. Depends on how it goes, really. Usually legends like this one  end up being nothing more than a big fish, or even just natural conditions in the water – we debunk more than we believe in to be honest."

The barman said nothing as he continued his polishing, a small, but deep, crease forming in between his eyes.

"Hey, you just going to let me sit there whilst my beer gets warm?" Piers asked. Mags suppressed a little jump; she hadn't heard him get up.

"Ah, no – sorry. Just got chatting to, uh…" she paused, inviting the barman to supply his name. That he hesitated before supplying it spoke volumes to her.

"Henry," he said. "Henry McCormack."

"Chatting with Mr McCormack here about the legend."

Piers raised his glass and took a long swallow before nodding at McCormack in approval. "One hell of a legend you've got here, you know? Harder than hell to find anything about it, though. All we have to go on are vague tales of something to do with lights in the water and some kind of floating blob, which led us to even vaguer stories of pacts with the Big Guy Downstairs and then the church being drowned… We were up by the loch this afternoon, and I tell you, even if the legend turns out to be complete shit, that church spire sticking out of the water like that has to be one of the creepiest things I've seen in a while – and, believe me, I've seen a few creepy things in my life time." He took another pull of his drink. "So, off the record – what d'you think? Does the devil live in the loch, or is it a load of crap?"

Mags often marvelled at Piers' ability to do that. She could be brash and more than a little opinionated, but compared to Piers, she was an amateur. That's what had attracted her to him in the first place, she supposed. Shame he turned out to be such a shitty boyfriend, really. The barman was obviously marvelling too, because it took him a good minute before he could respond.

"Well, you're nae backwards in coming forwards, are you?" The barman forced a chuckle. Mags noted a hint of nervousness to it. "Do I believe? That's a loaded question, make no mistake. I suppose, like most people, I grew up around here and so on that level, the myth is real. But do I think the devil lives in the loch?" He smile ruefully. "'Course not. They allowed that church to flood because it would've cost more to save it, I suppose. The valley was perfect for building a new reservoir to supply water to the bigger towns further inland, and something as insignificant as a little church wasn't going to stop them."

"Water for the other towns?" Piers said. "Weren't there enough lochs around here to do that already?"

"Wheesht, you're talking to the wrong man, so you are. Something to do with us having lots of rain but nowhere to store it – water tables and the like, I think. I don't know. I suppose they needed to supply the towns and the new industries they brought with them, and this valley was slap bang in the middle, so it must've made sense to someone. Anyway, it's not important now. The loch is here, and it isn't going anywhere."

"Still weird, though," Piers persisted. "It's not as if there aren't a load of other lakes around-"

Mags nudged him sharply in the ribs. She didn't know if he'd noticed it or not, but the barman's expression had hardened and turned hunted, and something told her that if they continued down this road, they'd be thrown out.

"So, you haven't seen anything?" she said, hoping this might subtly steer the conversation down a different route and mollify him.

"Me? No. Apart from Malcolm Allen, you'd be hard pushed to find anyone who would say they have. It's like most of the villages around here – folklore keeps coming up as fact. Which, incidentally, is why you probably can't find much in the way of research – 'cos there isn't anything to be found." He gave them both a satisfied nod, as if that cleared up that mystery once and for all. "So, you having another drink or what?"

Mags shot Piers a look. Leave it be. No point upsetting the locals by prying. Whatever it was that rattled them, it'd come out sooner or later. Anyway, getting testimonies on tape was such a small part of what they did, even if they were popular with the viewers. They'd find out for themselves tomorrow, if all went well and good. She turned her attention back to the barman shook her head.

"We're fine."

Another customer approached the bar and the barman left to serve him. The newcomer muttered something and Mags swore they both glanced hatefully over at both her and Piers. She nudged him again and he nodded – he'd seen it, too. They drained their glasses, said their goodbyes and left, all the while unable to shake the feeling that they were being watched, scrutinised, judged as they made their way over to the exit.

Outside, Mags let go of a breath she hadn't been aware she had been holding.

"Phew," Piers said. "That was certainly... interesting. You okay?"

Mags nodded, more out of habit than anything else, then hesitated. She screwed her face up, unsure as to how to explain that uneasy twinge she felt in the pit of her stomach. She didn't even know why it was there; the barman's explanation was more than reasonable. But that was part of the problem. It was reasonable. No one was trying to spin anything – and that, Ladies and Gentleman, didn't happen in places like this.

"Look," Piers said, a heavy note of put-upon patience infecting his voice. "Spit it out. What's bothering you?"

It took her a long moment to gather her thoughts. "I'm not sure. It's just that every place we go to, every legend we've look into, every story, every myth... It's always been something the local people have embraced. Even if they know it's a big old pile of crap, they still sell it like it's prime ribeye steak, a real juicy morsel of fine forteana. They get their five minutes of fame and people come from far and wide to buy into it. So why not here? This is the only place we've been that has denied the existence of their legend, and that feels... odd." She shrugged, unsure of how else to describe her feelings.

Piers walked next to her in thoughtful silence. "Yeah... it is odd, but maybe they genuinely aren't interested in any kind of publicity. Not everyone likes tourists."

"I suppose so. But even then..." she trailed off, still struggling. "Something isn't right here. I think Decker feels it, too, which is why he's acting so strangely."

"Now that I agree with. He's worrying me a bit. It's like this place has sucked all the life out of him."

"Yeah, that's it! That's exactly what it's like. He's lifeless. No fight in him at all. Like... like he really didn't want to come here, but had no choice." She frowned. "Does that make sense?"

"Of course it makes sense." The answer didn't come from Piers, but from behind her. Mags turned and found an old man, maybe older than anyone she'd ever seen stood there, leaning on a stick.

"Uh, excuse me?" she said.

"Can't talk here," the old man said. "Eyes everywhere." As if to prove his point, his eyes darted to every corner, every shadow. "Give it a few seconds, then follow me."

Piers raised his eyebrows, looking amused. "Pardon?"

But it was too late – the old man had already hobbled off into the rising mist.

They paused for a moment, unsure of what to do. Mags then started forwards. Piers caught her by her wrist. "Hey, what are you doing?"

"Oh, come on... aren't you just a little bit curious?" she said, a mischievous glint in her eyes.

Piers looked heavenwards and sighed. "Yeah... of course I am. I wouldn't be here if I wasn't. Let's go and see what that old crackpot has to say."

# chapter Fiue

If anything, the back room was even shabbier than the shop. There were bits of broken electrical equipment and old stock-boxes everywhere. Pinned up on one wall were a load of fuzzy photographs, mostly black and white, all inexpertly taken on an ancient camera. They all had one subject – the loch.

As it turned out, Malcolm Allen was only too happy to talk to the camera. By his own admission, he was a big fan of "stuff like this, y'know, ghost hunting and all that" which made Yolanda smile ruefully to herself. She'd been a fan of "stuff like this, y'know, ghost hunting and all that" too, which was why she'd been so keen to join them on this trip. After spending an economy train journey (which she had paid for – no expenses paid in this set up) plus a long day's drive in an economy camper van listening to a range of choice music (everything from Dolly Parton to Slipknot), some of the magic had definitely been lost.

Allen handed out mugs of tea whilst Decker set up his equipment, which didn't really amount to much more than a Sony hand-held and a microphone. When they were comfortable, Allen leaned forward with almost obscene enthusiasm.

"So – what do you people want to know? There isn't much I don't know, so ask away"

Paul nodded and glanced to Yolanda. Was she ready to do this? Well, nothing like jumping in with both feet and seeing how far you could swim...

As Paul explained their procedure, Yolanda went through her questions in her head. Open, but a little bit leading. Keep them on topic. We can edit, but too much meandering makes it too obvious that stuff has been cut and people start to question the authenticity of the interview. Keep it simple, keep it to the point, keep them on topic. Easy, right?

Decker gave the nod and held up his hand. Yolanda settled in her seat and gave the camera her best newsreader face. Then she remembered Paul favoured a more naturalistic approach and faced

Allen instead, but this meant she couldn't see Decker's signals properly –

"Don't fret, lassie," Allen said, and laid a hand on her knee. Yolanda fought the urge to smack it away. "Just ask your questions and I'll answer them."

From the corner, Paul harrumphed. Okay, time to be professional. Time to prove to the world – or, at least, a small section of it that was interested in the paranormal, that she could do this.

"I'm here with Malcolm Allen, the owner of the Post Office in Dùisg a' Pheacaich. So, Mr Allen – have you seen the Bèist an t-Sluic, also known as the Beast of The Hollow?"

"Why, yes, I do believe I have." He reached behind himself and picked up a sheaf of photographs, so conveniently placed you might have thought he'd been expecting them all along. "This here's the loch – if you look there you can just about see the spire sticking up out of the water – and if you look to the left of it, you can see a mighty strange disturbance in the water."

They were all like this. All vague, all ill-defined, all exactly like the other photos that had been passed around at other meetings in other places just like this one. Despite this, Decker still diligently filmed each one, and Yolanda fought to maintain a straight face as Malcolm Allen told her with complete and earnest sincerity the story behind each blurred snap.

"Now, this one," Allen said with the air of someone sharing a very real and rare treat. "This one I didn't take. How could I? My Grandpa took this in 1941, eight years before I was born. The loch wasn't a decade old then, and yet he took this." He slid the photo over to them. "That's always been the biggest mystery here, y'see? Nothing natural about it, although I realise you probably already caught on to that, given there's a church at the bottom of it. The valley had been earmarked for a new reservoir since the '20s and they finished building it in 1931, ready to supply water to the growing industries nearby. By rights, there shouldn't be anything in there bigger than maybe a catfish or a carp, but look at that, eh? Look at that!"

He tapped the photo and gave them all a triumphant look. Yolanda didn't know how to react, because no matter how much she studied it, all she could see was yet another fuzzy picture of the loch, this one with what looked like the shadow of a cloud passing over its sepia-tinted surface.

"Uh, Mr Allen – sorry, Malcolm – what is it? What are we looking at?" The clipped edge to Paul's voice said it all, but Malcolm Allen obviously took it as awed interest, because he beamed at them.

"I don't know!" he said. "It don't make sense, and that's the point! It was a sunny day that day, or so my Grandpa, may the Lord rest his soul, said. So what's making the shadow? People try to decry it, tell me it's fake or whatever, but I swear my Grandpa took that with his new Ensign camera, and to the day he died, if anyone spoke to him about it, he shook like a leaf in an autumn storm." He stabbed his finger in the air, as if to punctuate his point. "Like. A Leaf."

"But that still doesn't answer my question," Paul said. "What is it? What did he think he saw?"

"Young man, you have eyes, don't you? Can't you see? It's the Beast, just below the surface of the water! What else could it be? Like I said, it was a sunny day, not a cloud in the sky-"

*Apart from that one,* Yolanda thought as she continued to study the photo.

"-so what else could it be? It's there, I tell you, brooding, waiting for unwary travellers..."

An unholy urge to giggle welled up within Yolanda. It was obvious the man was a few sandwiches short of a picnic. Where she saw passing clouds – there was one in the photo, for Chrissakes! - he saw monsters. It was beyond ridiculous. She smoothed a hand over her mouth to keep it in, aware that if he said anything else, she wouldn't be able to stop laughing. After taking in a few deep breaths, she managed to compose herself.

"So... how did it get in the loch, Mr Allen?" She chewed the inside of her mouth to stop herself from smiling.

"Well, there's been lots of stories about that over the years, all different but with one common thread – the church. In every tale, they say St. Machan's had been taken over by bad influences – corrupted, if you will – and rather than admit it, they allowed it to crumble and hoped it would just go away. But go away it wouldn't and the rumours persisted until the whole area became the byword for illicit goings-on, you know, witchcraft and satanic rituals and the like. People even wondered if the Church itself was involved in the end, which is the real reason it didn't stop – and why no stories got out. Because they were involved and wanted it all hushed up." He leaned forwards, as if worried someone might overhear him. "I reckon the old pastors must've been sending letters out to the bigwigs, telling 'em everything was fine and for the longest while, they must've been believed, because I don't think anything was done. But then, around the turn of the century, something changed. I don't know what it was – no one really does, as those who lived through it refused to talk about it, may the Lord rest their souls – but something happened in that church. Next thing you know, the construction wagon's in town and they're building a dam to flood the valley... and what remained of the church."

"So... what? They flooded the valley to cover up whatever was going on in the church?" Paul said.

"Aye." Malcolm Allen sat back, looking satisfied with himself. "That's exactly what I'm saying. You won't get many to admit it – I mean, this is a God-fearing town and to think our own clergy was consorting with dark influences... well, it isn't something we want to contemplate. It was the ultimate betrayal, which is why we don't like talking about it, usually-"

"Right. I see." Paul wasn't bothering to hide his disdain now. "Well, thank you, Mr Allen, for your time and your cooperation, but it's getting late and we don't want to take up any more of your precious time-"

"Oh, no, you're not doing that. I like to talk about this. I have more pictures..." He dangled the prospect in front of them like a fisherman with a particularly tasty worm on his hook, but Paul refused to bite.

"I think we have enough to work with," he said. "Thank you, and goodnight."

The finality in his voice made Yolanda stand up and offer a little wave. Decker, on the other hand, didn't move. To her surprise, he was still filming the photos, as if mesmerised. Paul nudged him and he jerked his head up. He offered them both a sheepish look and snapped the camera's little viewing window shut.

"Yeah... thanks," he mumbled and left the room. Yolanda followed him, with Paul bringing up the rear.

"Remember, if you need anything else, you know where to find me!" Allen called after them.

None of them replied.

oOo

"Well, *that* was a waste of time." Paul paced, seething. "It was all rubbish! Just random, badly taken photos of the loch!" He balled his fists up and rounded on Yolanda and Decker. "Ever felt like someone's playing you for an absolute fool?"

Decker gave him a reproachful look.

"Oh, no, no, not you – I didn't mean you. Really. I meant him. Allen. And that Kelly woman, for pointing us in his direction. They did this deliberately. Must be what they do – cook up crap and serve it up to idiots... well, I'm not an idiot, and I'm not swallowing it. They can try all they like, but I know when someone's bullshitting me."

"So... what?" Yolanda said. "You think there's nothing in this legend? That it's a hoax?" She felt something loosen in her chest. "Are we leaving?"

Beside her, Decker sighed, his shoulders slumped. He looked the picture of defeat. "Might as well," he said.

"No... no, Decks, no. I do believe you. I do." Paul wrapped an arm around Deckers neck and pulled him into a rough embrace. "It's not you. It's them. It's them I don't believe. They're playing some kind of game with us."

"What do you mean? What game?" Yolanda asked as Decker shrugged Paul off. Hurt flickered briefly across Paul's face

"I don't know what it is, or what they get out of it. But whatever it is, they're not chasing us off."

"But why play a game in the first place? Why even do that?" Yolanda said. "It doesn't make sense."

"I know. Which leads me to believe there is something going on, something else." Paul shot the sky a defiant look. "If there's nothing here, then why go to all this trouble to hoax us? And if you're going to hoax someone, why not go full on Nessie and embrace it? No... something's going on here, I can feel it – and Allen is not the guy to talk to about it. He's just there to play games, of that I am certain."

"If it's any consolation, the story he told about the church is the same one I heard when I was a kid."

Both Paul and Yolanda turned to Decker. Was he... was he defending Allen?

"So he was telling the truth about that," Paul said. "So what? The rest of it is obviously bollocks-"

"Is it?" Decker interrupted. "Yes, the photos are crap, but the rest of it... the rest of it is what I grew up with." He drew his arms around himself and shivered. "It's all coming back to me now. Slowly but surely, I'm remembering things I thought were lost. And as far as I can remember, Allen didn't lie. Okay, so he didn't give us what you wanted, but that's a long way from deliberately misleading us."

Paul went to snap back, but the naked fear in Decker's tired eyes made him stop. "Okay... point taken. So what do you want to do? Stay or go? Do you think it's worth pursuing?"

Decker paused, staring at the ground. He stirred the ever-present mist with one foot and shuddered.

"Yes," he said. "Yes, I do. I told you about this place, I told you about this legend, and I'm not about to run away from it again."

*Run away from it again. What a strange way of looking at it,* Paul thought, but didn't say anything. Instead, he simply nodded. "Okay, if that's what you want, then that's what we'll do. We'll stay. One way or another, we'll get to the bottom of this."*And maybe, just maybe, you'll be able to sleep peacefully again,* he added to himself.

# chapter six

"So, what are you saying? That those involved... killed themselves?" Mags asked, enthralled. The old man chuckled, an unpleasant, gargling sound. They'd followed him at a discreet distance before he'd headed off into the local park – although that was probably a bit of an exaggeration, since it was no more than a piece of scrubland with a rusted swing and a half-rotted wooden bench – where he'd led them to a quiet corner and he'd regaled them with tales of Dùisg a' Pheacaich, its origins and its legends – most of which they'd heard before, thanks to Decker's and Paul's research. But this... this was new. She wondered if Decker knew, or if this would be news to him, too.

"No, no, young lady," The old man said. He hadn't supplied his name and Mags got the impression he wouldn't have given it to her if she'd asked. His eyes constantly flickered this way and that, searching, as if the bushes might suddenly disgorge the villagers and force him to flee. "That ain't it. It ain't it at all. If anyone asks – not that anyone has, mind you – that's the official line. The name Sinner's Wake is supposed to hark back to the time when the folk here felt so bad some of them took their own lives than face up to what they'd been involved in. But that ain't the truth – not by a long stretch." He leaned in and lowered his voice even more, until it was barely even a whisper. Mags leaned in closer to catch what he was saying, and fought down the urge to cover her mouth and nose with her hand. Up close, the old man stank of cigarettes and booze – and something else. Something unpleasant yet oddly familiar.

Fear.

"So, what is the truth?" Piers asked. He sounded bored. Mags shot him a warning glance – this was not the time to play the fashionable cynic. She wanted to know what he had to say, and she didn't want Piers ruining it for her, like he had ruined so much in the past.

The old man coughed. Mags recoiled on instinct and she missed the first part of what followed.

"- did it to satisfy its needs, not to assuage their own guilt," he said.

"Pardon?" Mags said. "Sorry, I didn't catch all that. Can you say it again?"

The old man looked annoyed and cast fearful glances about himself once more. He swallowed hard, his reluctance plain.

"I said, those people who drowned weren't suicides. They did it to satisfy its needs, not to assuage their own guilt."

"They did it to... what? Satisfy who?"

"Not so much 'who', as 'what'. And what do you think?" The old man's eyes unconsciously darted to his left, in the direction of what Mags could only guess was the loch. "They've got to satisfy the demon, or it'll find its own satisfaction. No one knows for sure what its ultimate purpose was or why old Pastor Decker-"

"Uh, what? Pastor *Decker*?" Piers interrupted.

Despite her own curiosity at this, Mags glared at him. *Shut up, Piers – let the old man speak. This might be our only chance.*

"Aye. Pastor Decker. He was in charge of the church afore they got the plans to flood the glen. Last one, he was – last one to do anything there before it was abandoned in 1892."

"1892? I thought they said it had laid empty for years before that?"

"Aye, that's what they say, but no – that church had a flock right up to near the turn of the century."

"So why lie?" Piers said.

"It's like I said – shame drives people to do strange things." He now sounded breathless, as if excited. "The government at the time gave the say-so for the dam shortly after Pastor Decker disappeared. They said it was for purposes of industry, but we knew different. All of us do, whether we want to admit it or not. The shadow down there... it is but a part of a whole, which is why it is weak." The old man leaned in even closer to Mags now, so he could whisper in her ear. Around them, the wind picked up, rustling the dry autumn leaves from their branches. Mags held her breath. "It is weak, so they have some control. Blood controls it, for blood has power. They raised it, but they were stopped afore they could finish. And now it floats there in the water, caught between oblivion and freedom, darkness and light, waiting for its time, when they can open the doors again and all of it can enter... By blood they'll do it, young lady – you mark my words. By blood, one way or another." He sat back and gave Mags a knowing look. "By blood."

A cold trickle of dread tracked Mags' spine. "You mean... sacrifice?"

The old man said nothing, just nodded. Piers snorted, but Mags ignored him,

"Aye, sacrifice. And the time is coming round again. If I were you, I'd be looking to pack up and get yourself as far away from Dùisg a' Pheacaich as possible. You and your friends."

"What, so if we stay, we're going to be sacrificed to a lake monster?" Piers sounded amused. "Like, hasn't that been done before? I'm sure D'Argento did that in the seventies at some point-"

"Shut up, Piers," Mags said, quietly. Piers rolled his eyes and let out a sarcastic chuckle, and yes, he was right. It did sound stupid, and it did sound corny, but he wasn't sitting close enough to see the naked terror in the old man's eyes. Whether it was true or not didn't matter; the old man believed it.

In the distance, the clock struck five. Had they really been out for that long? Each tinny 'bong' vibrated round Mags' head, making it throb. As if answering her unspoken question, the old timer pushed himself to his feet, and without another word, shuffled off.

"Hey..." said Piers. The old man did not look back.

"Let him go," said Mags.

"You seriously don't believe him, do you? I mean, come on... Sacrifice? Demons? Please. He's having some fun with us, indulging in his own personal five seconds of fame."

"Oh, really? Then why didn't he insist that we film him? Why didn't he tell us his name?"

"Uh, because we didn't ask him?"

"No... no. It was more than that. Didn't you see? Couldn't you tell? He's terrified. I don't know what it is, but that poor man is scared shitless of something."

"So, what? We turn tail and run? All because an old man's scared of something that might just be a product of his senile imagination? Come on, Mags… give me a break. We've come across crackpots before, enough to know that they're fucking everywhere and that they'll do anything to get us involved in whatever their own personal crusade is. So, he was scared – I don't doubt that. But whatever he's scared of is inside his own head. Please… human sacrifice? A government cover up via the formation of a reservoir? I mean, a *reservoir*. It's so ridiculous it's not even funny, it's just sad."

Mags had no choice but to agree. It was sad. But that didn't stop her wondering – or, indeed, thinking that the old man was closer to the truth than Piers ever would be when it came to this place.

"Look, why don't we just go back," Piers said, his tone softening. "Paul said we'd meet back up at six, so they won't be long. It's a long shot, but maybe that Kelly woman knows of a decent restaurant nearby. I don't know about you, but I could do with a steak."

o0o

Dùisg a' Pheacaich was as quiet as ever when Mags and Piers walked back to the guesthouse, though Mags swore she saw at least one pair of curtains twitching as they passed by. She tried to imagine the people behind them and turned the old man's words over in her head. In a way, she was relieved. She'd picked up on something – she had a talent for that, although most people just laughed at her when she spoke about it – but now she felt vindicated. Piers didn't believe her, but then again, he never did. Quite why he was involved in this kind of gig in the first place often baffled her, but hey, here he was, a part of it, so who was she to judge? From that, a kind of unspoken agreement had sprung up between them: she believed, he didn't and if they didn't talk about it, there was no need to argue. And for that reason they now walked in not entirely comfortable silence.

Although it was barely past five, the door to the guest house was locked. That was a bit of a surprise. She'd always thought

42

rural types prided themselves on their ability to never have to lock a door, but there it was. Piers offered her a facial shrug as she raised a hand to knock, but before her knuckles struck the wood, there was a jingle of keys and the sliding back of bolts from the other side of the door. It opened to reveal a not-entirely happy looking Mrs Kelly, who frowned at them like a school-marm of old.

"Uh, sorry," Mags said. "We, uh, didn't realise you locked up early."

"Early? Maybe for you city-types, but I close at five o'clock. I've got dinner to prepare," Mrs Kelly all but snapped. Before either of them could continue their apologies, she turned and strode off, leaving Mags and Piers feeling like a couple of naughty teenagers breaking curfew.

The others were in the lounge, drinking tea. Mags had hoped to grab another beer before bed, but given Mrs Kelly's attitude, she figured alcohol would likely be off the menu. They all looked a little subdued, especially Decker, who looked positively worn out. Paul raised his mug as they joined him, and Yolanda shuffled over on the large couch so they all had room to sit down.

"So... anything?" Mags asked. Paul let out an annoyed sigh whilst Yolanda took another sip of her tea and Decker stared into space.

"Not really," Paul said. "Nothing new, anyway. If I didn't know better, I'd say we'd just been given the Official Line disguised as some big revelation. Still, not many people know about the legend, so having a local relay it is always good viewing. We can use what we have, so it wasn't a total waste of time. You?"

Mags shot Piers a look. Should she tell them here? Normally she wouldn't have waited for an opening but the town's indefinable 'something' still niggled at her. That and the thought of Mrs Kelly sitting in the next room with her ear pressed to the wall, listening to them, bothered her.

"Maybe something," she said as nonchalantly as she could. "But probably nothing. Nothing worth losing sleep over, anyway." She widened her eyes and shook her head slowly, hoping Paul got the hint that she didn't want to talk about it here. He frowned but nodded back and mouthed "now?" at her. She gave her head the slightest of shakes then looked up. "Later" she mouthed back. At this, Paul nodded.

"Well, we were just discussing plans for tomorrow. Up early, get down to the loch, sort out the boat. Hopefully that won't take too long, so we should get a dive in before lunch if we're lucky. Just a prelim one this time – scope it out, see what the conditions are like, maybe take a few shots of the submerged church... That sound okay to you and Piers?"

"Yeah, that sounds fine to me," Piers said. "What are we doing about the connection problems?"

"Not sure. Seems to be something that affects this whole area – no that it bothers the local much. Suppose you don't know what you've got 'til it's gone, eh? Mags – any ideas?"

Mags should have had plenty of ideas, but she was too preoccupied with the old man and so his question caught her off guard.

"Uh, um, what? Sorry... I wasn't listening."

Paul frowned disapprovingly at her "I said, have you any ideas about our connectivity problems? Going to be hard to stream live footage if the issue with connectivity runs to your Go Pros."

"Oh, yeah, sorry." She shook all thoughts of the old man's warning out of her head and endeavoured to concentrate. "The radio should be fine- I've got that new rig that allows us to relay messages as long as we don't swim too far off. It does mean the boat needs to be near enough above you most of the time so we'll need to anchor off the church itself, but we should be able to get audio streaming quite easily. All you have to do is keep hold of the probe and keep it as still as possible in the water. We'll just record the visuals – no point in even trying to sort that out if there's no connectivity. I know that means we run the risk of them being a bit crap since we don't know what the visibility is like down there, but we can always adjust it for the second dive."

"That sounds excellent." Paul lowered his voice. "And you're okay going down there?"

Mags just nodded. She was fine going down there; oddly enough, the loch didn't bother her as much as the town did and since going there meant not being here, she was almost looking forward to it.

Almost.

They continued honing their plans for nearly an hour, until the clock struck six. Mrs Kelly entered the room and announced that dinner was ready. They shared a look, but no one had the nerve to say they were going to try and find a restaurant. Instead, they traipsed after her like children and sat around a large table before helping themselves to a rather grey steak and kidney pie, over-boiled vegetables and a thin, tasteless gravy. She watched them grimly before leaving, remaining absent for the majority of the meal, coming out of the kitchen only once to bring them a jug of water. This actually suited them fine; the last thing they needed was her tutting at them as they pushed their carrots around their plates, debating whether they could dump them in one of the nearby pot plants without her noticing. They kept their conversation light and when they were finished, Paul announced he thought it was a good idea if they all turned in for an early night. Or, at least, that's what they said out loud. Both Mags and Paul had come to the same conclusion – time for another, more private meeting upstairs.

oOo

"Sacrifice?" Yolanda sounded more than a little incredulous. "I mean, come on… really? You bought that?"

"I'm not saying I bought it, just that's what the old guy said. He was really nervous, always looking around to check no one was watching us. He warned us to leave, too," Mags said.

"Malcolm Allen didn't mention anything like that," Yolanda said. "I think you just ran into the local nutcase, Mags."

"Well, yeah, obviously I thought the same… but what if there's something in it? What if there is something going on here? It would explain a lot – the attitudes of the locals, the lack of coverage, the weird feeling that something isn't right here…"

She turned to Paul, expecting him to scoff, but instead found him looking thoughtful.

"Yeah, I know what you mean," Paul said. "That Allen guy spun us a load of crap. All the photos were amateur rubbish at best and his so-called big score ended up feeling more like he was just trying to hoax us. Usually I would say we should just leave and write this place off, but it's like you say. There's definitely something not right about this place. Why are the locals so hostile to us? If they're trying to hoax us, they should be welcoming us with open arms, trying to get us to part with as much of our cash as possible and get more people to come here... but they're not. And that simply doesn't make sense to me-"

"Look, guys... please, just stop." Everyone turned towards Decker. He hadn't spoken in ages, which was unusual in itself. He looked harried and like he could do with a good night's sleep. "I'm sorry I ever mentioned this place. I should have kept quiet. Stupid childhood tales being taken seriously... sheesh! If I'd known it would come to this, I would never have said anything." He pulled his legs up under him and wrapped his arms around his knees, as if protecting himself. "Let's just go. In the morning. Just leave. Get out of here and forget I ever mentioned it."

"What? Are you crazy?" Piers said. "I'm the first one to admit I think the whole thing is probably horseshit, but that church? Footage of that alone will bring in advertising revenue beyond our wildest dreams! Add in a loch monster legend and we might as well be given blank cheques! Come on, people. You're looking at this all wrong. Whether the legend is real isn't the issue here. So what if the locals are acting contrary? Seriously, who gives a shit? We're not here to untangle their problems – we're here to bring a relatively unknown story to the fore, to spin it out, to dive down and investigate that church... pull that all together and we're made! It won't matter if there's nothing down there, people are going to love the mystery of it all regardless. We *can't* leave now."

An uncomfortable silence followed. Paul shot Decker an apologetic glance. "Look, man – he's got a point. We can do this in a couple of days, max. We've got some local colour - all we need is some interior footage of that church. Think about it. Some moody shots of the surroundings and some dark, pensive footage that may or may not show the potential lair of something mysterious... we get that and we're golden. Piers is right. It would be madness to leave now."

Decker's body folded in on itself, shutting out the world. Paul shared a worried look with the others. By silent mutual agreement, everyone left, leaving them alone. Even then, Decker refused to uncurl himself; instead, he continued to sit on the wing-backed chair by the window, his head down, his back to the room. Paul hesitated. He wanted to comfort him, to ask him exactly what was bothering him, but something stayed his hand.

"This is a mistake," Decker muttered after a long pause.

"Why is it a mistake?" Paul asked, gently. He crouched down in front of him and dared to lay a hand on his knee. "What is it that's bothering you so much?"

He felt Decker's muscles tighten under his palm as he withdrew from him. "Nothing."

"Really? It doesn't look like nothing. To me, it looks like something. Something bad. Something big. Brandon... what happened here, when you were a kid? What is it you're trying to run from?"

Decker lifted his head enough to let Paul see his shadowed eyes. Their cadaverous appearance startled him and he fought down the urge to snatch his hand back. This was Decker – was Brandon, the man he loved, his soul-mate and best friend – not some imagined monster. He was just upset, nothing more.

"Nothing," Decker said again. "Forget I said anything. Go get your footage. I'll be okay." He bent his head down again and buried it once more into his knees, hiding those haunted eyes. Goosebumps skittered across on Paul's skin, making him shudder.

"Okay... we'll get the footage, then we'll leave. Try to be out of here by tomorrow evening. That's fine. I can live with that."

"I hope so," Decker said. "I hope so."

# chapter seven

Paul left Decker alone after that. He'd never done anything in all the years they'd known each other to scare him – well, okay, maybe apart from that time they went to Manchester for the weekend and Decker had taken way too much speed and declared he was having a heart attack – but even that hadn't chilled him the way his words chilled him now.

They undressed in silence and lay back against hard pillows that smelt of lavender and damp. Usually, they both relished this time together; a time where they could just be, without any of life's pressures intruding, but tonight Decker wouldn't even look at him; he just rolled over, pulling the blankets up so high that they nearly covered his head. A lump, bitter with disappointment and hot with worry, rose in Paul's throat. He reached over and tried to gather Decker closer to him, to try to at least imitate their usual intimacy, but everything about him was as if made of stone, unyielding and cold. The lump expanded, making it hard to breathe, and Paul couldn't help wonder if they should just call it off. Do what Decker suggested and leave, because it wasn't worth this.

Paul lay on his back and closed his eyes. The dark seeped in and, surprisingly, sleep found him pretty easily; it wasn't long before Paul was snoring.

oOo

A short while later, Decker raised his head and looked over his shoulder. He paused for a moment, checking to make sure that Paul was truly asleep before sliding out of the bed and grabbing his clothes off the nearby chair.

He wasn't really sure what it was that bothered him. The dreams were vague but filled with menace, and they were getting worse. He didn't even have to be asleep now for the darkness to find him; merely resting was enough. He shivered. The darkness.

What a crap name for something that scared him so much. But what else could he call it? He couldn't see it, couldn't define it, but it dogged his every moment, a tight suffocating certainty that something was out there, watching, waiting for... what? Him? It had to be him. Otherwise, why would he be so afraid? But afraid of what? An acute sense of unease and a strong desire to get the fuck out of here? And so his thoughts went, around and around, until he feared they'd never stop.

That's why they had to leave. He couldn't tell Paul, because Paul would think he was cracking up... and he'd be right, because that's what scared Decker the most. That he was cracking up. Going doolally, crazy as a shithouse rat, or even worse, crazy as his mother with her constant mutterings about how the demons lived in the water, and how he had to avoid it at all costs...

He crept over to the door and slowly turned the handle. It squealed, making Decker wince, sure it would wake Paul up, but he just kept snoring right on. Finally, there was a deep clunk and the door gave, allowing him to open it just enough to slip through.

Well, he was going to find out what it was that seemed so determined to drive him to the nuthouse. This place was doing something to him; he had no doubt about that. He'd been fine before they'd arranged this trip, fine until he'd told Paul that Sinner's Wake existed. Ever since then, he had been plagued by nightmares and vague, dread-fuelled anxieties which left him unable to eat or sleep comfortably. Well, now it was time to find out why.

Good job he knew of someone who might be able to explain.

He took the stairs carefully, measuring each step to ensure no-one would hear him. The old guesthouse had taken on a second life in the dark; what had once seemed twee and harmless by day now looked creepy and wrong in the moonlight. He shivered and the darkness inched closer. His vision swam as his heart quickened, forcing him to stop and clutch at the handrail. It took a good few minutes to pass, and he spent each one convinced someone would burst out of a room and demand to know what he was up to, he knew better, stay inside, stay safe, never question, Old Nine Eyes would know –

He stopped. What? Old Nine Eyes? Who was that? His pulse banged in his ears and for a moment, he thought he might be sick. Where was all this coming from?

Old Nine Eyes... Yes, he had heard that before, somewhere... but where?

Where?

*Where? Why, here. Here is where you heard-*

His fingers clenched around the handrail, his teeth gritted.

*Where I heard what?*

Nothing.

Outside, something shrieked. It was probably no more than a fox, or a hunting owl, but to Decker's subconscious, it was a warning.

Something was coming.

He crept downstairs as quickly as he dared. Something was coming. Not now, maybe not even tomorrow, but it knew he was here, knew he was back. He paused by the bottom of the stairs and listened again. All was silent: no vengeful Mrs Kelly swooped out of the kitchen, demanding to know what he was playing at, Paul didn't appear at the top of the stairs telling him to get back to bed, Old Nine Eyes didn't slither across the lobby and smile a jawful of jagged teeth at him, willing to him follow. He padded over to the reception desk, let himself through the counter and opened the desk drawer. Inside was a ledger, a mess of papers and a small, battered address book. Despite himself, Decker grinned. He knew she'd have one – all old ladies in small towns did. He leafed through it, daring not to breathe, until he found what he was looking for. His grin widened, and had Paul seen it, he would probably have run to the hills.

*Sadie Decker.*

He knew she'd been lying.

He grabbed a scrap of paper and scribbled the address down.

One way or another, he was going to find out what was going on here.

And he was going to stop it.

# chapter eight

*25 years earlier...*

Even in high summer, the mist is there. It hugs the ground as if it is afraid to leave it, afraid that one day it won't be there. Brandon stirred it with his toe, making it swirl into shapes that reminded him of smoke and ice cream.

He looked up at his father, who smiled at him and jiggled his hand playfully. The small boy smiled back. A boy and his daddy. What could be more perfect?

"Now, Brandon," John Decker said. "Today is an important day. An important day of many more yet to come." He hunkered down in front of his son, who regarded him with a solemnity only small children and priests are able to achieve. "You're a big boy now – seven, at last. That means we're going to trust you more."

"Does that mean I get a key?" Excitement fizzed through him. David Fenton had a key to let himself into his house after class, because his father was gone and his mother worked. They'd all passed it around in awe, small fingers caressing its jagged teeth, marvelling at the way it shone in the sunlight until David had insisted on having it back. He kept it on a piece of string which he put around his neck so he wouldn't lose it. He said it was his Big Responsibility. Brandon wondered if this was going to be his Big Responsibility. He wiped his damp palms down the sides of his trousers, just in case.

"You know where we're going?" his father said.

"Aye. The loch."

"Aye. The loch," His father paused and wiped his mouth with the back of his hand.

"What's wrong, Daddy?"

"Oh, nothing. I'm just surprised at how quickly this day has come around, I suppose. Now, you know the loch? How you're never going to go near it?"

"Yes, I know that. Everyone knows that." Brandon rolled his eyes. Was this it? Another lecture about never going near the loch?

"Yes, and you've been a good boy about that. Some boys aren't so good about it, but you are. You are so very, very good."

John Decker leaned forwards and pulled his son into a rough hug. Brandon hugged back, confused. He sensed something in his father – a nervousness; a fear, even – but he didn't know what it was about. And now he'd brought him here, telling him it was important… just to tell him something he already knew? He hugged his father back, as if he might squeeze the confusion out until John rubbed his son's back one last time and stood up.

He sniffed and passed his hand over his eyes. Brandon frowned. Was his father crying? A little bubble of unease popped, sending shooting stars of fear burst in his tummy. Why was Daddy crying? Daddy never cried. Mummy did… but Daddy? Never.

Not until now, anyway.

# chapter nine

The next day dawned bright but cold. The air held that tang only autumn brought. It always reminded Paul of the beginning of the university year, and he felt a pang of nostalgia. Had it really been eleven years since they'd left? He glanced over at Decker, who looked like hell. Poor guy must've had even less sleep than he had. He kept getting woken up by weird noises on the edge of his hearing, undefined and unsettling. He supposed this was his city-boy sensibilities kicking in; give him sirens and the roar of a local train, and he'd sleep like a log. Silence, though... silence unnerved him, made him feel an irresistible urge to fill it with noise. Nature was even worse, which was kind of ironic when you considered he spent so much time in remote places like this, chasing dreams and nightmares.

They parked up on the side of the road, on the opposite side of the loch from the day before. The shore was still a fair way off, but they could at least see the slaty expanse of water from here – all they had to do was head down a rutted path and they were there.

The camper rumbled up behind him and disgorged three dishevelled looking passengers. None of them looked like they'd slept particularly well. He offered them a wan smile and a wave. Only Mags returned it.

"You okay?" she asked.

Paul nodded.

"Decker still..." she didn't need to finish the question.

"Yeah. He is," Paul said.

"Is he ill?" she asked.

"I don't think so. Just didn't sleep very well. Something is really bothering him, but he won't tell me what it is."

"Maybe we should, you know..." she gave him an apologetic look.

"I don't know. Maybe. We'll see how today goes."

Paul wandered over to where Decker gathered his camera equipment and helped him pile it up in the back of the camper. They figured it was better to only risk one vehicle to the muddy track, but it wasn't long before they regretted choosing it over the Astra. The Astra might have been smaller, but its suspension was definitely better, and more than once they winced as it rock and rolled its way down. Finally, they spied the water's edge and their spirits lifted. The view was beautiful – almost uncannily so, and even Decker seemed buoyed by it. He climbed out of the VW to take some establishing shots, and Piers managed to turn the camper around so they could ease their boat off its trailer and into the water with little trouble. The way the light refracted off the early morning mist that clung to the edge of the loch gave it an ethereal quality, a faerie grotto of legend bordered by drooping pines and the odd deciduous tree just turning a glorious gold. After a few minutes, Decker finished filming and they continued on to the water's edge, where Yolanda gave the obligatory introductory speech whilst Piers and Mags ducked behind a nearby tree to pull on wetsuits.

"Hey... have you seen this?" Piers emerged from behind his tree, his wetsuit dangling from his torso. He held something large and round in his hands. Paul rolled his eyes and called cut.

"Piers, how many times? Don't interrupt filming!"

"Oh, sorry, man – but you've got to take a look at this."

He offered Paul a rounded lump of grey stone, about the size of a brick, carved into the shape of a face. It had staring eyes and a round 'o' for a mouth, reminding Paul of Edvard Munch's 'The Scream'. It was a crude approximation of a human expression, but it unsettled him enough to refuse to take it from Piers when he offered it over.

"Where on earth did you find that?" he asked.

"It was on the floor, just over there behind the tree." Piers jerked a thumb over his shoulder. "I wonder what it is?"

"Hey... I think there's another one over here!" Mags' voice floated over from the trees. She was fully suited up, a splash of violent colour crouched amongst the earthy tones of the surrounding trees. Both Paul and Piers wandered over to join her, Piers' fingers still caressing the lumpen features of his find, and indeed, there was another one, sitting amongst the bracken, its sightless eyes facing the loch. Mags continued her search as the two men compared sculptures, pulling the undergrowth back until she let out a low whistle.

"Yep, another one... what the hell are they?"

She bent down to touch this third one, but was stopped by a bark from Decker.

"No! Don't... don't touch it." He came running over, his equipment forgotten. "Please, just don't-" He stopped abruptly when he saw Piers holding one.

"What?" Piers said. "I was just looking at it."

"Put it back." Decker's request was quiet; he didn't shout, he didn't swear, but Paul couldn't help feeling it might have been better if he had. Piers shrugged and ambled over to where he discovered his little head and set it back on the ground.

"Face it the right way," Decker said.

"For God's sake," Piers muttered, but did as he was told nonetheless.

"What are they, Decker?" Paul asked.

Decker paused and looked to the ground. "Just a local superstition. They... they protect us. From the Beast. They're always watching."

"They're weird," Piers said. He dusted his hands on his thighs and switched his attention to Mags. "You ready, partner?"

Mags nodded and threw the stone near her feet one last, almost hateful look. "Yeah, I'm ready."

Together they manhandled the boat into the water. Without a jetty it was a bit of a struggle, but they managed it. Usually they hired boats from the locals as they tended to be larger and sturdier than their little motorised dinghy, but after asking Mrs Kelly, they'd discovered there were no boats for hire at all in Dùisg a' Pheacaich. It seemed a little odd, but Paul hadn't been willing to push it, so they'd decided to stick with their own and make do.

Decker was to stay on the shore with Yolanda whilst Paul operated the probe that allowed Piers and Mags to communicate with them as they dived. In the past it has always been Decker in the boat, but Paul didn't have the heart to send him out there, so he's offered to go instead.

The water was bitingly cold as they waded out, guiding the dinghy out into deeper water. One by one, they clambered aboard. Mags took hold of the tiller and they motored out to the middle of the loch, a few feet shy of the church spire. At this distance, they could see its weather-stained surface, mauled and pitted by the ravages of time. No weathervane graced its top; judging by the chunk of stone taken out of one side, it had been torn free many years ago, probably so it could be sold for scrap. Out here, all was quiet, the only movement the occasional gust of wind that stirred the waters, shattering its surface into a million glittering fragments before it calmed back to glass once more.

Undeterred, Paul took the probe and dangled it over the side of the dinghy before switching it on. Both Piers and Mags then pulled on their full face masks so he could check and see if he could pick up their frequencies. It wasn't perfect, but after some fiddling he managed to tune in so their voices were at least louder than the background hiss of interference.

"I don't know what's up with it – must be atmospherics, or something," he said. "When you're down there, keep talking – even if it's just to sing 'Mary Had a Little Lamb'. I'll need to know you're there, so if I do lose you, I know it's time to start tuning again, okay?"

Both Mags and Piers nodded.

"I'm looking to you to get some good footage of that church and get out," Paul added. "Don't take any risks, stay together and don't go inside. Last thing we need is for either of you to get stuck down there-"

"Yeah, yeah, we know the drill," Piers said, grinning. Every dive, the same pep talk. He'd heard it all before.

Paul pulled on his headphones and pulled the radio-mic close to his mouth.

"You hear me?"

Piers nodded. "Back at you."

"Yep, I read that. Mags?"

"Yeah, I can hear you,"

"Good. Looks like we're going to be okay."

Mags and Piers shuffled over the edge of the boat and plopped backwards into the water, where they hovered for a second, gaining their bearings. That done, they both gave Paul a thumbs-up and disappeared into the depths. As always, Paul watched them go with a mixture of trepidation and awe.

This, as the old saying went, was it.

oOo

Decker stood a little way from the water's edge. He dare not go closer. Even though he knew it was stupid, that the warning only applied to children, something deeply ingrained within him made him stop.

It had taken everything he had to stop running up to them, to beg them not to go. Now he watched helplessly as the dinghy powered out to the middle of the loch. The hum of its little motor filled the glen, drilling into his head, giving him a headache. Then, finally, it stopped and they were motionless, tiny dolls atop a child's bath toy.

A familiar, coppery tang spurted in his mouth. He dragged his attention from the loch and looked at his fingers. He'd bitten them to the quick; one was bleeding.

*Blood.*

The word loomed over him, important and heavy. He swallowed hard and tried not to allow the memory that howled behind the prison-door of his mind a chance to escape.

"Are... are you okay?"

The way Yolanda spoke, hesitant and awkward, told Decker she was concerned. And of course, why shouldn't she be? She had been left here, with him, a man who trembled at nothing and bit his fingernails until they bled. He tried to offer her a reassuring smile, but it wouldn't come. Instead, he nodded and continued to stare out over the water.

Two little figures were now sitting on the edge of the dinghy, their backs to them. Decker mouthed the conversation they would be having: one about safety, about communication, about sticking together and not taking risks. He knew it by heart, because he was the one who usually gave it. Not today, though. No, today neither love nor money could get him in that boat. A shiver chased its way down his back. He hadn't gone, but he'd let Paul go. Paul, the one who mattered most to him, was balancing precariously near the edge, dangling the probe that would pick up the divers voices into the water.

He'd let him go.

He took in a shuddering breath and raised his gaze, finding a spot on the other side of the loch. There, a small gap in the cliff side held his attention and finally, the long-buried memory slipped its leash.

All Decker could do was watch.

# chapter Ten

They sat together, their legs dangling precariously over the edge of the cliff. This was something else the children of Dùisg a' Pheacaich had been forbidden from doing, but Brandon supposed that if it was your Dad you were doing it with, it was okay to sometimes break the rules. A hundred feet below, the loch stretched out as far as he could see, and at its centre, St Machan's spire rose.

No one bothered them. But then again, why would they? Most of the time, the villagers avoided the loch, and no outsiders ever came here, despite its beauty. The whole place felt wild and lonely, but the isolation that might crush another soul did not affect Brandon. It was all he'd ever known, after all.

His father didn't say anything for the longest time; he just sat, one arm around his son's shoulders, the other steadying itself against the grassy edge of the cliff. When they had first approached, Brandon had hesitated, scared of Breaking the Rules, but his father had smiled sadly and beckoned him on nonetheless, saying it was okay and what his grandmother didn't know wouldn't hurt her.

"I want you to promise me something, Brandon," his father said, shattering the fragile silence between them.

"Okay, Daddy." He answered immediately, because no matter what he wanted, Brandon would do it. He looked up at his father, who was gazing over the loch, his expression caught perfectly between awe and fear.

"I mean it. No matter what happens, you must keep your promise."

A lump, unexpected and fiercely hot, rose in Brandon's throat. He swallowed; he didn't want Daddy to see him crying, not so soon after he'd shed a few tears of his own. Rather than speak, he nodded his head vigorously. No matter what Daddy asked, he'd do it. He had to. He was father.

John sighed heavily and pinched the bridge of his nose.

"Promise me you'll look after your Mammy."

Now the lump expanded, making his eyes water. Look after Mammy? Why would he need to do that? Of course, if he had to, he would… but why would he? Daddy was here. Daddy was here to look after both of them.

John shifted his attention from the loch to his son. "Brandon?"

"Yes, Dad?" he croaked.

"You promise?"

"I do."

"Say it. So I know you mean it."

"I… I promise that I'll look after Mammy."

He ruffled Brandon's hair and planted a kiss on his forehead. "Good boy. I believe you."

A question rose, monstrous in its insistence, but before Brandon could ask why his father needed this promise, he stood up, pulling him to his feet as if he had sensed it coming and wanted to head it off at the pass.

"Come on – we should get going. Mammy's cooking something special tonight, so we don't want to be late."

The question sank back down. He'd ask it later.

# chapter eleven

It took the divers a few, heart-stopping seconds to get their bearings and begin filming. Water conditions were reported as good, which came as a surprise. Paul fiddled with the feed, hoping to strengthen their signal, but it wasn't to be. All the while, both Piers and Mags kept up a kind of holiday-guide type commentary, talking about plant life and fish – or indeed, the lack of them. Sure, it was never like it was in the movies where great shoals of silver circled the heroic divers, but you at least expected to catch sight of something. Down there, though, it seemed like there was nothing. Well, nothing apart from the church.

"Whoa," Piers breathed. "You guys have to see this."

"Yeah, Piers, thanks – gonna need more detail than that," Paul said into his own radio mic. "What can you see?"

"It's not just a church – it's more like a cathedral. Must have been built in a hollow or something, because this baby has to be at least eighty feet tall."

"Yeah," said an equally awed Mags. "I wasn't expecting anything like this. This is... this is *awesome*. We are made, guys – fucking made."

Envy twinged Paul's gut. Not for the first time did he wish he'd insisted on going on the first dive, but he knew Piers and Mags had more experience than him and worked together in perfect harmony. It was as if they could pre-empt what the other was thinking, a precious gift in a new and potentially dangerous environment. Still, it didn't stop Paul from being a little jealous and wishing he was there to share their obvious awe first hand.

"Where are you?" he asked.

"We're going down, filming the exterior... This isn't set into a hollow. I think... I think it sunk into some kind of crack in the earth. It seems to be sitting on a ledge set inside it. The crack itself just keeps going down. I don't even know if we can reach the bottom."

"What do you mean, if you can reach the bottom?" Paul asked. Their equipment was good for up to 500 metres, way more than they should require.

"Hey, Mags, you see that?" Piers said.

"Yeah. Windows. Broken ones. Must've happened when they flooded the place – No, Piers – what are you up to? No going in there Piers… No! No going in there!"

"Piers – she's right," Paul broke in. A cold bloom of dread shoved aside any lingering envy and clawed at his chest. "Stay out of the church."

"Aww – just a little peek? Not to go in, just stick my head in, have a look around…"

"Piers," Paul said, his tone low and forbidding. "We agreed."

"Yeah, but you're not down here. Believe me, we need this footage. The audience is going to shit itself when it sees this. So will you when you see the footage. I promise. And I promise I won't go in… Just let me poke my head in."

"No," said Paul. "Stay out. Don't go near it. External footage only. You don't know what's in there."

Piers snorted in derision. "What, like some kind of lake monster? Come on, man. Mags is with me. She'll stop me doing anything stupid."

Paul sighed heavily and pinched the bridge of his nose. Truth was, he was dying to see what that church looked like, and actually appreciated the fact that Piers was asking him. Once upon a time, he would have just done what he damned well pleased and hang the consequences.

"Okay. Poke your head in. But just your head. You don't go in. Get some interior footage and then surface. I think we've got enough to play with this morning. And Mags?"

"Yeah?"

"Make sure he does as he is told."

Paul heard the grin in her voice. "Sure, boss."

Both divers fell silent, apart from the eerie, almost mechanical suck and blow of their breathing, which got noticeably faster as they approached the broken window, or so he assumed.

"Piers… Mags… speak to me…"

Neither replied. The cold feeling sank into Paul's belly and began twisting his guts around.

"Piers. Mags. Report. What is going on?"

"Jesus," Piers whispered.

"Jesus what?" Paul asked.

"You will not believe what is in here. It's... it's huge. A huge room. And... I dunno. An altar? In the middle. But there's something on it... Something moving..."

"Piers?" It was Mags, sounding concerned.

"Just a few more seconds – I need to make sure I catch this..."

"No – Piers... Behind us. Look. What the fuck is that?"

Paul's heart jump started. "What is it? Mags? Are you okay?"

"Holy shit!" Mags exclaimed, and if she said anything else, it was obscured by a violent screech of feedback.

The line went dead.

"Piers! Mags! Answer me!" Paul yelled. He twisted the little knobs that controlled the feed, desperately seeking another frequency, but it was no good. Out of sheer desperation, he raised the probe and dropped it over the other side of the boat, looking for that elusive sweet-spot, but still there was nothing. His heart crashed around his rib cage, making him feel weak and shaky. What had happened? Had they moved too quickly? Or was it simply atmospherics? If it hadn't have been for Mags' last exclamation, he might have been able to convince himself, but now his imagination ran rampant. He spared the shore a glance; standing there were two figures, waiting for them to return, happy in their obliviousness. He now selfishly wished he had insisted Decker do this, like he usually did, because Decker would know what to do, he would know what to press-

Another blast of feedback heralded the return of the radio connection.

"...aul? Paul? Are you there?"

It was Mags.

"Fuck! Yes! Mags – are you two okay? What happened down there?" The joy of sudden relief made him want to laugh.

"I don't know... there was a ... a... shadow. I can't describe it any other way. Maybe a big cloud passed overhead and it freaked me out." She sounded sheepish. "Sorry."

"No – don't apologise. I'm just thankful you're okay. Is Piers with you?"

"Yeah, boss, I'm here. We're making our way back up now. Be with you in five."

A tense few moments passed before tell-tale bubbles broke the surface. Piers grabbed the dinghy's gunwale and dragged himself and out of the water and pulled his mask off whilst Mags prepared to join them.

"Fuck, yeah!" Piers said, grinning. "You have got to see this... seriously, it kicks ten shades of shit out of anything else we've ever filmed!" His enthusiasm was dampened by a sharp intake of breath behind him. "Hey... you okay Mags?"

Paul frowned and leaned over to her side of the boat. She was no longer trying to pull herself out of the water, but was instead holding on to the gunwale with one hand, her face contorted in pain. Piers' grin disappeared, and both men grabbed her arm and hauled her into the dinghy.

"What's wrong?" Paul asked. Mags just shook her head and grimaced whilst Piers hunkered down beside her leg. He let out a pained hiss.

"Paul, you'd better get the first aid kit out," Piers said. "What happened, Mags?"

"I don't know," she said. "I think something bit me."

"Something... bit you?"

"Yeah. I don't know what it was, but it got me good. Hurts like a bitch."

"I can imagine. It's gone right through you suit," Piers said. He pulled off her boot and began rolling the leg of her wet suit up as gently as he could, but that didn't stop Mags from wincing and biting back a yelp of pain. Blood and water trickled down her leg and pooled in the bottom of the dinghy, staining it red.

"What the hell... what could do that?" Piers breathed.

Paul shook his head. Just above her ankle was a perfect circle of needle-like puncture marks, about an inch and half across. Each little wound welled blood every time Mags moved.

"It hurts," Mags said. "Like it's burning."

"Well, whatever it is, we'll need to sterilise it," said Paul. He peered at the wound. "It doesn't actually look that deep, but we'll get it cleaned up and dressed properly when we get to shore."

Piers hauled in the probe and Paul whipped the motor on. All the time, Mags face went through every pained contortion it could as the dinghy skipped over the surface of the loch and back to shore. As soon as he cut the engine, Piers jumped out and guided them to solid ground, shouting for a first aid kit. Together, they manhandled Mags out of the boat. Yolanda rushed forwards with the kit and Paul told her to prepare sterile cleaning pads and some distilled water, which she did without question. He tried to ignore the fact that Decker did nothing and focused entirely on Mags.

"You're up to date with your shots?"

"'Course I am," Mags said through gritted teeth. "Holy crap! That hurts. Why does it hurt this much? Shouldn't do... I've taken sea urchin spines to the foot, for chrissakes." She tried to grin, but it looked more like a grimace. "Must be getting weak in my old age."

Finally, the blood stopped beading and Paul felt confident in dressing the wound properly. At first, he and Yolanda tried to help Mags out of her suit, but pulling it down over the bite proved too painful so he let her keep it on as he wound the bandage around her calf. He looked back at Decker and scowled; he was sitting back, fiddling with his laptop, all but ignoring them. What was wrong with him lately? Okay, so he had some issues with this place to work through, but ignoring a friend in need – an injured one at that – really stretched the limits of his sympathy.

"What's up with him?" Mags murmured.

"Oh, nothing a good slap upside his head couldn't cure," Paul replied. Mags laughed, which made Paul feel better. If she could laugh, then everything would be okay.

He finished dressing the wound and helped Piers lug her tanks back to their makeshift station whilst Yolanda offered her arm as a crutch. Mags smiled, but declined the offer, and instead hobbled back up herself. Decker barely raised his eyes from his screen as they approached and Paul had to stop himself from slamming the equipment down in front of him out of sheer annoyance.

"You got the footage?" Decker asked. Piers shot him a look.

"Yeah – good stuff, or at least I hope so." Piers unhooked the little camera clipped to the side of his mask and handed it to Decker, whilst Paul did the same for Mags. Decker didn't say anything else, just plugged it into his laptop.

"Aren't you going to say anything to Mags?" Paul asked.

"Mags?"

"She got bitten!" Paul fought down the urge to wrench the laptop from under Decker's fingers.

"Oh," said Decker.

"Oh? Is that all you're going to say?"

"It's all right, Paul… just leave it," Mags said. "It'll be fine. Feeling better already, actually. Let me rest it for a while and I'll be back underwater in no time."

Ever the optimist, Paul thought. Even though he was annoyed – no, make that bloody furious – with Decker, he couldn't help the warmth he felt for Mags bleeding through. She was one of the good ones, and no mistake.

"Okay – here we go," said Decker. He had the courtesy to offer Mags his seat, at least. They all crowded round the monitor as the slightly grainy footage flickered to life. At first it was like any other dive footage they'd shot – a wide expanse of greenish grey water, occasionally bordered by various water plants, which gradually darkened as they went deeper. So far, so normal.

That all changed when the church loomed out of the murk.

At first, no one spoke. No one breathed until Yolanda let out a low whistle.

"Wow, that has to be the creepiest thing I have ever seen."

Piers nudged Paul's back. "Told you, buddy. People are going to go nuts when they see this."

Neither age nor water had done anything to dull St Machan's majesty. Its Gothic carvings were still intact, if a little green from the algae that clung to them, and its unbroken spire swept upwards to pierce the surface that twinkled so far above them. Huge stained glass windows, miraculously still largely intact, were dark holes in the side of the buildings, their colours muted and turned shadowy by the depths. As Piers swam closer, the pitted surface of the limestone used to build this place betrayed its age. To Paul, the church wouldn't have looked out of place in Medieval saga, and wondered why such a magnificent structure had been allowed to be drowned. It seemed almost sacrilegious to him.

They watched in silence as Piers' camera swept back and forth, drinking in its silent grandeur. Occasionally the light would catch one of the windows and make it sparkle. You didn't need any form of lake monster down here to start a legend – the whole place was a legend. Just some commentary over the top and they were sorted.

"Whoa – what was that?" Yolanda pointed at the screen. Decker paused the footage and rewound a little, and all five of them craned forwards.

"There, there!" Yolanda exclaimed. "Just like Malcolm Allen said! Did you see it?"

Paul and Piers shared a look. It was good to see her finally getting in on the act, even if she was just misinterpreting shadows.

"Just something passing overhead," Decker said. He sounded bored, which only heightened Paul's annoyance with him. "See? Mags just swam into view. It would've been her shadow. Nothing else."

"Still, we might be able to use that as a probable hint at something being down there," Paul said, more to mollify Yolanda than anything else.

"You mean, lie?" Decker said, his tone dripping with sarcasm. "Gee, like we've never done that before…"

"Hey man, what has gotten in to you?" Piers said. "Ever since we got here, you haven't done anything but mope around-"

Decker snorted and stood up. He looked like he might say something, but instead shook his head and stalked off.

"What the fuck?" Piers asked.

"I don't know. Just leave it. Let me speak to him."

"And the footage?"

"It can wait for a moment. Give me five, okay?"

The others didn't look happy about it, but that didn't bother Paul much. What did bother him was Decker. They'd been together long enough for him to know something wasn't so much bothering him as eating him alive. He jogged after him, only to find him crouching at the base of a fir tree a few hundred yards away, his face in his hands. Was he... crying? The anger he had been nurturing since they'd come off the boat melted away, replaced by worry.

"Hey... you okay?" He knew it was lame, but what else was he going to say?

Decker snorted again and followed it with a small, disdainful laugh. "Yeah. I'm peachy. You?"

Paul crouched down beside him and peeled one of Decker's hands from his face. He laced his fingers through his, and gave his hand a squeeze.

"We don't have to stay here, you know," Paul said.

"Yes, we do."

"No, we don't. Not if you don't want to. Brandon... I thought it was bad enough yesterday, but today you're falling apart at the seams. I don't know what history you and this place have, but it isn't doing you any good-"

"Paul... please. Even I can see that footage is pure gold. We'd be stupid to leave now. Usually I would be jumping with the rest of you, but... but..." He trailed off.

"But what?" Paul asked gently.

Conflict battled across Decker's face. "Nothing."

"Nothing? Sure doesn't look like nothing from where I'm standing. Come on, Decks. If you can't tell me, who can you tell?"

Decker took in a deep breath and blew it out hard, as if he was psyching himself up for something big. He flexed his hand around Paul's fingers once, twice, three times, steeling himself as if for confession.

"You know I have family from this town, right?"

"Yeah. Your Dad's family."

"That's right. And you know my Dad died when I was seven, and since then I never went back because my Mam didn't get on with my grandmother."

"Yeah, you've told me all that before, even before all this lake monster shit started up."

"Right. Y'see... y'see..." he stopped and went to start again, but his mouth flopped open and shut like a fish taken out of water.

"Brandon... what is it? You obviously want to tell me, so why don't you just get it out there? It can't be that bad."

"Can't it?" Decker chuckled bitterly. "Paul… You know I said I hadn't told you about the legend of Dùisg a' Pheacaich because I thought it was a load of mis-remembered nonsense? Well, that's a lie."

"Oh." Paul paused, unsure of what to say next. "What's the truth, then?"

"I'd completely forgotten everything to do with this place. Oh, sure, I remembered the name because of my Dad, but the rest of it? If you'd asked me six months ago, I would've told you to stop being stupid. Because I hadn't just forgotten bits – I'd forgotten all of it. I suppose you could say I repressed it. I don't know, I'm no psychologist. But being here, being by the water…bits are coming back. Not much, but bits. And it isn't a nice feeling."

He paused to bite at the skin on the side of his free thumb. Paul didn't speak; he was right about it being a confession and he didn't want to break whatever personal demon Decker was trying to drive out.

"My Dad," he continued, eventually. "My Dad used to take me up here as a kid. We sat up there, on the cliff, over looking the water. I remember him warning me not to go near the lake. And I don't mean a 'because you can't swim for shit, son' thing, I mean a real, heartfelt plea. The loch scared him. And now I remember that it… it scares me, too. I'm sorry. It's irrational, but I can't help it. There, I've said it. I'm scared, Paul. I'm scared of this place."

Paul didn't know what to say to that. He disentangled his fingers and stood up, running a hand through his hair as he did so. This was something he felt Decker should be telling a shrink, not him. He knew he had unresolved Daddy issues, but boy, this was way out of his remit.

"I… I don't know what to say," he said. "Just that whatever you want to do, I'll go with it. I mean, we can go and, uh, get you someone to talk all this over with-"

"You mean a psychologist, don't you?" Decker asked. He sounded amused. Paul wasn't sure if that was a good sign or not.

"No – no, of course not. Well, okay, maybe. If these memories are causing you this much distress, then we can postpone the shoot, or pad out what we've got and use that – I mean, the footage of the church is nothing short of awesome-"

Decker smiled, derailing Paul.

"You're the sweetest, you know that?" he said. "Here's me, freaking out over something I half-remember from over twenty-five years ago and you're willing to chuck it all in just to make me happy. No... you're right. I'm being silly. Of course I am. Come on – let's go see the rest of that footage and get on with this. The sooner we get it sorted, the sooner we can get out of here – and the sooner you can cart me off to the nearest nut-house if you want to."

Decker straightened up, kissed Paul on the cheek and wandered back to the others. To a casual acquaintance, he might have looked happy; at peace, even. But Paul saw the slight hunch to his shoulders and the way he crammed his trembling hands into his pockets so no one would see the mess he'd chewed his fingernails into. He was trying to suppress his fear to make him happy, and that made Paul feel even more wretched. He glanced back over the loch and felt a powerful, conflicting tug. Fame and fortune were potentially buried there; everything he'd ever wished for. Everything *they'd* ever wished for. Could he throw all that away, based on Decker's nebulous fears?

He sighed. Once upon a time, he would have said yes, of course, no issue... but now they were here, faced with this dilemma, he wasn't so sure. Oh, yes, of course he'd made the offer, but that's what you did, wasn't it? You made the offer and hoped that your significant other would say no and you'd get your own way, guilt free. But it didn't feel guilt free. What kind of bastard was he to make the one who was supposed to mean everything to him go through this?

Round and round the arguments swirled, churning Paul's guts until he felt physically sick. He trudged after Decker, no closer to an answer.

o0o

It was a testament to their shared friendship that no one said anything – not even Yolanda – when Paul and Decker joined them again.

"Right," said Piers, gesticulating at the screen. That he was now talking with his hands betrayed his excitement. "This is where it all gets really fucking interesting,"

They all crowded around the screen. No one spoke as the footage sparked up again. Video-Piers now swam closer to one of the windows. It didn't blink silver at him, which indicated it was probably broken. He looked back and caught a glimpse of Mags floating behind him, recording his progress. A raised thumb appeared just in front of the lens. Mags reciprocated.

He turned back and swam over to the opening. The glass was long-gone and the hole it left more than enough to allow him to enter. He paused – Paul guessed this was when he tried to convince him to let him enter – and instead just took a good, long look at everything in the room.

Paul craned his head further. This was it. The interior. Just as Piers had said, the room was huge – much larger than he had anticipated. As far as he could see, the pews had been torn out, as had the cloisters, creating a massive space. At the centre sat a slab of black stone, covered in what looked like graffiti. Upon this altar was one, solitary thing. It was small, too small to make out at this distance, and it looked like it was... flickering? It was too dark to tell against the black of the altar, but whatever it was, Paul couldn't take his eyes off it – and judging by the way Piers was filming, neither could he.

Suddenly, the camera whipped around. This was it, Paul thought. This was when the signal had failed. The limitations of their equipment meant they had no sound and so could not hear their conversations, but his mind filled in the rushing sound of water as Piers frantically searched the area for whatever it was Mags had seen. But it was gone; Piers had not captured it.

Good job Mags probably had.

No one wasted time speculating what that thing on the altar might be. That could come later. Now, all anyone wanted to see was what Mags had captured. Paul fought the desire to tell Decker to fast forward through their descent, but knew it was unprofessional – what if they missed something? – and so they sat through an agonising minutes of near-identical footage until Mags hung back when Piers swam ahead to investigate the broken window.

The church lost none of its imposing magnificence on a second viewing, and Paul found himself jumping at every shadow, every ripple. Was it there? Were the tales true? If they could prove it... Jesus... He daren't let himself think of the consequences, but visions of fast cars and expensive holidays still intruded on his thoughts, driving out Decker's fears and his own dilemma. Had someone slowed the footage? It seemed to creep past as Mags continued to watch Piers, her view shifting every now and again as she drifted on an unseen current-

"There!" Mags exclaimed and jabbed her finger at the screen.

Paul's heart leaped into his throat. Something dark hovered on the edge of Mags' vision.

"I didn't notice it at first," she said by way of explanation. "But-"

She didn't get to finish.

"What the hell is that?" Yolanda breathed.

No one answered her.

No one had a clue.

It was elongated, but indistinct. Like a snake in pain, it curled around itself; sometimes it even looked as if it poured *through* itself. The distorting effects of the water meant it was hard to tell how big it was as it hung there in the water, writhing, watching them.

Then, before anyone could look closer, it vanished.

"Could be... could be some kind of weird shadow pattern from the water's surface," Piers said, but he didn't look convinced.

"Back it up. Watch it again," Paul said, which Decker dutifully did.

On the second viewing, things, if anything, got weirder.

"I can't make out any actual solid structure to it," Paul said. "No head, no limbs... unless the... the wavy bits are limbs... but who knows?"

No one else said anything. What could they say? But whatever it was, they couldn't shake the feeling that it had been watching the divers. They watched it a further three times, rewinding, pausing, rewinding again, trying to pinpoint areas of recognition, to be able to slot it into a more comfortable place in their minds, but they couldn't. It wouldn't fit into any box; not fish, not reptile, mammal, even invertebrate. An awkward thought tapped Paul on the shoulder: *maybe Malcolm Allen was indeed telling the truth, after all...*

"We need to get more footage," said Piers. Paul nodded eagerly, but Mags shook her head and Decker simply went white.

"I... I don't know," Yolanda said. "I mean, yeah, more footage would cement our success here, but shouldn't we at least try to find out more about it? Maybe... maybe we should go and talk to Allen again. He might know something else. I mean, we have no idea what we're up against-"

"Exactly," Paul interrupted. "That's why we need more." That, and there was no way he was going to crawl back to Malcolm Allen; not yet, anyway. "Come on, you guys – we have real, proper, bona-fide footage of something truly weird living in this loch! This isn't hearsay, or... or some whack job's eyewitness account. This is real. It's there, and it's real! If we can get more, then no one will be able to question its authenticity." His eyes saucered as he finally allowed his dreams of riches to run riot. "Fucking hell, guys – this could be it. This could be the thing that makes us!"

"I don't know, Paul... going back in there feels foolish." Mags unconsciously scratched at the bandage on her leg. "Say that is a real entity and not just some trick of the light-"

"Come on, that's no trick of the light. You caught the footage yourself! You're the one who told us about it!"

"Yeah, I know, but even so, we're jumping to some pretty huge conclusions here. Doesn't anyone else feel it's all a bit convenient? How many times have we spent days filming and seen squat? Then we're here and kerching, one day in and we're seeing so-called proof-"

"What? You're complaining because we actually might have something this time?"

"No! No... more that it doesn't feel right. If it is the so-called monster and it is that easy to find, then why haven't other people?"

"Why haven't other people? Listen to yourself, Mags! No one else has found it because no one else has come looking. We have potentially found something special. It doesn't matter why we saw it – fate, divine intervention, Mars being in ascension or whatever – all that matters is it's there, we're here and we need to get back in there and see if we can track it down before we waste this golden opportunity that has been so kindly gifted to us."

"Yes, Paul, I take your point." Her tone turned clipped, and she stared at him the way a furious mother stares at an unruly child. "All I am saying is maybe some people," her eyes flickered towards Decker, "might like time to coordinate something a little more coherent than 'let's go back and hunt it down!!'"

Piers made to say something, but a swift nudge in the ribs from Mags shut him up.

Decker was staring at the ground. He might have said he was okay with all of this, but it was pretty clear now that he wasn't. He swallowed audibly and then looked up. "What are you guys looking at?"

"Uh, no one's looking..." Paul said. "We just want to know what you think. You're the nearest thing we have to an expert here. Do you think that's the creature, or something else?"

It took Decker a long while to gather his thoughts. All of them, even Piers, sat and waited politely for his response. The seconds stretched to the longest minute Paul had ever experienced. Then Decker sighed, long and drawn out, and ran a hand over his face.

"I... don't know. The part of me that fears the loch says 'hell no, this is something we shouldn't be messing with', but that part of me is, like, seven years old and I need to get a grip on that." He hesitated again, obviously steeling himself. "So... yeah. Let's go back down there. Let's hunt this sucker down and make us millions. Fuck it."

"Are you sure that's what you want, Decks?" Mags looked genuinely troubled by Decker's response. "Really? You're not just saying that to keep us all sweet, are you?"

"No – I mean it. Thanks for your concern and all, but it's like I said to Paul earlier – I've got to get over this. If there's something in this loch – and it now looks like there might be – it seems only fitting that I should be the one who has a part in uncovering it.

That bastard's given me nightmares for years – it's about time I got some pay back."

# chapter Twelve

They all agreed that the footage should be backed up multiple times, just in case, even though it meant they had to delay going back into the water until after lunch.

"I reckon that thing's lair is probably in the church," Piers said, through a mouthful of sandwich. "That's where we should start looking again. We can also go and get a closer look at that altar. There's definitely something going on there, too."

Paul nodded, but Mags said nothing, just kept picking at her sandwich, letting the crumbs fall into her lap.

"You not hungry?" Yolanda asked.

"No, not really. Must be, I don't know, nerves or something," Mags replied.

Paul frowned, and Decker looked up from his laptop.

"You look a bit pale," Paul said. "You feeling okay?"

"Yeah, yeah, I'm fine. Just not hungry." She bent over and scratched at the bandage again.

"Hey… do you need to see a doctor?" Yolanda said. "You've scratched that a few times now."

"No, no, I'm fine – the, you know, bite, or whatever it is, is fine. Really, it's okay. It's the dressing. I think I might be developing a sensitivity to Elastoplast, or something." Mags smiled weakly, and then as if to prove her point, took a massive bite out of her sandwich. "See, I'm fine. Seriously."

"I dunno, babe… maybe you should get it checked out," Piers said. "Not now, but later. You know how bites can be. Remember when Chuck got bitten by that rat? It was only a small one, but it went really nasty really quickly."

"What happened?" Yolanda asked.

"Not sure I should tell you when you're eating," Piers grinned. "But let's just say the physical bite isn't the issue – it's all the bacteria and crap that lives in its mouth that causes problems."

"Yeah, runny, pustular problems," Paul said.

"Eww." Yolanda made a face. "I don't think I need to know any details, thanks. But in the light of that, maybe you should get it checked out later, just to be on the safe side?"

Mags sighed. "Okay – I'm sure this place isn't so backwater that it doesn't have an on-call doctor's service. I'll ask Mrs Kelly when we get back. Does that satisfy your concerns?" She smiled, trying to make light of the situation, but everyone noticed the way her hand involuntarily made its way to worry at the wound again. She stopped herself just in time, and crammed more sandwich into her mouth.

"Yeah, that sounds fine," Paul said. "But one more thing – you're not diving this afternoon."

"What?" Mags was outraged. "You can't expect Piers to go down there alone. Anyway, I shot the footage, so I should get to be the one who goes looking-"

Paul held up a placatory hand. "Look, I know and I respect that, but going back into the water might worsen the wound. And yes, I know, the dressings are waterproof and yada yada yada, but I still don't want to risk it. If we can find a GP and they pronounce you fit, then tomorrow, by all means. But this afternoon, I'll go down with Piers. No arguments."

"But-"

"I said no arguments. You forget, I may not have half the hours you've clocked up, but that doesn't mean I'm a complete novice. I've done my fair share of wreck diving and I figure this is no different. Piers and I will go into the church – you can man the relay on the boat. We'll get some more footage and see if that... mass turns up again. Then we'll head back and get you seen to, okay?"

"Huh. Seen to? I'm not a dog, you know."

"Oh, I don't know..." Piers grinned. Mags kicked out at him with her good leg.

"Hey, guys – I'm just going to head back up to the Astra to store the back up and to put my laptop back on charge for a bit, okay?" Decker said.

"All right," Paul said. "You need help?"

"No, there's not a lot here. I left a couple of back-up cameras in the boot, so I'll fetch them, too. They should be all topped up and ready to rock."

"You left them in the boot? Why didn't you put them in the camper?"

"Because I'm not risking nearly a grand's worth of kit in something that doesn't lock properly." He smiled. "You enjoy your picnic. Let the man work."

At that, Piers let out a bark of laughter and turned his teasing on to Paul, with Mags heckling him. Yolanda watched them in bemused bafflement. Decker shook his head and grinned to himself. Whatever happened, they were good friends, and he should never forget that. Sure, they get a little over enthusiastic sometimes, but they'd never actively do anything to harm him. He had to trust that.

He shoved his kit into his rucksack and wandered back up the path to the car. The weak autumn sunlight dappled through the trees, painting the ground in shades of light and dark. Above him, a bird took flight, rustling the branches. His heart jumped and started to race and his childhood fear, the fear he had been trying to suppress all day, reared its head again. It was just a bird, he knew it was just a bird, so why did his mind try to populate this little bit of scrub with monsters from his childhood? He hoisted his pack higher on his shoulder and straightened his back, an arrogant gesture meant to instil some confidence, but no matter how much he tried, how hard he fought, the fear would not back down. To his shame, by the time he spied the Astra he was almost in tears. Seeing it did bolster him, though; the car was something solid, something normal, and the lump in his throat allowed itself to be swallowed down.

He dug his keys out of his pocket and unlocked it. The thunk of the mechanism rang out, making him jump again. Jesus, he really had to get a hold of himself. At this rate, he was going to have a heart attack before the weekend was over-

"Afternoon," a voice said from behind him.

Decker span around, his eyes wild, his heart thumping.

A policeman stood there.

"A...after... afternoon," He managed. He took note of the stripes on the policeman's epaulettes: a sergeant. "What are you doing here, Officer?"

"Well, I could be asking you the same question," said the sergeant. "This your vehicle?"

"Yes, it is," Decker replied.

"And may I ask what you're doing up here? Nothing much for tourists up here, so what you up to?"

"Nothing illegal, Officer." Jesus *Christ*, he wished his heart would calm down and let him think straight. "Just making a short documentary about the loch."

"Aye, that so? I'd heard as much." The sergeant proceeded closer to him. He was a man of middling height and older years, but there was something about his bearing that commanded respect. His uniform was also out of date by at least 20 years, so much so that he looked like something out of a prehistoric episode of The Bill. "I've been receiving complaints from the local inhabitants all morning of you people going around upsetting them. Say you want to cash in on the legend and aren't respecting their right to privacy."

"Right to privacy?" Decker was genuinely confused. "All we've done is asked a few questions. We've made it clear from the beginning exactly what we're doing – hell, we even brought contracts with us that people can sign beforehand so they know exactly what's expected of them, so I'm not really sure how we're upsetting people-"

The sergeant raised a hand to interrupt Decker. "Be as that may, I'm here to tell you this is going to stop. No permission was given for you to film here."

"No permission? Of course there's no permission – there's no one to ask! I researched it – no permit is needed because there simply isn't one to obtain."

"That's no' the point. If the local population doesn't like it, then it doesn't happen. I'm here to serve them, and they say it needs to stop, so I'm here to stop it."

"That's ridiculous. There is no law in this land that says we can't film here. You have no right-"

"Och, don't I now? You might think that, coming from whatever big fancy English city you hail from-"

"Big fancy English city?" Decker felt his anger rise through him like a plume of magma. "I'm actually a local, officer. I'm Sadie Decker's grandson, and John Decker's son. I was raised here – which is why we're filming here. I'm exploring my own roots, my own heritage."

"Aye. Tell me something I don't already know." The sergeant was calm in the face of Decker's wrath, which gave Decker cause to pause.

"You know? How do you know?"

"That isn't any of your business. All you need to know is that I know. I also know you left this town a boy of seven, which hardly gives you the right to trample down on the lives of people who've been here for more than seventy. So I'll ask you again, nicely. Pack up and leave. No more filming. And if you make any of this public, then be expecting an awful lot of solicitor's letters. People like their privacy around here. You need to respect that."

A million retorts pile-drove towards Decker's mouth, but sheer incredulity stopped him from spitting them out.

"So... what you're saying is we're being run out of town?"

The sergeant sniffed and rubbed the side of his nose with one finger. "Aye, I guess that is what is happening here. But it doesn't matter what you want to call it – either which way, you're to leave. Soon as possible. Do you understand?"

"No," Decker said. "I do not understand. We're not doing anything illegal, nor are we stirring up any trouble."

"Well then, I guess we have a problem," the sergeant said. He pulled his cap on his head and subtly squared his shoulders.

"I guess we do," said Decker. His stomach fizzed a little. He was standing up to the Filth. Wow. He'd never done that before. This was definitely one for the bar-bragging book.

"Okay. As long as we understand each other, Mr Decker. If you're wise, you'll move on. If not, then I guess I'll be seeing you later today when I bring the rest of the station down with me." He leaned forward so that his nose was just a hair's breadth from Decker's. His breath smelled of tea and stale cigarettes. "Please don't make it come to that" He leaned back and tipped his cap.

"I'll be leaving you now. Remember – be out of here by the time I get back."

"Or what?" Decker dared shoot back.

"Or else," the sergeant said.

oOo

For a moment, Paul was lost for words.

"Run that by me again?"

Decker sighed and ran a hand over his face. "The copper said we've got the afternoon to clear out. Well, no, not the afternoon as he didn't specify an actual time frame, but he wants us out of town asap."

"On what grounds do they think they can do this? I mean, all we have to do is run to the press. We could make some real trouble for them if they do this," Yolanda said. "Why bother threatening us? Wouldn't it just be easier to ignore us and hope we just go away?"

"Not if you've got something to hide," said Mags, and gave them all a significant look.

Yolanda inclined her head towards Mags. "True. But even so, they don't know we've potentially found anything."

"Well, that kind of makes sense," Mags said. "At the moment, they think we're just a bunch of hacks after a story. They probably reckon we haven't been out here long enough to uncover anything and so want us out before we can do any real damage."

"But that's just stupidly over the top," Paul said. "Threatening Decker like that? Why bother? It's incendiary behaviour. Local policemen acting like thugs and all. The police have had enough bad press recently as it is. Why risk more?"

"This isn't London, Paul," Decker said. "I seriously doubt they care up here. It's also my word against his and I'm guessing he knows it."

"But they don't have any right to do this," Paul said. "There are no laws that prevent us from being here. This isn't private property. We checked. No permit to dive was needed. Sure, that might simply be because no one has ever thought of diving up here, but it still stands. No court in the land would uphold this."

"I don't think that's an issue around here, Paul," Decker said. He sounded tired. "Small isolated communities like this one operate by their own laws. They don't give a damn about what comes out of Holyrood, let alone Whitehall. Up here, whatever the sergeant says, goes. Mark my words. They will be back."

"Then we'd better get into the water as soon as we can," said Piers. He'd been unusually quiet during the exchange. "We get out there, we get into that church, we get the footage and then we scarper. We'll be well away in a couple of hours. There's nothing they can do about it. They won't even know where to find us.

To this, everyone but Decker nodded.

"Is it worth moving? That way, they won't know where we are. Might buy us some time," said Yolanda.

"I'm not sure that will actually help us," Paul said. "We've got, what, an hour or so before the good old Sarge calls in the cavalry and hightails it back here? If we get back into the water now, we can do a good half hour dive. That gives us plenty of opportunity to explore the church and get some more interior footage. After that, we can just pack up and go. If we pack up and move now, we're looking at, what, quarter of an hour to pack up, then half an hour's drive, then unpack and dive? Just to buy us a little more 'catch me if you can' time? I don't think it's worth it."

"Then there's the fact that they probably know these roads like the back of their hands," Piers added. "What takes us half an hour to find will take them ten minutes. Let's just get in the water, shoot the interior footage and then get the fuck out. Don't look back."

"And our stuff at the guesthouse?" Yolanda asked.

"Paul offered her a shrug. "I don't know about you, but there's nothing there I'm particularly attached to. I can always buy a new toothbrush."

"Speak for yourself," Yolanda said. "I've got an iPad back there. They're not cheap, you know."

"Don't you worry, sweetheart. I'll buy you a gold plated one once this footage goes viral," Piers grinned. "Come on, what are we waiting for? Let's shut up and get in!"

o0o

Mags still wasn't too happy at being the one left in the boat, but didn't kick up a fuss given their time constraints. In a matter of minutes, Paul had his suit on and they were motoring out to the centre of the loch again.

Even through his wetsuit, Paul felt the thrill of the cold water. Visibility was still good which allowed him to find his bearings quickly. He kicked off after Piers, who was swimming as if someone had strapped a rocket to his back. They'd agreed that they had enough locale footage and so didn't bother with wasting any time obtaining any more of that, which was a bit of a shame. Home to a terrifying demon-thing or not, the loch was a beautiful place: clear water with an abundance of weed, the light from above dappling through both to make everything look like it had been gilded. As before, the only thing lacking was any real presence of wildlife. In Paul's experience, even the grottiest of pools still had fish in them and so to look upon this wondrous vista and not spy the odd flash of silver felt strange to him.

Paul's heart kicked up a gear as they swam closer to the chasm the church was nestled in. It yawned wide below him, a deep slash in the earth. Compared to the almost airy expanse of water behind him, this felt forbidden; wrong, even. The change in temperature raised gooseflesh through the thick neoprene of his suit, and he couldn't help but let out a gasp. Mags chuckled in his earpiece, but she couldn't disguise the nervous twang to her voice when she quipped, "Scared?"

"A little," he admitted.

"That's going to be on tape, you know," she said.

"Yeah, I know. To our viewers – yeah, this is real, and yeah, I'm shaking in my boots out here. And that's the reason why. Would you look at that..."

Even though he'd seen the church on the screen, nothing could prepare him for this. The footage simply didn't do it justice. Piers swam straight over to the broken window, but Paul took a moment to hang motionless in the water and stare. It would've been impressive standing out there in the fresh air, but down here, under the water, the whole thing took on an almost mystical edge.

"They don't build 'em like that any more, huh?" Mags said.

"You're right there," Paul agreed. "They do not."

With Piers out of sight, Paul shook himself out of his awestruck stupor and picked up the pace. Swimming through the broken window proved a cinch – it was easily as large as a conventional door, and all of Paul's previous anxiety about being snagged, or worse, trapped evaporated away.

It took him a moment to adjust to the gloom of the church's interior, and again he was blown away by the sheer size of the place. When Decker had first told him about it, he'd pictured a quaint little countryside chapel; in reality, St Machan's was easily the grandest he'd seen outside of the city, and even then, it gave some of them a run for their money. He couldn't help but stop and wonder why such an impressive structure had been built here, way out in the middle of nowhere. Even back in the day this area had been a backwater, so why spend all that money to build something so... so... *huge*? He felt a little embarrassed at resorting to such a lame description, but he really was lost for words. Even if the legend turned out to be grade A bullshit, this place was a gift. No, it was more than that. It was a lottery win.

Small particles of matter swirled in the dark water as he swam through it, reflecting the light of his headlamp, filling the room with little sparkling motes. Now he was physically there, Paul could see all the little details Pier's footage hadn't picked up. He looked down over the room, carefully angling his head so his camera would catch everything: the pews might have been ripped out, but the statues, hidden from casual view in their dark niches, hadn't. They still posed piously, their once-angelic expressions worn away first by time, then by water. Paul swam over to the nearest one, entranced. As he drew closer, he realised its face wasn't so much worn as obliterated deliberately, replaced by something far more sinister. Deep grooves ran vertically over its lips, cut into the form of crude teeth, and its eyes had been hacked out. Instead, a large central orb had been carved into its forehead, flanked on each side by four smaller circles so that they wrapped around the statue's head until they almost touched its ears. Each circle has a vertical line cut into them, slashing through like the pupil of a cat's eye. He reached up to touch it, tracing his gloved fingertips over the grooves.

"Nine eyes..." he murmured to himself.

"What?"

Paul jerked his hand back, his heart skittering around his ribcage. A thick plume of bubbles erupted as his breathing quickened, floating up to the hidden ceiling. He'd forgotten Mags was listening. "Nothing," he said. "Just some weird modifications to the statues. You'll see when you watch the footage."

A flicker of movement below him caught his attention, but it was only Piers.

"You okay, buddy?" Piers asked. His voice sounded strange – tight and slightly higher than normal, and it wasn't just down to the mask. Piers was excited... and something else.

"Yeah, I'm fine. Have you see this?" Paul said. "Why would they do this? What does it all mean?"

"I don't know, but I think they're all like it. Nine eyes and mad teeth."

"Do you think it might be a cult thing?"

"Another thing you assumed that Malcolm Allen bloke was lying about, eh? Maybe we should go back and have another chat with him."

"Maybe we should do the same with your mad old bloke," Paul shot back.

"Yeah... maybe. Anyway I'm just about to go and take a look at the altar. You coming?"

"Oh. I thought you might already have done that," Paul said.

"No... no, not yet." Again, Piers voice thickened and Paul realised he'd misjudged him – Piers wasn't excited at all. He was frightened. But why? Last dive, that was all he had been interested in. So what had changed? "Come on. We don't have time for this. Let's go look and then get the hell out of here before Deputy Dawg gets back."

Paul swam down after him, marvelling at the church's state of preservation. Besides the vandalised statues, the place was almost pristine; they could drain this reservoir, dry this place out and hold sermons within a month, he was sure of it.

Still they continued down.

Surely they'd reach the altar soon. Paul peered ahead, through the gloom. The particles still hung there, unmoving even as he swam through them like tiny pinpricks of projected light.

They still swam.

Paul's brows drew together. Surely this wasn't right. They'd been swimming down now for a good minute now. The floor didn't go down that far. It couldn't have done. From Piers' footage, they'd been able to see the altar from the broken window.

He stopped, hanging in the twinkling water.

"Did you see the altar when we swam in?" he asked Piers.

"What?" Piers stopped and looked back.

"When we saw your footage from the previous dive, you could clearly see the layout of this room, with the altar in the centre. I don't remember seeing it when we entered. My attention was on the statues. Did you see it?"

"No," Piers said.

"No? But... but you went straight down. That was what you were interested in."

"Yeah. I… know."

The stream of bubbles that emanated from Piers mask told Paul everything he needed to know. He had tried to swim down to investigate, but couldn't find it. This was it. The thing that had bothered him. A tightness grew around Paul's jaw and crawled up the sides of his skull, making him feel dizzy. He fought off the desire to shake his head and peered down.

He still couldn't see the bottom.

"This isn't right," he said.

"I know," Piers said.

"What's going on?"

"How would I know?" He raised a hand to the side of his mask. "Hey, Mags? You still there?"

There was no reply.

Now the tightness seized Paul's throat. "Mags?" he croaked. "Mags? Are you there? Please reply."

"Mags!" Piers all but yelled.

There was still no reply.

"That relay has a good five hundred foot range on it," Paul said. "I should know, I paid for it. This loch, whilst deep, isn't five hundred feet deep. She should be able to hear us. She should be able to reply-"

"Hey, man – calm down," Piers broke in. They were treading water now, hanging in a black void, their headlamps the only light source. Even the little motes had disappeared. Panic gave Paul's throat another little squeeze. They weren't that deep – even inside, there should be something, some illumination, something filtering down. He dared to glance up.

Nothing.

"What the... Piers. Piers, look up. Where's the church?" He had to force the words out now. "What is going on? Just what the fuck is going on?"

"Some kind of light anomaly," Piers said. He was trying to sound calm, but his rapid breathing gave away his true feelings. "Remember, we're in a building, so light won't necessarily filter in-"

"Light won't necessarily filter in? What do you mean? It's pitch black up there! No... no, we have to go now, get back up... something is not right, not right at all. Fuck this. That altar wasn't so far away. Hell, we could see it from the window! We need to get back to that and find our bearings. We need to know where we are."

Something deeper than mere instinct drove Paul on. It had been his idea to go down here again, but now he was here, every bit of him screamed to get out. He kicked up, hoping he'd soon see something familiar, a carving, a part of the crenelated balustrade that ran around the raised gallery, even one of those defaced statues, anything that would allow him to find his bearings, but with each powerful kick of his legs, all he found was more darkness.

Panic bubbled through him, spreading to every part of him. He was lost. But how could he be lost? Sure, the church was big, but it wasn't *that* big. He should have been able to swim across it in under a minute. Same went from floor to ceiling. He kicked again, muttering to himself, hoping that someone, anyone, would reply, but the relay remained stubbornly silent.

Something brushed up against his leg and he screeched. It echoed around his mask, intensifying it to the point of pain. He kicked out, randomly, wildly, trying to shake off imagined fingers of grasping unseen horrors, but it crept up his leg and managed to catch hold of a tiny fold in his wetsuit. His heart, already in high gear, kicked up a notch and he felt as if he might faint.

"Paul…"

*Oh god, oh Christ, oh shitting fuck, it didn't only have hold of him, it knew his name…*

"P-Paul…"

Paul gibbered under his breath, twisting and turning, trying to shake off the thing that ensnared him. He batted at his leg the way he might a sudden spider, all panicky jerks and disgust, but it held on, dragging him down, down again into the indeterminate depths.

"P-Paul… please…"

He looked down, frantically scrabbling at his leg for his knife, but he stopped when he realised the horror was, in fact, Piers.

Piers' face was white behind his mask, his eyes staring. He'd managed to grasp Paul's suit with one hand; the other dangled, useless, behind him.

After that, Paul had no idea what he was looking at.

Whether it was because he couldn't work out what had ensnared Piers due to him not being able to see it properly or whether it was because he simply couldn't – or wouldn't – comprehend it, he'd never know. The darkness had gathered beneath them, or more correctly, gathered beneath Paul, for Piers was half consumed. Tendrils of black oil crawled over him, boiling around him, slithering over his skin until nothing but blackness remained. Below Piers, a sense of pressure built and Paul thought he caught a fragmentary glimpse of a huge eye, dull red in colour with an elliptical pupil staring up at him before the seething mass of its dark, incorporeal form subsumed it again.

Panic now turned to white-hot terror. Paul lost all sense of propriety, all sense of loyalty, and tore Piers' fingers away from his suit. Piers' eyes widened even further at this final betrayal, this final act of self-preservation, before he was yanked back into the blackness below.

Time stood still. Nothing moved, and reality took on a brittle quality. Paul hung in the void, his breath coming out in short, sharp bursts that made his chest hurt. Then the water around him began to vibrate, and something floated up beside him.

A diver's mask.

Piers' mask.

That shattered the spell. Paul kicked up and kicked hard, away from the building sense of pressure below, away from the shadowed creature that laired there. He had no idea if he was going in the right direction; what as important now was 'away'. The vibrations increased the pressure around him until his ears sang and his nose popped, but he still swam. Up, up, up, never stopping. That was important. Must never stop. Ever.

He felt like he'd been swimming for hours as his supply of fear-induced adrenaline ran low. How deep had they been? But such questions had to wait. He couldn't stop, not now, not when his life depended on it. He struggled up, praying he was going the right way until finally, a tiny shaft of light filtered down. There, at last, was a beacon of hope. Using the last of his reserves, he kicked hard. His head broke through the miasma into the interior of the church. He was near the bottom – the floor should only have been a foot or so below him. Instead, a deep chasm yawned wide – and whatever dwelt there was rushing up, rushing up to drag him back down and never let him go. He could feel it, feel something huge gathering in the black waters beneath him. He looked up, frantically searching for the broken window, which was just eight feet above him. Relief flooded through him. At last, he knew where to go! He tried to claw his way up, but something snagged his foot, dragging him down, trying to drown him in darkness.

He thrashed his legs, trying to shake it off, and bolted for the window. He felt a moment of resistance as the matter twined around his ankle stretched, then broke and he shot upwards and out of the church.

"-ere the fuck are you? For God's sake – say something!" Mags' terrified voice almost deafened him. Paul winced, his teeth gritted against the sudden sonic barrage.

"It's okay! I'm here," he panted as he careened upwards, away from the church and towards the murky light of the surface.

"Paul! Oh my god, Paul... what happened? Why didn't you respond?" Mags said, her voice thick.

"I... I..." A huge sob welled up within him. "Oh, Mags... He's gone. Lost. Piers is... gone."

"Gone? What do you mean, gone?"

"I don't... I can't..." His body sagged. Everything felt very heavy and all he wanted to do was stop swimming; stop moving; stop everything.

"Just get up here," Mags said. "I'll try Piers' radio again."

Wearily, Paul forced his legs to move. He didn't bother to correct her. She'd find out soon enough.

From under the water, the boat was easy enough to see. It sat on the glassy surface, a dark bruise on an otherwise flawless complexion. He struck out for it, not daring to look back. Whatever had tried to ensnare him wasn't following, he was sure of that, but looking back felt like tempting fate. He didn't protest when Mags hauled him on board; he just lay there, exhausted whilst she pulled his mask off. The air planted a chilly kiss upon his wet skin, but he didn't care.

"Where's Piers?" she asked.

"No time," Paul said. "We have to go. Get off the water. Get off the water before... before..."

"Before what? Paul, where's Piers?"

Paul stared up at here. Hadn't she heard him? He staggered to his knees and yanked at the motor's cord, but no matter how hard he pulled, he couldn't make it fire. Tears ran unchecked down his face. Why wouldn't it fire? He pulled it again, grimacing when he felt something in his shoulder pop.

"Paul! Where is Piers?"

"No, we need to get away... why won't it go? Don't just sit there – help me!"

She gave him an angry hiss and took the cord from him. One, hard yank and the motor sputtered to life. Paul fell back into the boat. At last, they could leave.

"What happened down there?" Mags said. All anger had fled her; only naked fear was left.

He didn't reply. He *couldn't* reply. How could he? He didn't know what had happened. How was he supposed to even begin explaining it to someone who hadn't been there?

"Paul... seriously. You have to tell me. What happened? Where is Piers?"

Paul shook his head. He tried to piece things together, to find a way of expressing just what he had experienced, but once again came up empty.

"I don't know," he croaked.

"What do you mean, you don't know?" Mags said, her anger returning. "You're supposed to know. That's why we dive in pairs, so we can look after each other. That's the whole point. You were with him, ergo, you know. So I'll ask you again, Paul. Where is Piers?"

Tears welled in his eyes again. "I... I don't know. We were in the church... and... and..."

"And what?" Mags' face flushed red.

"It got him," Paul sobbed. He couldn't help it. He wasn't usually one for tears, but he simply couldn't stop them from flowing. "We dived down, down so we could take a look at the altar, but things... things *changed.* It's deep. Deeper than you think. Deeper than it should be. And then it went dark, and it rose up and... and... it *engulfed* him."

"Wait... what? What do you mean? What engulfed him?"

"It did," Paul whispered. "The... the darkness. The *creature.* In the church. Only there is no bottom. It's endless, and it lives in it. It took Piers." Paul reached up and grasped the front of Mags' life jacket. "It took him. I tried to... it... I couldn't... It took him! It took Piers!"

"No. That's... that's madness. You're mad. You can't have been looking out for him properly." Mags' eyes were wild in disbelief. "We need to go find him – there'll be enough air in those tanks to sustain him for another twenty minutes-"

"Mags, you have to believe me. You have to listen." Just the thought of her entering the water again made Paul feel sick. "You can't go in there. You said it yourself – there's something wrong here. You were right. We have to get away, as far as we can."

"But, Piers-" Mags' eyes glittered with tears.

"If I thought for one moment there was a chance for him, I'd be down there like a shot. But there isn't. I saw it take him. I saw...

saw it..." He swallowed hard. "I saw. He's gone, Mags. And so will we be, if we don't get the fuck off this loch."

She glanced back to St Machan's spire peeking above the surface of the water. It looked peaceful; idyllic almost, ready to lull other unsuspecting visitors into a false sense of security. Paul shuddered. Mags' attention remained on the church, and for a heart-stopping moment, he thought she might ignore him and jump in the water. Instead, she closed her eyes and nodded. He let out an exhausted sigh and lay back as she kicked the boat's little motor up a gear and guided it back to shore. He risked a quick peek over the side only once and shuddered as the surface of the water sparkled back at him. Behind them, the church spire dwindled into the distance until it was once again more than a speck.

A frown creased Mags' brow as the shore drew closer still. Paul did not look up; adrenaline debt had left him as weak as a kitten.

"What is it?" he mumbled.

"Blue lights," Mags said. "Up there."

"Blue lights?" Paul forced himself to sit up and followed her line of sight. Sure enough, in the distance, a blue light strobed through the trees.

"Shit," he said.

"Yeah. That's one way of putting it. How did they get back so quickly?"

"The sergeant must've already had them on alert." Paul buried his face in his hands. "How could we be so stupid. We should have left straight away. We should have just packed up and got out of here when we had the chance."

"Paul, what are we doing to do? How do we explain..." She trailed off, reluctant to say it out loud.

"I don't know. I don't think there is anything we can do."

Mags steered the little boat in the natural cove with ease. Yolanda and Decker made to run to them, but two burly police officers held their arms out and stopped them.

"Paul!" Decker yelled out, his voice cracking. "What's going on? What happened out there? *Paul!*"

Paul took in a shuddering breath and tried to compose himself. Forget the police. They didn't bother him, not really. How was he going to explain this to Decker? They'd been friends with Piers for years. Hell, he'd even been instrumental in getting them together. He'd introduced them to Mags. Now he had to explain that Piers – wonderful, vital Piers – was gone, out of their lives forever.

Mags didn't say anything as she helped haul him upright. She couldn't even bring herself to look at him. It took all of his strength to clamber out of the boat and stumble through the shallows. All he wanted to do was allow Decker to wrap his arms around him and tell him everything was going to be okay, but he was denied even that small comfort.

"Now then. What's going on here?" the Sergeant said. "I thought I told you people to move along. Now it looks like I have been given no other choice but to take you all in."

"Fuck you," Paul mumbled.

"Pardon me?" the Sergeant said.

"I said, 'fuck you'."

"Paul, that doesn't help," Mags said.

"I don't care." Paul said.

"Where's Piers?" Decker asked.

Paul could tell by the tension in his body that all Decker wanted to do was run to him, but the policeman stood next to him held his hand just close enough to his baton to stop him from doing so. Bitter bile stung the back of Paul's throat and fresh tears blinded him as he shook his head. He didn't have to say anything else.

"No…" Decker whispered.

Paul simply nodded. Beside him, Mags sniffed and let out a small but desperate sob.

"Now, you people better be telling me what's going on here," the Sergeant said. "I was told there was five of you – two lasses, three lads. Now there's only four of you. Where's the other one?"

"I don't know," Paul whispered.

"What's that? You best speak up."

"I said, I don't know. We… we went for one last dive. We were going to pack up and leave, I swear, but we just wanted some more footage. That's all."

The Sergeant's expression hardened. "More footage? You risked everything for more bloody footage?"

A furious heat erupted in Paul's chest, but Mags jumped in before he could gather his thoughts and form a response that wouldn't get him arrested on the spot.

"Risk? What do you mean, risk? Decker said we had to leave because people didn't appreciate us being here. No mention of risk." She squared up to the Sergeant. "Are you telling us you knew something like this might happen?"

"I think you need to calm down, lass," the Sergeant said. You could have bent iron around his tone. "We still don't know what's happened here. But your... friend here was about to tell us, weren't you, 'friend'? So why you keep nice and quiet and let the laddie speak."

There was no disguising the disgust Paul felt towards the Sergeant. His mouth puckered in a sneer, and it took everything he had not to launch himself at him and wipe the smug look straight off the Sergeant's face. Instead, he satisfied himself by clenching his fists and fixing him with his best glower.

"Mags has a point," Paul said. "No one said anything about 'risks'."

"It's just a turn of phrase," the Sergeant said. "Nothing more. Now, I'm asking you one last time. What has been going on here?"

The fight fled Paul like someone blowing out a candle. What was the point? He dropped his mask. Someone nearby dodged forward to catch it, but he didn't register who. He gave long, defeated sigh and raked his fingers through his still-damp hair.

"Piers is gone. I don't know where. We dived into the church and this... this *shadow* rose up. I didn't even realise what was going on at first, but something in the darkness pulled him down." He paused to swallow. "I don't know what happened to him. But I never saw any hint of him again."

Well, apart from his mask floating up, he added to himself, but for some reason he didn't want to admit that to the Sergeant.

"Didn't you look for him?" It was Yolanda who spoke, her dark eyes wide with shock.

"Of course I did," Paul said. "Well, I tried to... but then I saw... I saw..."

"You saw what?"

This was the question he'd been dreading. He had no idea how to even begin answering it. How could he? He didn't have the words to describe it; no one did. Human vocabulary just didn't stretch that far or delve that deep.

"I don't know," Paul whispered. "I don't know what it was. I can't describe it. There was... darkness. No, not darkness. More than darkness. It was like being in a black, empty space. And then I saw something red – maybe an eye? But it was huge. Then I felt... vibrations. A sense of pressure. All I knew was that I had to get the hell out of there."

Next to him, Mags' breath hitched. Paul looked up. She was crying again.

"So... what you're saying is, he's dead?" Decker asked. His voice had a hollow quality to it. Paul shrugged.

"I guess so. I can't see how he would've survived."

"Sounds like you lads bit off more than you could chew down there," the Sergeant said. "Why do you think no one comes up here? It's disorientating down there." He shook his head sadly. "And now you've lost your friend because you people can't do as you're told."

Mags stared at the Sergeant, her reddened eyes blazing. "It's disorientating?" she said. "You think that's all that went wrong down there? That he got disorientated? Piers isn't a tourist. He's an experienced diver. He's been down on reefs, in lakes, in caves... this would've been a piece of piss for him."

"Over confidence kills, Miss," the Sergeant said.

"Over confidence? Seriously? You have got to be kidding me! Diving in a simple building like that – it's only one room, for Christ's sake! That's beginner stuff compared to what Piers is used to. There's no way he would've got lost, or... or..." she trailed off. "Why are you guys looking at each other like that? What's going on here?"

The Sergeant sniffed and gave his fellow officers a little nod.

"You said it yourself. This would've been an easy dive for him. Leaves us with only one course of action."

Paul's head snapped up. "What do you mean?"

"I'm sorry, but you were warned. And now the worst has happened. This isn't something we can ignore. We can't make it just go away. You're all going to have to come with me."

"But… but… no!" Paul said. He stood up and the two constables took a threatening step towards him. He raised his hands, more out of instinct than showing he wasn't a threat. "No, we have to call someone, get someone in, someone who can go and… go and find-"

"Find what?" the Sergeant asked. "Your friend's corpse?" He gave Paul a calculating look. "But maybe you already know where that is, hmm? It's like your friend here said – it was an easy dive for him."

It took Paul a few moments for him to realise what the Sergeant was insinuating. "Excuse me? Are you really saying what I think you're saying? That I… that I… did something to Piers?"

"It's an avenue of investigation we will have to pursue," the Sergeant said.

"You're insane!" Mags leapt to Paul's defence. It didn't escape Paul's notice that Decker remained silent and he shot him a vicious look. He would have at least expected him to stick up for him. Instead, Decker was staring at the ground, looking pale. No… that wasn't right. He was starting at the ground, looking terrified. Beside him, Mags continued to rage.

"I can't believe this. I can't believe you'd think that. Piers was Paul's best friend – they've worked together for years, built all this up together…"

All the way through her rant, the Sergeant kept quiet. The two constables shot him occasional questioning looks, like two dogs seeking their master's permission to attack, but the Sergeant's eyes never left Paul. What was he looking for? Some glimmer of guilt? A twitchy mouth that might give him away? He didn't know, but he was damned if he was going to be intimidated by it. Instead, he stared right back, determined not to give the good Sergeant the satisfaction. Finally, Mags began stumbling over her words as her fury ran out of steam. Fresh tears sprung to her eyes. They might have split up because Piers was a lousy boyfriend, but that didn't mean she'd stopped caring about him. He had still been her friend.

"Okay now, lass – have you finished?" The Sergeant sounded bored. "I can understand your strength of feeling, I really can, but you've got to see this from our point of view."

"What point of view is that?" Paul said, icily. "That the loch is a dangerous place for out-of-towners, or that you think I might have taken this opportunity to drown a dear friend?"

The Sergeant's face turned to stone. He raised a hand and flicked his fingers towards them. His officers sprang forward like eager rottweillers, pulling their cuffs off their belts as they went. The Sergeant then pulled his out own pair and forcibly turned Paul around.

"You do not have to say anything," he said as he snapped the cuffs on Paul's wrists. "But anything you do say will be taken down and may be given in evidence-"

"Hey, hey! I can't believe you're doing this! What is the charge? What the hell are you doing?"

Next to him, Mags started struggling.

"Miss, I really wouldn't do that if I were you." The smile on the constable's face said he was enjoying this more than he should be; Paul guessed they didn't get much in the way of trouble out here, so the chance to play the Big Cop was something he welcomed.

"Mags – calm down. There's no point,"

"But we haven't done anything!" Mags said.

"Oh, really?" the Sergeant said. "Trespassing; diving without permission; a missing person, presumed dead... Put yourself in my shoes. Would you let me just walk away?"

He had a point and judging by the scowl Mags shot at him, she could see it, too. The second constable finished handcuffing Yolanda. Decker had actually turned around and offered up his wrists like a lamb to the slaughter. Soon, the four of them were traipsing up the wooded path toward three ancient police cars.

"What about our equipment?" Decker asked in a dull voice. Paul couldn't help but feel a little hurt. He'd said nothing to support him, but worried about his kit.

"Don't you fret about your toys," the Sergeant said. "We'll pack them up. They're evidence now."

Evidence? Paul glanced at Decker, but he was still staring at the ground. He snapped his attention to Mags. Judging by the look she shared with him, the same thought had crossed her mind.

Was this all about getting hold of their footage?

He stole one, last look at the loch. Its surface was as calm as ever. A bird soared above it; some kind of bird of prey, given its size. Above it, the clouds coiled upwards into meringue-like peaks. Everything looked perfect – too perfect.

As if taunting him, the water churned and a dark shadow bloomed on its surface. Paul's heart thudded heavily in his chest as something emerged and rolled slickly over. As quickly as it appeared, it slid back down into the depths, leaving the loch as smooth as glass once more.

He didn't mention it to the Sergeant, though.

He had a feeling the Sergeant already knew.

# chapter thirteen

Sergeant O'Toole pinched the bridge of his nose and sat down behind his desk.

This was something he really didn't need.

His hand hovered over the telephone.

Should he call her?

Well, of course he should call her. It was his duty to. He'd sworn to that when he'd taken charge of the station. But if he called her, he'd have to explain what those idiots had been up to and why he hadn't stopped them. And that was something he really wasn't looking forward to. To put it bluntly, he'd fucked up... and she didn't tolerate fuck ups. She couldn't afford to.

But what would happen if he didn't tell her? Those stupid townies had woken it up early. Yes, he knew the time was coming; he'd seen the portents and had the dreams, but they weren't anywhere near ready to deal with it. And to top it off, they'd fed it. He ran a trembling hand over his face. Although he knew he'd have to deal with this at some point soon, he hadn't thought for one second this was how it would go.

It was no good. He picked up the phone and dialled. It rang a few times before it was picked up.

"Yes?"

"It's happened. You'd better come down here."

"Come down? Now why would I need to do that?"

"Because..." he took in a deep, steadying breath. "Because it's awake. They woke it up."

The voice on the other line fell silent, but Sergeant O'Toole didn't dare fill it.

"I thought I told you to move them on?"

"I know. I tried to. But they..."

"But they, what?"

"But they ignored me. I'm sorry, Sadie, I really am. I was trying not to raise suspicion-"

"Not to raise suspicion? They're already suspicious. That's why they're here. So they woke it?"

"Yes."

"How?"

This was the one question O'Toole dreaded above all others. He swallowed hard, as if that would steady his voice and calm his nerves.

"Diving. They were... diving. In the church."

"Diving?" The flat tone of her question made Sergeant O'Toole wince. "In the church? I see."

"It, uh, it gets worse," he said.

"Worse, you say? Worse than trespassing in its lair? And what could be worse than that? Unless you mean..."

She didn't have to say it. He knew exactly what she meant. He found himself nodding, even though she couldn't see him, his eyes closed, his heart pounding.

"I see," she repeated. "Call a village meeting. We need to deal with this now. We can't risk waiting until the meddlers are dealt with. Where are they now?"

"Locked up."

"I see. Is he with them?"

Sergeant O'Toole frowned. "He?"

"Yes. Him. My grandson."

"Oh, him. Yes. He is.

"Let him go."

"Sadie – Mrs Decker – do you think that's wise?"

O'Toole almost heard the creak as Sadie Decker smiled on the other end of the line.

"Yes, I do, for the Lord works in mysterious ways, you see. You think they woke it up. I'm wondering differently. "

"Differently?" A horrible, sinking feeling hollowed out O'Toole's belly.

"You heard me. Send Brandon my way. We have to move quickly now, and with any luck, all of this might be over before they even realise what's going on."

"And what do you want me to do with the others?"

"The others? Leave them where they are. We'll deal with them later."

# chapter fourteen

Sometimes, later never comes.

Dinner smelled delicious. It was Daddy's favourite: roast beef with roast tatties and all the trimmings. They usually only enjoyed such fayre on special occasions, and Brandon wondered for a moment why Mammy had gone to such lengths. What was so special it warranted this kind of attention? He didn't ask anyone, though. For some reason, he got the impression that such a question would not be met with joy. So he waited with his parents until Grandma Sadie joined them.

In contrast to his parents' subdued demeanour, Grandma Sadie positively glowed. Her usual stiff greeting was now full of smiling pride, and rather than nod at him as usual, she enveloped his father in a warm hug. She whispered something to him, and he hung his head, his eyes glittering. Whatever she was proud of, it upset his father and that in turn upset Brandon.

He'd never really liked Grandma Sadie all that much. Theirs was an insular community, cut off from the rest of the world by distance and attitude, and Sadie Decker was at the centre of it all. Some might say that put Brandon at an advantage, but if anything, the opposite was true. Where the other children were allowed to go out and play together, Brandon was often forbidden. Even on the rare occasions he was allowed out, Brandon always felt cut off from them, a soul apart from their games and their laughter. It wasn't as if they treated him badly, more that he never truly felt a part of the group – and for this, he blamed his Grandmother.

She ruled their community with a fist of iron. No Outsiders. No leaving the town unless she decreed it. No wandering the moors. And, most important of all, no going near the loch.

Obviously, small boys being small boys (and quite a few small girls, too), curiosity often got the better of them. He remembered the afternoon last year when they had sneaked off out of town, down the hill and through the thickly-growing pine trees to the edge of the forbidden lake. All the way down, the children had whispered excitedly, daring each other to throw stones, or maybe even dip a toe in its chilly water, but once they were stood before it, all their bravado evaporated away. They'd seen it from the near by cliff edge when going out for Sunday walks with their parents, but never this close up. Close up, it stretched out forever in front of them, as still as a mirror and as quiet as the grave. At its centre, they could just about make out the spire of the drowned church.

Some grown-ups said it had happened naturally. Erosion had weakened the thin strip of land that protected it from a tarn higher up the mountains, and a landslide had breached its walls during heavy rainfall, flooding out the valley. Others swore, quietly and furtively so others might not hear – that the Government had allowed the valley to be flooded, but no one really knew why. A new reservoir was often bandied around, but here? In Scotland? Where it rained non-stop for six months of the year? They questioned that logic and came up with a far older, darker reason.

They drowned the valley to seal in the evil that dwelt in St Machan's.

Even thinking about it sent a flurry of goosebumps up Brandon's arms.

No one talked about that, at least not when the children were around, but the legend was so pervasive they absorbed it anyway. By instinct, they knew not to talk about it in polite company, but when they were together with no grown-ups around they liked to whisper about it to scare each other, coming up with tales so lurid Brandon sometimes had trouble sleeping.

The Devil lived down there, in the depths, or so the older kids said. Old Nine Eyes, they called it. The loch was bottomless, leading straight down to Hell. Brandon often wondered how that worked – surely, if it led to Hell, then it couldn't be bottomless? - but he never asked, instead choosing to keep his mouth shut and listen to the tales as they grew wilder and wilder, involving sacrifice and fire and blood.

No one dared tell those tales when they were stood next to the water, though. All of a sudden, it felt wrong. They'd told the stories to frighten and titillate, but now they were here, standing on the shore, gazing out over its surface to the drowned church beyond, those tales didn't feel so ridiculous. The air stirred, sending the pine needles skittering across the floor, and the loch shivered. A dark shadow bloomed upon its surface, and as one, all the children of the village turned and ran. No one screamed; no one spoke – they just ran as fast as their small legs could carry them, away from the loch and back to the safety of Dùisg a' Pheacaich.

Well, what they had thought was the safety of Dùisg a' Pheacaich. Brandon wasn't so sure now. Grandma Sadie released his father from her embrace and stalked past him to grasp Brandon by the shoulder. Her skeletal fingers bit into his flesh, and he smelled talcum powder and rot.

*Please don't hug me, please don't hug me* he thought as his body stiffened, waiting to be smothered by his grandmother, but thankfully she let him go. Grandma Sadie didn't believe in being soft with children; 'spare the rod, spoil the child' had always been her world view, and this time he was glad of it.

Brandon's mother indicated that they should all sit. Her face was expressionless, like a mask, and he didn't like it one bit. Usually, she was so animated, so full of life, but in recent weeks she had grown quieter, more withdrawn, as if something was coming, something she didn't want to face. Wordlessly, Brandon and his father waited until Grandma Sadie took her seat and then followed suit. His mother set down a huge platter of roast meat and tatties, and a bowl of veggies on the side. Usually, Brandon's mouth would have been salivating when faced with a feast like this, but tonight just the sight of it was enough to make him feel sick.

Grandma Sadie nodded at his mother as she sat down to join them and held out her hands. With practised obedience Brandon took one, and with the other, took his father's. He could have sworn his mother shuddered slightly when she copied him.

They sat holding hands in a circle around the food. Grandma Sadie closed her eyes and said;

"We shall pray."

His mother and father closed their eyes, but Brandon rebelled, lowering his lids just enough to prove that Grandma Sadie wasn't the total boss of him.

"Oh Lord, take this as thanks for all you have provided; for keeping us safe from harm when times grow difficult; for keeping us true to your purpose; and for Your Guiding Hand in everything we do. Amen."

"Amen."

In an unspoken agreement, everyone waited for Grandma Sadie to serve herself first. She took a piece of meat and put it on a plate, which she set aside. She winked at Brandon, a gesture so unusual that he had to stop himself from recoiling. She seemed excited about something, almost girlishly so, and it frightened him.

"A piece for Old Nine Eyes," she said. "So he goes for that first, and not for your soul."

Brandon looked to his father for reassurance, but instead found a new source of fear; his father's expressionless face drained of all colour, just like mother's.

"Well?" Grandma Sadie said. "What are you all waiting for? The Good Lord didn't provide all this for us to stare at it. Get stuck in!"

# chapter fifteen

Decker lay on the hard bench in his cell and stared at the ceiling. It had seen better days; in one corner a large water stain dotted with black mould leered, making faces at him in the dim light. In the other corner, on the floor, stood a rusted bucket encrusted with filth.

His parents stared down at him from that stain, their expressions grim and unmoving. The memory had been crystal clear, almost frighteningly so. Why was all of this coming back to him now? Why not sooner? A sense of something lurking ahead, of something waiting wormed its way into him, making his skin itch.

He should have called her. He should have plucked up the courage to see her earlier, before they'd gone to the loch. Then maybe all of this wouldn't have happened. If only he'd had the backbone to confront whatever it was she represented. But he hadn't. He hadn't, and now they'd paid the price, like innocents to the slaughter-

A heavy clunk roused him from his despair. The handle on the door of his cell turned and the Sergeant stepped inside.

"Well, now," he said. "What a mess, eh?"

"Excuse me?" Decker said.

"All of this. A mess. Didn't need to be, mind you. If only you'd done what you were told."

"You think I haven't already thought that?" Decker turned away from the Sergeant, curling himself up into a ball as he did so. "Leave me alone."

"Why did you bring them?" the Sergeant whispered. "Why?"

"I don't know."

"You weren't supposed to."

"I know."

He heard the Sergeant sigh. "Come on, laddie, we have to go."

"Go?" Decker raised his head from the protective cocoon of his body. "Go where?"

"I think you know."

He nodded. He did know.

oOo

"Well, don't just stand there and stare. Sit down."

Decker couldn't help himself. He fumbled for the chair and sat heavily in it, but he couldn't stop staring.

"I knew you were still alive," he said.

The old woman sat opposite him, her expression stony.

"Why did she lie? Mrs Kelly?"

"She lies because she doesn't have much imagination," Sadie Decker said. "I don't think she fully appreciated what was going on. Plus, your friends were there. And we don't talk about this stuff with outsiders. Outsiders ask questions they have no way of understanding."

"And I do?"

Sadie nodded. "You do."

She was a thin woman with an air about her that commanded respect. There was nothing soft about her; she seemed to be made of angles, all sharp edges and straight lines. Now she was sat in front of him, more memories of Sundays spent in her company came flooding back: the soggy, over boiled vegetables and cremated meat she served for lunch; the dirgy hymns she made them sing as she played the old piano; that horrible, sinking feeling that you were never quite good enough, despite only being seven years old. She'd been a hard woman to please, and Decker didn't remember her smiling. Well, apart from-

He blinked rapidly as his mind shut down that particular line of thought.

"You know, those mental barriers you've constructed... you're going to have to find a way of lowering them." She picked up her mug and sipped her tea, watching Decker all the while. "You're here for a reason. You know what that reason is. You just have to let yourself know it."

Decker screwed up his face. "No, I don't. I... I don't know what is going on."

For a fleeting moment, Sadie Decker looked impressed."You've a strong mind," she said. "Stronger than your father's, I'd wager. Which is odd, given how weak your mother was."

"Not too weak to escape this place," he said.

"Yes, well, I'll give you that one. Maybe I did underestimate her. Do you know why she took you away after your father died?" Sadie hesitated for only a fraction of a second before saying 'died', but it was enough for Decker to notice. He gave her a long, cool look. She might be his grandmother, but he didn't like her very much.

"To get away from you."

Sadie chuckled to herself and took another sip of her tea. "So that's what she told you. Maybe she was also wiser than I gave her credit. I suppose she told you never to come back here?"

"She did."

"But still you came."

Decker faltered. "Yes. I did."

"And I'm betting you don't really know why. I'm betting you ask yourself that question every minute you're in this town."

He said nothing.

"I thought as much," she said, and made to stand up.

"I... I have dreams," Decker admitted. Sadie stopped, and sat back down. She steepled her fingers in front of her face and regarded him for a long, painful while.

"Dreams?"

"Yes. Some don't make sense. Others... Others do. But one thing connects them. They all take place here."

"I see," Sadie said. "Tell me about them."

Decker stared at the mug in front of him. It was filled to the brim with tea, a drink he didn't really like. Wisps of steam wafted from its surface, curling about themselves, forming strange spirals before they disappeared as they climbed higher into the cooler air of the room. The weight of Sadie's expectation lay heavily on him. Should he tell her? In a way, she probably was the best person to tell. She was family, after all. If anyone might understand the strange portents that bothered him so much, it would be her. But telling her was admitting to them, and admitting to them made them real. And Decker wasn't sure he was ready for them to be real.

"Come on, Brandon. Tell me. I might be able to help you."

That was certainly a seductive prospect. She could share his burden. He could ask her – ask her about the truth. The truth about his father. The truth about Dùisg a' Pheacaich. But every time he thought he'd found a way to ask her, a way to frame the questions in a way that didn't make him sound like he was losing his grip, doubts set in, blasting them apart into incoherent fragments.

"I see." Sadie did get up this time. She wandered to the window and spent a moment looking outside. Decker followed her line of sight; past the pristine net curtains, the clouds were thickening, darkening, growing impatient. A storm was brewing, mirroring the one growing inside him. "All right," she said with her back turned to him. "I'm thinking you have been having dreams about water. About fire. About a black place. And about your father. About a wild night, with wind and lightning. But it's all just snippets, a jumbled mess that makes no sense when you wake up.

Decker sat, stunned. How could she know that? He hadn't told a soul, not even Paul. Unless...

"Yes, I know what you're thinking. I'm right. I don't have to look at you to know that. I have the same dreams, Brandon. We all do." She turned away from the window. A sole shaft of sunlight broke through the clouds, outlining her in white. For a moment, she didn't look like a harsh old woman, but rather like an angel. Not the wishy-washy angels of modern times, but those true to the legends of the Old Testament, all swords and vengeance and cleansing fire. "The time is nearly here and you're the only one who can stop it, Brandon, like your father and your grandfather before you. I sensed it first, the stirrings, the dreams it projects, and I knew you'd feel it too. For you are of my blood, of its blood." She took a step closer to him, her eyes blazing with righteous indignation. "You feel it, and you've come. Deep down, you know what to do. You try to deny it, try to ignore it, but you know. Given your actions since you've been here, you know you now have no choice. The machinations of the Beast means things are now certain and we are on the path – there is no way of stopping it peacefully now."

"What? How could I... no." Decker tried to speak clearly but his words came out as a feeble whisper.

"Oh, but yes, Brandon. You know. You offered it sacrifice." She raised a clawed hand and pointed it at him. "You brought them here and delivered that boy to it. Whether it was intentional or not, that sacrifice was accepted. So now you have no choice. You have to silence it and seal the gate that you opened, or everything we have sacrificed will be for nothing. And I, for one, am not willing that to be the case. Do you understand me?"

Decker took in a long, shaking breath. His mind bubbled as long-repressed memories burst and revealed themselves. Tears pricked at his eyes, and terror erupted in his belly. Part of him wanted to run, run far away from this mad woman and her equally mad followers, but he knew it was futile. Because she was right. His mother might have tried to protect him, to break the cycle that had claimed every male Decker for the last century, but she might as well have tried to bottle light to stop the night. There was no stopping this, only appeasement and blood and family.

"I do," he said. "But please, let them go. They are innocents."

"We're all innocents, Brandon. It is not up to me. Even if they were to walk out of here now, they wouldn't be able to leave. None of us can. No one ever has, apart from you and your mother. Due to her selfishness, the pain will be spread across all of you, not just borne by those who understand it."

"At least let them go," Decker whispered. He didn't know why it was important; it just was.

Sadie bowed her head. "All right. This one request, I will grant. But don't expect them to understand. They won't. It was wrong of you to bring them here."

"I know," was all he could say in reply.

# chapter sixteen

Paul had expected at least a little bit of interrogation and was surprised when there was none. Instead, they had all been thrown into individual cells – Paul had been surprised the station had enough, given he couldn't imagine the crime rates being that high – and left to their own devices.

Was this a tactic to catch them out? Well, they'd be waiting for a long time. He still didn't know what was going on here, not really. The sight of... of... what? He didn't even have a word for it. Appendage? Hump? Lump? Whatever it was, it played on his mind. His sensible side kept trying to change it into a wave, a reflection, or simply a mirage, but his imagination, forever the traitor, only allowed it to grow, grow until it was so huge that it filled his head until it threatened to burst. He'd been to enough tourist traps and investigated enough of their glorified puddles to know that this was the real deal – but instead of celebrating, they'd managed to get one of their crew killed and themselves arrested.

He felt a painful twinge in his throat at the thought of Piers. Instinctively, he tried to avoid the subject, but it was useless. He was here because of Piers. Piers, so full of life... now dead. Well, presumed dead. No – dead. How the hell could he be expected to survive that? But he hadn't seen a body, so maybe there still was a chance...

Paul shook his head to dislodge the swirling morass of questions, hopes and suppositions. He wiped his eyes – he hadn't realised he'd been crying again – and stared at the wall opposite.

Whatever was going on here, he was going to get to the bottom of it. His dear friend's death would not be in vain. He was going to blow the lid off this place and make millions and dedicate the lot to Piers. He'd do everything Piers had vowed to do when they'd made it. The Bahamas. A super yacht that would put Qatar royalty to shame. Hell, he'd even hire a bunch of midgets to water ski around it for his own entertainment, sipping expensive champagne out of a diamond-cut glass-

The lock chinked and the door creaked open, shocking Paul out of his daydream.

"You're free to go," the police officer said.

"Pardon?"

"You're free to go."

Paul didn't stand up, just squinted up at the constable in cynical disbelief.

"Just like that, eh? No reason, no explanation. Just 'you're free to go'."

"Aye." The constable's expression was blank.

"No apology?"

"No."

"I see. And my friends?"

"Already waiting for you in the lobby."

"So, none of us are being charged?"

"Not yet."

"Not yet? What does that mean?"

"Means you're not being charged with anything. Yet."

"I could sue you for wrongful arrest."

A glimmer of amusement touched the corners of the constable's mouth. "I'd like to see you try, sir." He turned away without waiting for Paul's reply. Paul stared at his back through narrowed eyes before standing up and following the deputy along a darkened hallway. He wasn't stupid. He knew something else was at play here. You didn't get arrested for nothing then get released without charge a few hours later. They'd wanted them out of the way for a while. That was the only conclusion he could draw, and he was determined to find out why.

As promised, the others were waiting for him in the lobby, where they stood in sullen silence. The room was a joyless, government issue beige. In one corner a dying pot-plant squatted, and a poster tacked to a huge pin board was the only decoration.

*Only you can help stop crime. If you see anything suspicious, call 8413.*

8413?

Odd. Why not 999? Did the community think itself so cut off from regular society that they couldn't rely on 999? And what a number to remember in an emergency. 999 was nice and easy. Even little kids could remember it. 8413? Nonsense.

"Hey," Mags said as he approached. Yolanda offered him a weak smile.

"Where's Decker?" Paul asked, his chest feeling tight.

"I don't know," Mags said.

"You seen him?" Paul asked Yolanda. She shook her head.

"Hey – officer. Where's our friend? Brandon Decker?"

The constable said nothing.

"I said-"

"Your friend is fine," the Sergeant said. His sudden arrival made Paul jump. "He's got a little business he needs to sort out. You know he has family from around here, don't you?"

"I, er, yeah, of course I know that. I just would've expected him to want to make sure his friends are okay first." Paul didn't know why, but he wasn't too keen on letting the Sergeant know exactly how much Decker meant to him; it was something that could be used against him, against them, and he didn't want to hand it to him on a plate.

"Well, it turns out he needed to square some things with his family first. Don't you worry. He'll be back soon. In the meantime, you're free to go." The Sergeant leaned forward. "But I'm warning you – do not try to leave. Our investigations are ongoing, and you're still caught up in this-"

"That's stupid. Why are you really releasing us?" Mags asked. "If there's still an investigation going on, you can legally still hold us for another day or so. Why even bother with this charade? Unless, of course, you know we're innocent and don't want to lose face."

The Sergeant sighed and pinched the bridge of his nose. "Y'see, this is why I don't like outsiders. We're doing something nice for you people, ensuring you don't have to spend the night in those cells, and yet you to question it. Always a conspiracy. Never that we're just showing you some kindness."

Mags looked a little sheepish, but Paul refused to be bought. Kindness? He seriously doubted that. This had nothing to do with 'kindness' and everything to do with... whatever.

"What about our stuff? Our equipment. Our Camper. Can we have those?"

"No. Not right now, anyway. Those things are evidence." The Sergeant shook his head sadly. "If only you people had listened, eh? You wouldn't be in this mess. Now a man's dead. Such a shame."

Paul's heart quickened. "So you've found a body?"

The Sergeant paused. "No... no we haven't found a body. But it stand to reason. You said it yourself – he drowned."

"No... I said he disappeared. Not that he drowned. There's a difference."

"There's no difference to me," the Sergeant all but snapped. "Man disappears underwater, it's pretty damn certain he drowned. Now, you people are going to go back to the guesthouse, and you're going to stay there until further notice. I do not want to hear tales of you wandering around, upsetting people with your questions. If I hear one peep that you're doing so, then I am locking you all up again. Do I make myself clear?"

"What about Brandon?" Paul asked.

"When he has finished reacquainting himself with his family, I am sure he will join you. But until then, it's back to the guesthouse for you. Play some Monopoly, maybe. Read a book. Shag each other raw. I don't care, as long as you stay in and you don't upset anyone any more. Understand?"

Paul gave in. "Yes."

"And you girls?"

Both of them nodded back.

"Good." The Sergeant turned to the constable. "Take them back in the car. Audrey Kelly is expecting them, so you don't need to stay. Okay?"

The constable offered a curt nod in reply and left the room without a further word. Paul, Mags and Yolanda trailed out after him like naughty school children after their headmaster. None of them looked back, so none of them caught the Sergeant sigh and smooth his moustache out of relief. Or maybe, just maybe, out of fear.

# chapter seventeen

The atmosphere in the guest house was muted, as if something had laid a blanket over it to smother any life that might exist there. Mrs Kelly's demeanour was as brusque as ever and all questions were met with a stony glare. Realising asking her anything was futile, the three of them gave up and trudged to their rooms.

Even though they had only spent one night, the floor Paul had shared with Piers and Decker felt eerily empty. He paused by the door of Piers' room and looked in; the bed had been made, but everything else was still a mess. Piers seemed to have an almost supernatural ability to create chaos wherever he went, no matter how little time he had spent there. Paul took in a deep breath and the lingering scent of that god-awful aftershave Piers insisted on wearing made tears scald the back of his eyes again. He would've done anything to have him here now, as infuriating as he was. But that would never happen. Because Piers was dead.

Paul turned away from the room and headed to the one he'd shared with Decker. Again, the beds had been made – Decker had pulled them apart after they'd slept, muttering something about small-town attitudes and how he didn't feel like having to explain himself to people who'd known him as a child. That had annoyed Paul – why should they hide the love they shared? – but he'd allowed him to do it anyway. Decker could be funny like that, like he wasn't truly comfortably in his own skin sometimes, and over the years he'd found it easier to indulge him. He sat down on the bed and stared at the wall opposite, fighting down wave after wave of despair.

They'd come here to find their fortune. Paul had even been annoyed that Decker had kept this place from him. Now he wished he'd kept it to himself. He glanced towards the door, willing Decker to slope into the room in that old, familiar, round-shouldered shamble of his, but it remained resolutely shut.

Where was he? The Sergeant had said he was visiting family, but Mrs Kelly had insisted she didn't know his grandmother, that she'd never heard of her. Why lie about that? Paul gnawed on a hangnail whilst the question gnawed at his mind. Why did she lie? And if she wasn't lying, then why was the Sergeant? He let out a heavy sigh and flopped back, his mind full of thoughts of Decker, of where he might be and what he might be doing.

A soft knock at the door broke through his brooding.

"Paul? You okay?"

It was Yolanda. This surprised Paul a little; he'd been expecting Mags, given she'd known him longer.

"Yeah, I'm fine. You can come in."

She opened the door hesitantly and gave him an uncertain smile. "I... I just wanted to make sure you're okay," she said. "Mags and me, we're going to have a drink and wondered if you wanted to, uh, join us?"

"Yeah, of course. Why didn't Mags come up?" Paul asked.

"She's just having a quick shower. I don't think she really knows how to deal with all of this."

Ahh, so Yolanda was the go-between, the neutral ground, so to speak. "I see. I kind of know how she feels. I have no idea how to deal with all of this, either."

Yolanda seemed relieved at this admission. "Me neither. So, you coming down? She said she wouldn't be long."

"Sure. Give me ten minutes to get out of this wetsuit and I'll be down."

oOo

Mags listened intently, her ear pressed against the door. In the distance, she heard Yolanda's footsteps fading away as she climbed the stairs to find Paul. She took in a deep, shaky breath. At last, she was alone.

Little tears gathered at the corners of her eyes as she limped over to the bathroom. It had been hard not to draw attention to the pain in her leg, but she didn't want the others fussing. In a way, it had been a good thing emotions were running so high. People were focusing on Piers and the mystery of his disappearance and not on her earlier injury and that suited her just fine.

She closed the bathroom door and locked it carefully, giving it a good tug to ensure no one could just wander in. Then she began to strip off her now-dry wetsuit, leaving her injured leg until last. How on earth was she going to get this thing off it without screaming down the house? In the end, she decided to take the easy way out. So, she was ruining a three hundred quid suit, but that was preferable to potentially tearing her foot off.

The scissors bit into the cloth and the release of pressure made her calf throb. Mags gnawed on her bottom lip. She wasn't going to cry out. She wasn't even going to hiss. She was going to see to this leg, inspect it, clean it, dress it and then she would take herself off to a doctor at a more convenient time. It did pass her mind that leaving it probably wasn't the best course of action, but the thought of someone from this god-awful little town going anywhere near her made her skin creep. Anyway, with any hope they'd be able to leave tomorrow; she'd stop off at a hospital then. At least she would be guaranteed half-decent service. Here, she wouldn't be surprised if they still prescribed trepanning and leeches to drive the demons out of her.

She kept up her internal monologue, trying to distract herself from what she had to do next. The wet suit now in ruined heap on the floor, she turned her attention to the bandage that swathed her ankle. It had an odd, rusty tinge to it. It must've been the water. Definitely. The thought of the wound seeping that colour made her stomach squirm.

She took up the scissors again and began to cut. The throbbing had stopped and, surprisingly, the pain wasn't too bad. Still, she clenched her teeth in anticipation of what she'd find and peeled back the edges of the bandage. It came away with a faint sucking sensation, and tendrils of red-tinged mucus spun down and spattered on the floor. Her belly convulsed, forcing her to swallow down an acrid mouthful of bile. What was this stuff? It was thick and smelled faintly fishy. She let out a low groan. Whatever it was, it was disgusting and she needed to get rid of it, so she stuck her foot in the sink and turned on the tap. The cold water shocked her skin, sending a fresh wave of goosebumps crawling up her spine.

She swallowed again and hesitated, reluctant to touch the wound. Instead, she let the stream of water wash over it and take that... stuff with it.

Slowly, pink flesh was revealed. That was actually a relief. A stuttering bark of laughter escaped her. Whatever that stuff was, it wasn't hiding a horrendous form of gangrene, eating into her flesh. No necrotising fasciitis feasted there. No strips of skin gave way, revealing hideously rotted meat. Just skin. Pink skin, clean and healthy and-

She stopped. Her heart gave one, heavy thud as her fingers brushed against something hard and crusted. A sense of dizzy detachment settled over her when she felt another, and another, and yet another... She snatched her hand back, her eyes huge, her heart racing. The water washed away the last of the clinging mucus to reveal a concentric ring of nine crusted growths.

No, not growths. Scabs. Little scabs, left by the bite. She picked at the corner of one. It tore away from her skin easily. Rather than revealing a wound, a long, sickly grey-pink tube flopped out and squirmed. As if on cue, she felt a tingling sensation in her calf and the other eight scabs erupted, leaving her with a ring of glistening, wriggling tails. Where they buried into her, the skin looked red and bruised. Again, her stomach twisted and this time there was no stopping it. She threw her head over the bath and puked. As she did so, the little tentacles writhed, stirring up a blizzard of pins and needles.

She glanced back to her leg, propped up on the edge of the sink. The desire to vomit raised its ugly head again, but this time she managed to struggle it down. Gingerly, she pulled her leg out of the sink. The stench of puke was almost unbearable, but it gave herself something else to focus on as she dared to inspect the bite again. Now cleaned, it didn't hurt, not really, nothing more than a strange fizzing sensation in her calf. Out of sheer morbid fascination, she went to touch one of the protrusions. It twitched and the fizzing started up again, this time reaching her thigh. Her breathing came in ragged gasps as she fumbled for the scissors once more. Fighting back her revulsion, she tweezered it between her thumb and forefinger and snipped it away from where it was buried into her leg.

Its response was immediate. Bright white agony infected her whole leg, sending an explosion of pain up her spine. It detonated in her skull, threatening to knock her out. She reeled, the stench of sick the only thing stopping her from passing out. She hissed through her teeth, her jaw welded shut by the ferocity of the attack whilst tears flowed unchecked down her cheeks.

Whatever it was, it had no intention of leaving her body. She sagged back, her head resting on the toilet cistern, and cried. The scissors dropped with a tinny clang from her hand, and the tiny dismembered tentacle spasmed next to it.

A tap on the door brought her back to her senses.

"Mags? Hey, are you okay? You've been in there for over half an hour. Yolanda and I are worried. You need help?"

Good old Paul. His single-minded idiocy might have got her into this mess, but he was a good friend, nevertheless. She took in a shuddering breath and tried to ignore the stump, no bigger than the eraser on the end of a pencil, as it oozed fluid down from her ankle and over her foot.

"Yeah, yeah, I'm fine," Mags said. It was a struggle to keep her voice level, but she thought she did a pretty admirable job. "I'll be out in a minute."

"You sure?" Paul said. She could hear his doubt. "Have you been sick?"

"Uh, yeah, I have. Sorry. Today… Today has been a bit much, that's all."

*Please don't remember I was bitten, please don't remember I was bitten, please don't remember I was bitten, please don't –*

"Oh, okay. As long as you're sure."

*Thank you, God.* "Yeah, I'm sure."

"Okay, then."

She heard a whisper of cloth against wood as Paul moved away, followed by the murmur of voices as he went to talk to Yolanda.

Right. No time to deal with this now. Mags turned the shower on and rinsed away the sick. A few stubborn lumps refused to wash down the plughole so she mashed them down with her thumb. The tentacle followed. Quickly, she rinsed herself off and then dumped half a bottle of TCP on her leg. Again, the eight remaining tails did their dance of pain, but she was ready for it this time. She set her jaw and breathed heavily through her nose, counting backwards as little fireworks of pain burst behind her eyes. When they subsided, she dried herself and carefully wrapped another bandage over her leg.

No one need ever know.

# chapter eighteen

The one thing this guesthouse lacked, Paul decided, was decent coffee. They'd decided by mutual agreement not to go down and talk in the common room, where the coffee was still dire, but better than the powered crap in their rooms, and so were now sat on the floor of the room Yolanda and Mags shared drinking bottled water and despairing.

"We can't stay here," Yolanda said, and not for the first time. "We need to get somewhere that has decent, reliable contact with the outside world. We need lawyers and an outside police force. Hell, we need the Met, or whatever the equivalent is up here. This place needs to be torn apart."

"I agree," Mags said. "But I don't think any of that is going to happen, Yolanda. I don't think they're going to let us go that easily."

"Oh? And how are they going to stop us?"

"They'll just re-arrest us again." She stared gloomily at the patterned carpet. "They'll say Paul killed Piers, and that I helped. They'll say you were in on it. Even though they know that isn't true, that's what they'll say. I guarantee it."

"But why would they do that? Why are they even doing this? Why do we have to stay here? Why?"

Paul held up his hand. Yolanda's constant questions were beginning to give him a headache.

"Why are you asking me? I don't know. All I know is Decker's not here, and we're not going anywhere until we find him. We know they're hiding something, and he's involved somehow. We can't leave him here alone."

Mags pursed her lips, but nodded. Yolanda, on the other hand, looked rebellious.

"Look, your dedication towards Decker is admirable and all, but I really do think we need to concentrate on getting out of here and getting help. They have no right to do this, to make us stay. We're victims. I mean, where is Decker? They say he's visiting family, but how do we know? They could've taken him anywhere..."

She trailed off and gave the carpet a sheepish look when she noticed the look of pain that crossed Paul's face.

"I'm sure he's okay," Mags said, softly.

"Yeah, I'm sure he is fine," Yolanda added.

"We don't know that," Paul said. His throat felt tight, his eyes hot. He blinked and coughed, as if that might ease it all, but it didn't.

"Maybe we should go and ask someone?" Mags said.

"Ha. Yeah, like that would work. Who would we ask? I doubt we'd ever get a straight answer, not here. They're all in on it. Remember when we first arrived here and Decker asked about his grandmother? Kelly said she'd never heard of her. But now, his family – the same family that aren't supposed to exist – take him off God knows where to talk to him?" A sudden spark of fury ignited within him. "And we're just supposed to take this. To sit here and take it all. You know, after we find Decker and we get out of here, I'm going to blow the lid on this place, blow the fucking lid right off and expose it for all to see. We'll make them pay. We'll make them pay for everything."

"Yeah?" Mags said. "And how are you going to do that? They confiscated our gear. We have nothing. No footage, no interviews, nothing. It was all in the Camper. We don't even have anything in cloud storage, since the internet doesn't work here. Let's face it, Paul – we're screwed. Either which way, the best we can hope for is just getting the hell out of this place alive."

"You really think it's that bad?" Yolanda asked, her dark eyes huge. "That they want to kill us? Murder us? Why?"

"I don't know about cold-blooded murder, but I do think they'll do anything to stop their secret from getting out. And since we don't have any hard evidence of anything any more, the point is moot... What? What is it?"

Yolanda gave Mags a self-satisfied smile, leaned over and pulled something small out from under her pillow.

"What is that?" Mags asked. "Is that... is that what I think it is?"

Yolanda nodded and handed it to her.

"It's the camera. You got the camera." Mags gave Yolanda an awe-filled look. "But how did you do it?"

"It was easy. When Paul dropped his mask, I caught it, unclipped the camera and palmed it. Everyone's attention was on the two of you and I could tell which way the wind was blowing, so I thought it might be a good idea."

"But... but they did a pat down when we were put in our cells. How did you hide it? You didn't..." Mags' nose wrinkled in disgust.

"What? God, no! I put it in my boot, down the side of my sock. I took a gamble that they wouldn't ask us to remove our shoes, given we weren't exactly suicide risks. That's why I shut up. I didn't want to draw any attention to myself."

Despite everything, Paul broke into a grin. "You're a bloody genius." He held the camera up and admired it. "This means we have evidence. We have it. We can do it. We can find Decker, get out of here and blow this whole thing open! We can do it!" He leapt up. "I'll go get my laptop. Hang on."

He thundered out of the room and up the stairs.

"He could've just asked to use mine..." Mags said.

She got up and went to her suitcase. After rummaging through her clothes for a moment, she frowned and started pulling handfuls of t-shirts and underwear out.

"Where is it? It's not here." More clothes were scattered on the floor. "My laptop. It's gone."

"Gone? Are you sure?" Yolanda crawled over and started sorting through the clothes that now littered the room.

"Yes," Mags said. "I always pack it in the middle of my suitcase so the clothes cushion it, plus it helps hide it a bit. But it's not there."

Both women looked up when they heard the returning thump of Paul's footsteps down the stairs. He burst into the room looking livid.

"Someone's taken my laptop," he said.

"Mine, too," Mags said.

"Bastards," Paul hissed. "They aren't taking any chances. Still, we have the camera – that's something. We can always view the footage later."

"Or we can use this," Yolanda said as she pulled her own suitcase open. From a hidden pouch, she pulled out an iPad.

"You hid that, too? Yolanda, you are fast becoming my favourite person." Paul took the iPad from her with one hand and pulled her into a crushing hug with the other.

"How… what… why didn't they find it?" Mags asked.

Yolanda shrugged. "When you've lived in a bad part of a big city for any length of time, you soon learn how to hide things properly. This bunch of village idiots didn't stand a chance." She grinned and disentangled herself from Paul. "I've even got the cables – look. Now we can see exactly what's going on."

The elated mood crumbled. That the camera hadn't been confiscated was something to celebrate, but the footage contained within it was not. Now they had the chance to confirm their version of events, they all suddenly felt reluctant to turn it on and view it. Because whilst it may exonerate them, it might also show exactly what happened to Piers and no one really wanted to see him die.

No one moved. No one spoke. They just stared. In the end, Paul cleared his throat.

"We owe it to him," he said, his voice hoarse.

Yolanda and Mags simply nodded in response.

"Okay. Are you ready?"

They nodded again.

Paul took in a deep, steadying breath and wished Decker was there to support him. But he wasn't, so he had to do this alone.

"Okay. Give me the cables."

"You want me to do it?" Mags asked.

"I think I can figure out how to plug in a camera," Paul said, with a watery smile. "Don't need an electrician for that."

The cables sorted, he handed the tablet to Yolanda. She quickly logged in and located the footage. She glanced at both Paul and Mags, and clicked on the 'play' icon.

Everyone held their breath. At first, the footage was much like before – largely soundless bar the gurgle of the water, showing the sweeping underwater vista of the loch and the looming presence of the drowned church. Paul's breathing quickened. On the screen, he could see Piers up ahead, a dark phantom floating against a backdrop of worn stone. His throat constricted when film-Piers turned around and gave him a thumbs up before swimming through the broken window. Beside him, he heard sniffing and realised Mags was crying again, but he did nothing to comfort her. He simply couldn't. Nothing he could offer would soothe away this particular pain – nothing other than maybe time, and even then that looked a little shaky.

Film-Paul followed Piers, and the camera drank in the interior of the church once again as he took his time to take it all in. The memory of this moment had Paul reliving it – the sheer awe he felt at discovering such a place wasn't something he would soon forget. But this time fear lurked, intermixed with his awe, sullying the experience. Because he knew what was coming next.

"Are those the statues?" Mags asked.

"Yeah," Paul said.

"They look really creepy," Yolanda said. "Why mess with them like that?"

Paul shrugged and leaned in. The camera picked up every detail of those stone faces, re-carved to look like monsters. An ugly shudder crawled down his spine when his hand floated into view. He'd forgotten he'd touched one.

They continued to watch with bated breath as film-Paul's attention was drawn away from the statues and over to Piers, but just as they started to dive down, the footage stuttered and began to break apart into little blocks of grey, white and black.

"What the... no!" Paul whispered, struggling to find his voice. "No... what's happening... why – why is it doing that?"

"I don't know." Yolanda stopped the footage and restarted it once, twice, three times. In the end, she gave up and let it run. Every now and again, a frame would clear and they would spy something that might have been a carving, or might have been a beam, but the rest was electronic nonsense.

Whatever was down there, it didn't want to be filmed. Or maybe it couldn't be filmed. Paul remembered the yawning black chasm that had opened up when he and Piers had gone to investigate the altar, and he turned cold. In a way, this just confirmed it for him. The church wasn't just a building, and the so-called monster wasn't simply an animal. There was something else in the loch, something detached from what they all understood as reality – and it had killed Piers. The jumble of static and tumbling blocks continued on the screen as the camera tried to make sense of this new altered state, but it was futile. Normal rules didn't exist in that place. Paul was now certain of this.

"What's up with it?" Yolanda asked. She sounded croaky, like she was trying not to hiccup. Paul glanced at her. Her body was rigid, her pulse fluttering wildly in her neck.

"I don't know," he said. "I think… I think it's trying to film something it can't interpret."

"What do you mean, it can't interpret?" In contrast with Yolanda, Mags was angry. "How can it not interpret it? It's a fucking camera! You point it, it shoots. It's not exactly complicated kit. Maybe the footage has corrupted. That must be it. Something is wrong with the machine. Maybe its housing is cracked and water got in, or something. Or maybe its memory has gone. I don't know. We'll have to ask Decker. He's the tech geek. He'll be able to clean it up."

Paul wasn't so sure. He wondered why he hadn't thought of data corruption. It certainly was the most sensible interpretation of what they were seeing, but something deep within him knew that wasn't it. He'd been in that abyss. He knew.

As quickly as the footage had disintegrated, it sprang back to life. It showed his flight through the window, only to fall apart again when he chanced a glance back into St Machan's. When he turned his head back to the surface, the footage cleared once more and never fragmented again, right up until he was dragged back into the boat by a panic-stricken Mags and it was switched off.

"Still think it's just corrupted?" he asked Mags, quietly.

The look Mags gave him was hateful. "Screw you," she said, and clambered awkwardly to her feet.

"Where are you going?" Yolanda asked.

"Out," Mags said. She stormed away.

"Without any shoes on?" Yolanda called after her.

"Leave it," Paul said. He ran an exhausted hand over his face. "She'll come back."

"Corrupted footage, huh?"

"I know. I think she needed to believe that."

"The middle section… could still just be corrupted…"

"Yeah, it could be. But do you believe that?"

Yolanda paused. "No."

"Neither do I. She wasn't down there. She didn't experience it."

"Paul… what did happen down there? I mean, I know you tried to explain before, to the Sergeant, but it didn't make much sense."

Paul sat back and sighed. It didn't make much sense? How did she think he felt? He hadn't really allowed himself to think about it. Not just Piers' death, but all of it. He simply didn't have the words to describe what had happened to him. That yawning gulf… the impenetrable darkness… the *thing* that dragged Piers down… it was beyond anything he'd ever experienced. It was probably beyond anything anyone had experienced.

Something else bothered him, too. He dragged the little bar at the bottom of the video back and watched the footage through again.

Down in the dark, it'd felt like an age. Sure, he had no cues to help him mark the passage of time, but he couldn't sworn it had been a good quarter of an hour, possibly even longer.

According to the timer, it had been a scant minute and a half.

He leaned forwards and rewound it again, stopping it just before he had dived down to look for the altar. This time, rather than trying to make sense of jumbled mess the footage, he kept a close eye on the corner of the screen, where the date and time was displayed. It was hard to keep track of it given how much the picture skipped and stuttered, but eventually, after a few repeats, he had it.

Something deep within his chest clenched and turned icy.

"What is it?" Yolanda asked.

"I'm not sure. Watch the timer. It's hard, but watch what it does."

He rewound it again so she could see. She peered at it intently, but when it finished no dawning sense of understanding bloomed. Instead, she just shook her head.

"Sorry... I'm not sure what I'm supposed to be seeing. It's too fragmented. Sorry."

"It's okay. It is hard to see and I might be wrong – but hang on... wait a minute... damn, sorry... there – look." Paul fiddled with the footage until he managed to pause it at just the right point. The screen was still a mess of blocks and static, but in the corner, he could just make out the faint ghost of the camera's timer. Yolanda craned forwards until her nose almost touched the screen. Then she looked up in utter disbelief.

"That can't be right."

"I know."

"I mean, that really can't be right. It's impossible."

"It is."

"How... how does that even happen?"

"I don't know."

And he didn't. Because who could decipher constantly changing numbers that made up the time and the 00/00/0000 that made up the date?

# chapter nineteen

They found Mags in the sitting room, nursing a whisky. Judging by the frowns Mrs Kelly shot her as she bustled in and out, she did not approve. Judging by the glowering stares she threw her back, Mags didn't care.

Paul hesitated before sitting. Yolanda hovered behind him. Although he knew Mags well enough to blunder in on her in the shower – or worse, that one time after eating dodgy breakfast burritos in New Mexico, on the toilet – he felt awkward just helping himself to a seat. In the end, she rolled her eyes and waved at him to sit down, muttering 'Jesus Christ' under her breath as he did so. Yolanda followed his lead, but if the way she stiffly perched on the chair was anything to go by, Paul guessed she'd rather be anywhere but here right now.

"I'm sorry," Mags mumbled.

"Sorry?" Paul said.

"Don't make me repeat it."

"Oh, God, no. I didn't mean it that way." Paul reached over to touch her hand. She tensed, but allowed it to rest there long enough to reassure him that he wasn't the problem.

"You… you find anything else? You know, on the… on the…" She looked up and gestured with her head to their room above them.

"Not really. Nothing to help us prove what actually happened down there, anyway."

"But we did manage to isolate what looks like a time anomaly," Yolanda chipped in. Paul shot her an angry glance. This was not the time, nor the place, to be talking about such things. You never knew who might be listening.

"A what?" Mags said.

"It's not important," Paul said. Mags' brows lowered in confusion, but she still nodded slowly. She might not understand what they were on about, but she understood he was reluctant to talk about it – and why.

As if summoned, Mrs Kelly bustled over. "Do either of you want anything?" she asked. It was clear from her tone that she disapproved of Mags' early drinking; the yardarm must've been a lot later here than back home.

"Uh, yeah," Paul said. What could he ask for that might take some time to prepare? "Nothing alcoholic, though. Tea, maybe?" He didn't really fancy tea, but it took time to make properly, and if there was a woman who liked to do things properly, it was Mrs Kelly.

Mags must've caught onto his thinking, because she chipped in too.

"Yeah, that might be nice. Although, can I have a coffee? Take the edge off this." She raised her glass and clinked the ice against its sides.

Mrs Kelly growled under her breath and gave them a curt nod. "If you insist. And you?"

Yolanda shrugged. "I don't know. A Coke?"

"A Coke?" Mrs Kelly repeated, sounding like she'd never heard of such a thing before.

"Or tea. Tea will be fine," Yolanda said.

"Right. Two teas and a coffee. Milk and sugar?"

"Yes, please."

"Fine. I'll be back in a jiffy."

She turned sharply away and stalked off. They watched her leave the room and paused for a moment to make sure she wasn't lurking round the corner, listening in. When they were certain she had gone, Paul turned back.

"We saw some kind of time anomaly," he said. "After you left, Yolanda and I managed to isolate a frame that showed a random string of numbers where the time should be, and the date was a string of zeros. Have you ever heard of such a thing?"

Mags tossed back the last of her whisky, grimacing as she did so. "No, I haven't. But then again, I'm probably not the best person to ask."

At that, Paul couldn't help but glance to the doorway. If this had been a TV show, Decker would stroll in at this point, as if summoned by their collective need, but this was real life and the doorway remained resolutely empty.

"I'm sure he'll be back soon enough," Mags said.

"But what if he doesn't come back?" He hadn't meant to say that out loud, but it slipped out anyway. It was Mags' turn to reach over the table and squeeze his hand.

"I'm sure everything will be okay in the end," she said.

"I don't know, Mags... this feels different."

"We have to keep our hopes up. I know it feels like we're in the thick of it, but all we need to do is find the car and drive away. That's it."

When she put it like that, it did sound easy; almost childishly so. But none of the weight crushing Paul's heart lifted. If anything, it felt heavier.

"What about Decker? We can't leave him here."

Mags said nothing. She avoided his eyes and withdrew her hand, conflict scrawled all over her face.

"Paul, I know this is hard, but we have to think about getting out of here." Yolanda spoke carefully, as if trying to talk someone down for a ledge. "We're going to have to do something soon, whether Decker is with us or not. No, please, hear me out. I don't know what is going on here, but I definitely have the feeling things are only going to get worse if we stay."

"What are you saying?" Paul said. "No. We have to go and look for him. We can't leave him here."

Yolanda sighed, looking pained. "I hate to say this, but we have to be practical. Decker's from this town, so we can only hope that whatever they have in mind for us doesn't apply to him. I've been wondering for a while if that's the reason why they've isolated him, which is why we can't wait for him. If he gets back before then, fine – but we have to leave, and we have to leave soon."

"No. We can't."

"Paul... Yolanda's right," Mags whispered. "We can't stay here. We have to leave."

"But.. but... no! How can you sat that?"

"I'm sorry. I really am. But we don't have any other choice."

Paul's heart stuttered and died. He was all ready to argue, all ready to fight, but a small, rational part of him knew they were talking sense. The back of his throat grew gritty with the realisation.

"I'm sorry. I really am," Yolanda said. "I know you don't want to hear this, especially from me, but we have to be sensible. We can always send in the cavalry later, but right now we have to think of our own safety,"

"Mags?" He looked up, hoping to see something that might resemble sympathy to his plight. Instead, he saw sadness and pity. He withdrew his hand from under hers. She sighed heavily, her jaw clenched.

"Paul... please, don't do this. Don't withdraw. It's not him. It's not us. It's this place. I want to get him out as much as you do, of course I do, but we can't risk it, not now. We need to leave, and the sooner the better."

"But surely... surely we can go and look for him? Before we leave? I mean, we have to at least try. We can't just leave him here. We can't." Much to his shame, Paul's eyes blurred. Part of him couldn't believe they were even thinking like this, but another treacherously sensible part knew it was the only way.

Whether he wished to admit it or not, this was now a matter of their survival.

"I know this is hard," Yolanda said. "But we can't risk it. I know I don't know him half as well as you and Mags do, but in a way that puts me at an advantage. We all know something is going on here. Piers is dead... Decker is missing... what next? We can't afford to wait and find out. We have to go. It's already getting dark, so I say we wait until the early hours and then make a run for it."

"Yeah. I agree," Mags said. "We'll have more of a chance under the cover of darkness."

"That gives us a few hours to go and find Decker," Paul said. A glimmer of hope struggled upwards, through the despairing sludge that filled him. "We could go now."

"I don't think we can," Yolanda said. "If it's any consolation, I don't think he'd deliberately betray us, but he might say something to his family that would give them a hint. Plus, going out might raise suspicion."

The glimmer faltered. "Can't we at least leave him a note, or something?"

"And leave a clue for Mrs Kelly to find? I'm know this sounds heartless. Brutal, even. But we don't have much of a choice. If he gets back before we go then, of course, we can tell him, but we can't go looking for him. It'll make them suspicious. It might sound stupid, but I can't help but feel like we are in a lot of trouble here."

"I can only agree on that front," Mags said. "I felt it when we first arrived. I don't know what it is, but there's a definite... atmosphere here." She shivered. "Can't you feel it?"

Paul wanted to disagree with her, tell her that, of course he couldn't feel anything, but that would have been a lie. Because she was right. There was an atmosphere here that went beyond mere hostility towards strangers and into the realms of something truly unsettling. A sense of what he could only think of as pressure was building to intolerable levels, like the air before a storm, and at some point, it was going to break. What 'it' was, he didn't have a clue; the only thing he was certain of was that when it did break, it would be too late.

"So, how are we going to do it?" He tried to squash the sense that he was betraying Decker down to a deep place where it might suffocate and die. "This place is miles away from anywhere, and we don't have our cars any more."

"I think we're going to have to steal one," Mags said. "I don't know whether you've noticed, but all the cars here are old – even the police cars. I can get into one of those in two seconds flat, and starting one is a simple matter of wires. I'm guessing immobilisers haven't travelled this far north yet."

"You can hot wire a car?" Yolanda said. "I'm impressed."

"Hey, you aren't the only one with a misspent youth. Us smaller-town girls also had plenty of opportunity to get into trouble." She shared a grin with Yolanda. Paul didn't join in, but this time it wasn't thoughts of Decker that stopped him, but rather something Mags had said.

The cars.

The cars were all old. She was right. He couldn't recall seeing one modern model. Not one. If he was a betting man, he'd lay money on it. In fact, he'd go one step further. He'd lay money that they were all at least twenty-five years old.

Twenty-five years.

It had been twenty-five years since Decker had left Dùisg a' Pheacaich.

"You okay?" Mags asked.

Paul snapped his head up, unaware that he'd been frowning. "Uh, yeah. I'm fine. Just thinking, that's all."

"You didn't hear me, did you?" Mags said.

"Uh, no. Sorry."

"I was just saying I'm sure Decker is okay," Mags said. "I'm sure we won't have to leave him here."

Paul didn't agree.

*Twenty-five years...*

A clinking sound heralded Mrs Kelly's entrance. She carried a tray with two steaming pots and four cups. Paul was about to ask her why four, but before he could, Decker trailed in behind her. He looked tired. No, he looked *exhausted.* Paul's heart leapt and he jumped to his side, concerned, and went to embrace him, but something about his demeanour meant he stopped himself and only touched his arm instead. Decker offered him a weak smile in reply, and much to Paul's dismay took a small but very definite step backward. Paul frowned, and Decker dropped his gaze.

"Everything okay?" he murmured.

Decker gave a little shrug, but said nothing. Mrs Kelly set the tray down on the table behind them, her lips puckered, her stance disapproving. Usually such an attitude wouldn't have bothered them; they always maintained it said more about the person than themselves, but judging by his subdued entrance, Decker wasn't going to help him fight the good fight today. Paul felt something akin to anger flare up, but it soon died down and settled into an ashy mess of disappointment and worry.

Whether it was to break the uncomfortable silence or simply because she hadn't caught on, Yolanda smiled brightly at everyone and picked up the teapot. "Shall I be Mum?"

Paul and Decker exchanged one, last look. Decker's eyes were so full of defeat, Paul's heart broke.

"Tea or coffee?" he asked.

"I don't think-" Decker started.

"No… tea or coffee?" Paul asked again. He raised his eyebrows in the hope that Decker would pick up on his desire for him to stay. Decker let out a ragged sigh and all but whispered 'coffee' before perching himself on a chair next to Mags. Yolanda handed him a steaming cup, which he shakily added three sugars to. Now Paul knew something was wrong. Decker never took sugar in anything. Although he had a sweet tooth, he said diabetes ran in his family and it wasn't worth the risk.

Yolanda continued dishing out the drinks with a quiet question as to everyone's preference. When she finished, they huddled over their mugs as if taking solace in their warmth. On the other side of the room, the clock's incessant ticking deafened them. In the end, Paul could stand it no longer.

"Bran," he murmured as loudly as he dared. "I'm glad you're back. We've decided. We're leaving. Tonight."

Decker stared at the floor and took a long swallow of his coffee. "Good luck."

"Good luck? What do you mean by that?" Mags hissed before Paul could get a word in, but he didn't reprimand her. Despite his earlier objections to Yolanda's plan, Decker's response only confirmed his long-buried suspicions. Whatever it was that bothered him – that had infected him and stolen the life from his eyes – wasn't going to let go of Brandon Decker that easily. What disturbed him more was just how readily he had given in to it. The Decker he knew and loved would usually fight tooth and nail for what he thought was right… but this Decker had given up before it had all started. He thought back to the journey that had handed them all over to Dùisg a' Pheacaich on a plate. He should have realised then. Hell, he *had* realised then, but in his selfish eagerness to chase his personal ace, he'd sacrificed Decker back to this town.

The fire started up again within him. Well, he wasn't about to give him up without a fight. Fuck this town. Whatever it was going on here, it could find another victim. It wasn't having Brandon, because Brandon was his. Paul straightened up.

"You're coming with us," he said.

Decker sighed and shook his head. "I can't."

"You can't?" Paul fought down the urge to grab him by his shoulders and give him a damn good shake. "What do you mean, you can't?"

"You don't understand," Decker said. "None of you do. This… this is meant to happen. I have to be here. You guys don't. If you can get out, do it now."

"What are you on about, Decks?" Mags said. Her tone had turned gentle, as if she was talking to someone whose sanity was clinging on by its fingertips and didn't want to push them too far. "What's going to happen?"

Again, Decker sighed, but this time he grinned. Paul's blood turned to ice.

"You're staying, aren't you?"

Decker faced him. "I'm sorry, Paul. It's something I have to do. Something I'm *destined* to do."

Before anyone could say anything to stop him, Decker set his cup down and left the room.

# Chapter Twenty

"Sergeant?"

"Aye?"

"He's left."

"Did he say anything?"

"I don't think so. They all look a bit worried and shocked, but no one's getting up to make him stop, so I'm guessing he didn't go into details."

"I see. Are they still planning to leave?"

"As far as I know."

"Have you told Sadie?"

"I have."

"Then that is no longer your problem, is it? See you tonight, Audrey."

"And you too, Sergeant."

# chapter Twenty one

Brandon's parents had allowed him to stay up after dinner. That was a new one; bed times had always been something strictly applied in the past, but tonight, for some reason, it wasn't so important. Not that he wanted to stay up. Grandma Sadie's stories scared him and he couldn't shake the feeling that his mother and father wanted some time on their own, so once the novelty of passing bed time by had worn off, he'd whispered in his mother's ear that he'd quite like to go to sleep now. He'd heard her breath catch in her throat as she nodded. She glanced at his father with sad eyes before making excuses for him and following him upstairs.

Usually, he didn't want help getting undressed and brushing his own teeth was a small source of independence he prided himself in. He might do a shoddy job, but it was his shoddy job. Tonight, though, he was only too happy for his mother to help him, like he was once again a toddler. She tucked him into bed and then held him tightly, tighter than he ever remembered her holding him before, which frightened him more than any of Grandma Sadie's tall tales.

His father then appeared at the door and fresh tears spilled down his mother's cheeks. She dashed them away quickly and scuttled out of the room. His father hesitated, then offered Brandon a big smile.

"Goodnight, big boy." He knelt by the side of his bed and stroked his hair. Brandon smiled a smile he didn't actually feel.

"G'night, Daddy."

His father leaned over and kissed his forehead. "Remember what we talked about today?"

"What, about the loch, and about Mammy?"

His father nodded. "Yes, that stuff. Well, I forgot something."

"Oh?"

"Aye. That no matter what happens, you have a Daddy who loves you dearly. Never forget that."

Brandon sat up and flung his arms around his father's neck. He didn't know why, but a sense of dread so acute it almost suffocating stole over him. Something was going to happen, something bad. He didn't know what it was, but he did know there was no way he could stop it. He sobbed helplessly against his father's shoulder, wishing this day had never happened and dreading the next with all his heart. Judging by the way his father hugged him back and sobbed with him, he felt the same way.

# chapter Twenty Two

They ate a frugal meal of home-made stew. Paul's emotions swung from angry to desperate and back again so quickly he could only manage a few mouthfuls before it made him feel sick. Was he really going to leave Decker here? Just what the hell was wrong with this town, anyway? What was it that sunk its claws so deep into Decker that he couldn't wriggle free? His mind then turned to the loch and a black bloom of dread boiled in his chest. He dropped his spoon back into his bowl as he suppressed the urge to gag. It was all linked, that much he was sure. What was worse, he had a feeling Decker knew how and the fact that he wouldn't share this knowledge with him hurt the most of all. Was this really how it all ended for them? After all they'd been through together? After everything-

"Paul... you okay?" Mags asked. Paul jerked his head up and gave her a bewildered look.

"You've been staring at your dinner for, like, five minutes," Yolanda added. "Maybe we should just give this day up and go to bed."

She shared a significant look with both him and Mags. They both nodded wearily in return, left the table and trudged upstairs.

They'd agreed to leave at 2.00am. Cliché maybe, but it really was their best chance. This was hardly a party town and even the most persistent of night owls tended to be tucked up tight by 2.00am. It gave them long enough to take their time getting out and locating a car to steal, one preferably nearer the outskirts of town so to minimise the risk of anyone hearing them. Sad, sick little butterflies flapped in Paul's belly as he dragged himself to his room and threw himself fully clothed on the bed. His mind, so tired and full of grief, fogged over and he fell into the welcoming arms of sleep.

oOo

A deep, throbbing hum woke Mags. She blinked wearily and fumbled for her phone. It wasn't there. She sat up, groggy and disorientated, until she remembered her phone had been confiscated. Bloody pigs. She peered up at the clock on the wall, but the numbers wouldn't focus and the hands made no sense.

The hum rose to an enticing wail. Mags swung her legs out of bed and wandered to the window. She tore the curtains apart, and the universe spun in front of her. Great interstellar clouds of red and green boiled and vast fields of starlight glittered as she teetering on the edge of the cosmic gulf. She stumbled backwards and pushed the heels of her hands into her eyes, as if she could rub the vision from them. When she stopped, Dùisg a' Pheacaich swam back into focus. She took in a deep breath and let it out slowly. Everything was as it should be.

Except the hum. That persisted.

She peered into the darkness beyond the window. In the distance, pinpricks of light proceeded in a line that she would have recognised as the road had the street lights been lit. A fluttery sensation in her belly stoked her curiosity. She watched lights for a moment longer as a deep sense of yearning to join them rose within her.

Next to her, Yolanda slept. Not once did Mags consider waking her. She gave no thought to Paul upstairs, nor to the boots that lay in a haphazard pile beside her bed. The bag she had packed was forgotten, along with all the plans they had made to flee. All she knew was she had to join those lights. They meant something to her, something important, and she had to find out what.

She crept over to the door and hesitated. A sudden doubt assailed her. What was she doing? She blinked to try and clear the fog that blanketed her mind, and for a brief moment, she succeeded. This was stupid! She was supposed to be waking the others. They were supposed to be...

Supposed to be...

Supposed...

Her calf throbbed and her belly twisted painfully. Mags grunted and doubled over, and the fog returned. It seeped into her mind, smothering all other thoughts, leaving only the desire to follow the lights and join the source of the hum. Her insides relaxed and an enormous sense of well-being filled her.

This was the right thing to do.

She opened the door and slipped out.

The front door to the guesthouse was unlocked. Again, what remained of Mags' instincts told her this was wrong, but all doubts were soothed away by the comforting fog. She couldn't see the lights any more, but that didn't matter. She knew which way to go.

The streets were chilly and dripped with mist. Around her, houses leered, their darkened windows staring blankly at her as she hurried past. The hum was clearer now. It filled the town, rising and falling like a great beast breathing. In the distance, she spied the twinkling lights again. She hurried on to meet them, overjoyed that they had waited for her.

*Wait a moment.*

Mags forced herself to slow down. Again, a small section of her mind struggled free from the nebulous grip of the fog. What in God's name was she doing?

She looked around herself with new eyes. Barefoot in a silent town in the dead of night. This was not the behaviour of a sensible person. She shivered as the mist enveloped her like a damp shroud. It smelled of mud and rot, and she was sharply reminded of the loch. That was it – the town smelled like the exposed mud of a lake bed.

Again, her belly squirmed, a feeling not unlike menstrual cramps. She hissed and screwed up her face in pain. It wasn't that time of the month and he hadn't eaten anything strange, well, unless you counted Mrs Kelly's food as something strange-

Her heart gave a loud thump and dread chased away the last remnants of the fog.

Neither Yolanda nor Paul had woken. The front door had been unlocked. Even though they hadn't eaten much of it, the stew had been hearty and there had been plenty of it.

Had they known?

But how could they?

…But how could they not?

What had they been thinking? Of course the villagers would know. Had this all been part of their plan? Thinking clearly for the first time in what felt like days, Mags ran her hands through her hair, her eyes staring, her breath coming in short, sharp bursts. They should have just left, there and then. Screw the Sergeant – they should have just left and had done with it. Why had they felt the need for all this secrecy? Because whatever plot the inhabitants of Sinner's Wake were hatching, they were part of it. They'd manipulated them. Made them stay the night, even though they believed they had a plan to escape.

But to what end?

The hum rose again. Mags' calf throbbed. She reached down to touch the bandage and snatched her hand away when she felt something squirm under the tight wrappings.

This was the only thing they didn't know about. Unless Decker had told them, of course. Mags shook her head vehemently, forcing the thought out. No. She couldn't – she wouldn't – entertain that notion. Decker was as much a pawn in this game as the rest of them. She simply couldn't believe he was willingly involved, that he would betray them. And anyway, he knew nothing of what her 'bite' had transformed into. No one knew. No one would ever know.

The hum intensified and the desire to join the it reared within her again. She tried to steel herself against in, to force herself to turn back, to wake Paul and Yolanda and get the hell out now, this instant, but the lure of the hum was too strong. All she could do was follow and hope that she kept enough of her mind to hide so they did not know she had joined them.

She ran on, keeping to the shadows as much as possible. She needn't have bothered; the streets were deserted apart from the ever-present mist. As she passed through it, it stirred into tendrils that plucked at her legs, making the thing growing from her calf writhe and her stomach bubble. The lights were closer now, so close she could see they were candles held by a procession that marched in silence towards the Town Hall. Instinctively, she knew their destination had once been St Machan's, but as that was lost to them they made do with the next best thing.

By day, the Town Hall was small and quaint, a place that welcomed mother and baby groups and held bake sales. By night, it was transformed into something squat and voracious, devouring each villager one by one as they entered. No one spoke. Mags ducked down behind a car and watched until the last one entered and the door swung shut. She took in a deep breath that tasted of mud and salt and hurried over to the Hall, her heart thundering in her ears. As she pressed herself against the damp brick, she was sure someone would yell out, betray her position, but all was quiet and still. Except, of course, for the hum.

She crept along one wall until she spied a window. It was too high for her just to look into, so she searched around for something to stand on. An old fashioned waste paper basket answered her prayers – she lifted the solid insert out from its wire housing, praising whoever might be listening again that it was not locked in place. She scuttled back to the window, upturned it and clambered on top. It was still a little small and she was forced to stand on tiptoes so she could peer into the room beyond.

Like the church, it was one big room. Unlike the church, it was largely unadorned. No defaced statues, no stained glass windows to paint the wooden floor a kaleidoscope of colours, no intricately carved gallery to stand on; just an oblong room filled with cheap plastic chairs that looked like they'd been stolen from the local school. Hundreds of people were packed in: families sat together, some with infants in their arms and children sitting on their laps, rubbing their eyes sleepily. At the front a group of people stood, not clad in robes like Mags had been half-expecting, but in slacks and shirts, dresses and pumps, lending the whole affair a surreal edge. If it hadn't been the middle of the night, she would have sworn it was just a regular town meeting. Mags scanned their immobile faces, looking for any hint as to what this might be about, but they gave away nothing. Her gaze then fell on one figure sitting on a fold-out chair just behind the standing group and her chest tightened. It was Decker, his head bowed, his shoulders slumped. Beside him stood a tall woman whose face remained largely in shadow. Her eyes stinging, Mags clutched a hand to her mouth as the woman reached over to stroke Decker's hair. He did not respond. She then raised her other hand and the hum stopped, filling the whole town with the white-noise of silence.

The woman stepped forwards, revealing herself. She was old, but certainly not decrepit; her bearing was regal, her eyes unforgiving. There was no mistaking that she was in charge of this meeting, and there was no mistaking who she was related to. This had to be Decker's grandmother. The crowd watched her with palpable awe as she spent a moment surveying them, probably looking for non-attenders, and then began to speak.

Mags couldn't make out a word of it.

Frustrated, she inched herself up and craned her head as close to the window as she dared. All she could make out was the murmur of a voice; no actual words, just the drone of someone speaking. If only she could get in, she could listen and find out exactly what they were planning, but the thought of trying to sneak in made her feel sick. They all thought she was asleep, out of harm's way with her friends – what would they do to her if they found her amongst them? So she remained by the window, watching, trying as hard as she could to lip-read Sadie Decker's sermon. It was harder than she had thought, as Sadie was a remarkably restrained preacher: no shouting, no flailing arm gestures, no rousing the crowd to repeat what she proclaimed. Instead, she looked like a woman giving a sober speech to the local Women's Institute on their fundraising ideas for this Christmas. Every now and again, Decker's shoulders would rise and fall in a huge sigh, but apart from that, he didn't move. Neither did the congregation, who sat in enthralled silence. Even the children behaved themselves, some deep instinct keeping them quiet.

Finally, Sadie raised her arms and stopped talking. Even from outside, Mags felt the shift in atmosphere. What was once tense yet quiet turned unbearable as every single person hunkered down in their seats. Parents clutched their children close to them and a sense of quiet dread settled over the whole town. A breeze kicked up, bringing the stench of the loch with it, but the mist remained undisturbed. Mags shrank back against the wall, her attention now on the outside – the outside she was in. The hum started again, and Mags peeked back inside. One of the standing figures blew upon a complicated horn that belched out a deep, low note that made the ground tremble and her belly roil. Behind her, the mists thickened and the sickly stench of rot and sulphur made her turn back. Unearthly lights now flickered, like faerie fire, and Mags swore she saw shadowy forms writhe. The hum continued, scrambling her guts, blasting out over the town. She now had no doubt it was a summons… but what it summoned, she could only guess.

The air felt heavy around her, tasting metallic, as it did before a storm. In the distance, she heard a schlupping sound, like someone wading through deep mud, and from out of the heavy curtain of mist, a single figure shambled. Mags was too far away to make out any features, but she guessed from its height, it was probably a man.

It staggered down the path and out of Mags' sight. A moment later, she heard a booming knock on the door of the Town Hall. She scurried back up to peer into the window; the whole congregation now stared at the door, their eyes round with fear. A few people's mouths were moving as if they were muttering prayers under their breath. Sadie Decker glanced at them all, and for a split second, her icy armour cracked. Whatever was banging at the door frightened her as much as everyone else, but Mags knew Sadie was the only one who could face it.

Decker sank further into his chair, but otherwise did not move.

Sadie Decker picked up an iron-wrought seal made of a complication of symbols that Mags didn't have a hope in hell of translating and held it out in front of her. She spoke a few words, bowed her head and stalked over to the doors. She took in a deep breath and pulled them open. Mist swirled in, its fingers caressing the door frame, and the figure took a step inside. Sadie held the symbol up again, and it stopped. Sadie said something else and it rose its head, giving her a familiar sneer. Mags breath convulsed in her chest.

It was Piers.

But it wasn't Piers. Piers walked with an easy grace and exuded a charm few could resist. She should know, she'd fallen for it more than once. This thing didn't. It might wear his body, but all she felt was a terrified revulsion at its presence. Sadie continued speaking, and the Piers-creature sniggered. Surprised, Mags went to take a step back and almost fell of her precarious perch.

She might not be able to hear Sadie, but she could hear that thing as clear as day.

"You bring me here?" it said, mangling Piers' easy going tones into something cracked and gravelled.

Again, Sadie spoke, but it just laughed again. This went on for a while, making it impossible to know the exact purpose of this meeting, but it was clear that Sadie wished to strike some kind of bargain. But what that bargain was…

Finally, the creature spoke again.

"They came. They moved the seals. They offered flesh. They offered blood. They sent a vessel. What else was there to do?"

It sounded smug. Mags' stomach twisted as if something buried there was trying to escape. She hissed and wrapped an arm around her waist, as if squeezing it might still it.

Something from within her pushed back.

She forgot the loch. Sadie Decker no longer featured. All thoughts of Piers fled. Mags moved her arm and pulled up her top. The flesh beneath rippled.

*It was inside her.*

Her breath came out in erratic bursts as her heart crashed around her ribcage.

*It was inside her.*

As if in answer, it pushed out, distending her belly. A scream bubbled up within her and her eyes bugled.

*It was inside her. Inside her body.*

And the thing inside the building knew it. She had no idea how she knew that, but she knew she was right. She heard the creature's gurgling laugh again. As if attached to strings, Mags looked back into the room.

"Yes… that's right. There is nothing you can do. I am everywhere. Why, I am even outside now. Look."

Every head turned.

Mags' pulse clanged in her throat as she ducked back and plastered herself against the wall. It was dark outside and light in there, so there was every chance she hadn't been seen. But she knew deep down that this wasn't the case. A cacophony of chairs being scraped back, followed by the clatter of footsteps confirmed this. In her head, the loch's emissary continued its cackling.

A jolt of adrenaline shot through her, waking her from her terrified stupor. She had to get away. It didn't matter where.

Or did it?

A hot, black dread pounded at her skull. Paul and Yolanda! What about them? She had to warn them. But how?

The laughter in her head was cut off with a hiss, followed by a litany of babbled curses. The footsteps had stopped, only to be replaced by the weight of expectation. They were waiting for Sadie to banish the demon back to the depths of the loch.

*This was her chance.*

Not caring about the pain in her leg and stomach, Mags sprinted away from the building, charging through the mist in the general direction of the guesthouse. No matter what happened, she had to get back there and wake Paul and Yolanda. As if sensing her desperation, Dùisg a' Pheacaich threw everything it had at her. As if from nowhere, buildings reared up in front of her, forcing her to change direction, making her dive down smaller and smaller alleyways until she was lost in a maze of grey, slate-roofed houses.

Her breath came in great clouds as the stitch in her side overcame the pain in her belly, which writhed within her like a nest of snakes. Still, she limped onwards, zig-zagging across deserted streets, trying to avoid open spaces as much as she could. In the distance, she heard a bubbling shriek and a crash as the doors of the Town Hall were thrown open. Nothing now stood in between her and the villagers.

She didn't stop to think why the creature would try to impede their chase. She could puzzle that out later. Now, she had to get away. Get to the guesthouse if she could, but if that proved impossible, then at least get out of town. Get out, find help, crack open this town like a ripe watermelon and scoop out the cancer- oh for fuck's sake! She stopped, panting. She'd been down this road. She recognised the house on the corner. When had she been turned around?

All around her the shuffle of footsteps haunted her. They must have split up. Mags gritted her teeth and wrapped an arm around her aching belly, but snatched it back when whatever was inside pushed back. Bile scorched the back of her throat. She swallowed hard and hobbled off again before anyone could catch sight of her.

Back down the road, turn left, down the alley and then – what? No... that couldn't be right. She knew it couldn't be right. She had a good sense of direction and knew she'd put a good distance between herself and the Town Hall...

So why was it here?

She turned back and ran down the alley again, this time taking the second turning. She carried on down that street, breathing hard, a deep, dull throbbing in her calf causing her to skip rather than run. Then down the next alleyway between two dark, silent houses. Down here the mist was thick; it clung to the walls, creating a tunnel of fog, dampening all sounds. She slowed, her eyes bulging, her heart racing, and peered into it. On the edge of her hearing, there was the muffled slop of footsteps on damp earth.

She froze. Someone was at the other end of the alleyway, possibly more than one, waiting for her.

She backed up and crept away. The footsteps did not follow her. Keeping low, she peeked out of the alley and spied a set of twinkling lights at either end of the road. They were there, waiting for her. Panicking, she spied the wooden cover of a coal store snuggled in between two houses. It was no more than a small shed, but it would have to do. She knelt down and grasped the bottom of one of its planks and pulled. The damp wood didn't so much splinter as crumble away, leaving her with a space just big enough to squeeze into. Her skin crawled as whispers of spider webs broke around her face as she pushed her way in. She made herself as small as possible, curling up into a tight ball against the mildewy floorboards in the hope that they'd pass by. Through the warped slats, she saw the lights grow brighter, closer, until she could make out the distinct forms of those holding them. No one spoke. Mags clapped her hand over her mouth to stop herself from letting out an involuntary squeak. They were close now, so close she could discern individuals, each one looking like they had just stepped out of an issue of 'Good Housekeeping', all sensible shoes and Arran knits. Ribbons of mist seeped into her hidey hole and began pooling on the ground. Nothing else moved.

"She must be around here somewhere," a female voice said. It was followed by a murmuring chorus of agreement. Something small loosened in Mags' chest and allowed her to breathe again. They didn't know where she was-

A hand burst through the rotten wood, snatching at her. Unable to help herself, Mags let out a squeal and slithered back, only for another hand to punch in and make a grab for her. More hands followed, filling the store, until there was nowhere left to hide. Mags screamed and tried to struggle free as the hands caught her ankles, her hair, her wrists. Bodies followed the hands, wriggling through holes in the broken wood to try and secure their hold on her. Her screams now echoed throughout the village, and more and more of its inhabitants converged on her location. She thrashed around, not caring that every convulsion brought agony; she had to escape, one way or another.

But it wasn't to be. The more she kicked, the more she clawed and bit and spat, the firmer the hands held her. Other people now joined in, tearing off the boards, dismantling the coal store until she felt the kiss of the night air against her brow. The hands then pulled her from the ruins of her hiding place and carried her struggling form to the road. Now revealed, a few people recoiled as Mags' belly distended and rippled for all to see. She let out an agonised shriek.

"We may be too late," the female voice said again. "Quickly, now. We must prepare her. If we are in luck, she may yet be saved."

*May yet be saved?*

Through the fog of pain and panic, Mags paused.

*Saved?*

She turned her head. Beside her was the woman who had been holding the meeting. The woman who had spoken to the creature. The woman who looked like Decker.

His grandmother.

"Where's Decker?" she whispered.

Sadie Decker's face remained strong. "Where he needs to be."

All thoughts of any other questions fled as her belly convulsed again and a thousand flaming brands writhed inside her. She screeched and found herself babbling, begging anyone to help her, to make it stop, to end the agony.

But no one helped her. Instead, they hoisted her upon their shoulders and bore her away into the mists, towards the loch.

# chapter Twenty Three

Despite being exhausted, Brandon found it hard to sleep. Instead, he lay back and listened to the drone of voices in the room below. He couldn't make out who was speaking, but there was no joy there, no laughter. Just a droning buzz, punctuated by long bouts of painful silence.

Eventually, he heard the front door close and it stopped. Two sets of footsteps trudged up the stairs. His parents, or so he guessed. They hovered by his door. Through his half-lidded eyes, he watched as they craned their heads around it. Someone stifled a sob, he guessed his mother by the pitch, and the heads ducked out.

Questions Brandon didn't have a hope in answering swirled around his head. Why was his mother so upset? Was it to do with him? Had he done something wrong? But if that was the case, why had Daddy made him promise to look after Mammy? That sounded like something was going to happen to him, not Brandon. Was Daddy ill?

Was Daddy dying?

Brandon buried his face into his pillow, unable to face the enormity of the thought. He was seven, just seven, a little boy… why was he having to face all of this? And if Daddy was dying, why did Grandma Sadie look so happy about it all?

Grandma Sadie. Bl- he stopped, then gritted his teeth. No. No, he was going to think it, even though he knew it wasn't allowed. *Bloody* Grandma Sadie. It was to do with her. It always was. Vague memories of darkness and salt and fire rose up, but they were too indistinct for him to make any sense of them. A tightness gripped him, crushing his whole body, forcing him to curl up into a little ball. He wanted his Mammy, wanted his Daddy, but couldn't think of a reason to leave his bed and bother them. An instinct, something that went deeper than mere rules and fears, told him they needed this night, this one night, together. Shivering, Brandon pulled his blankets around him. The shadows in his room twisted as he prodded the memories, trying to puzzle them out, but nothing more than a nameless, bone-deep terror spoke back in a language he didn't understand. The only thing he was certain of was that something was coming, and there was nothing he could do about it.

# chapter Twenty four

Paul yawned and ran his tongue along his fuzzy teeth. God, he felt awful. Like a hangover, only he'd only had one drink last night, and that had been water.

His brain gave him a nudge.

Last night.

*Last night?*

Oh, shit!

He jumped up and grabbed the clock off the wall. Its hands stubbornly pointed down, indicating it was 6.30.

6.30.

What the... No. No! He'd fallen asleep! How the fuck had that happened? He raked his nails down his face, willing his sleep-induced stupidity to disappear. What was wrong with him? He was usually okay in the morning, unless he'd been drinking-

Drinking?

Oh, God, there must have been something in the drinks. Apart from Mags' one whisky, they'd deliberately chosen non-alcoholic drinks to keep them awake, but he'd still given in and fallen asleep. He looked down at himself and sure enough, he was fully dressed. His backpack was packed and sat on the bottom of his bed. He'd been ready to go.

Now, it was too late.

He glanced at the window. There was no tell-tale smudge of light around the drawn curtains, indicating it was still dark outside. Maybe there was still a chance.

He stuffed his wallet into the pocket of his cargo pants and tore downstairs, not caring that he made a noise. It was early still. Mrs Kelly might be up, but what about the rest of the town? That might still be sleepy. He didn't bother to knock on Mags and Yolanda's door, just burst in to find them still in bed.

"Guys, wake up." Paul strode over to the curtains and flung them open. As he'd suspected, it was still pitch dark outside. He frowned and glanced over at the clock on the wall.

The hands pointed to 3.42.

3.42? Their clock must have stopped. He reached up took it off the wall.

The second hand ticked backwards.

He held the clock to his ear. Inside, he could hear the mechanism working, but sure enough, when he looked again, the hands went the wrong way. He almost dropped it when the big hand shuddered backwards. Now it was 2.36. Then it jumped forwards.

9.12.

A groan beside him shook him out of his shock. They didn't have the time to ponder possible temporal conundrums. They could do that when they were out of this godforsaken town. He put the clock down.

"Yolanda! Mags!"

Yolanda mumbled something and pulled the blanket over her head.

"Oh, no – you're getting up. Come on." He grabbed the blanket and tore it off her. Protesting, she curled in to a foetal ball and screwed her eyes up. Then, slowly, she unfurled herself and looked blearily up at him.

"Is it time?" she raised a hand to her forehead. "Jesus… I feel awful. We didn't drink that much, did we?"

"We were drugged," Paul said. "No other explanation. It's morning now."

"It's… morning?" she gave the naked window a confused glance. "But it's still dark -"

"I know. And no, I don't know how this works. All I know is we slept through both our alarms." He glanced over to Mags' empty bed. "Where's Mags?"

"Mags? I don't know. She went to bed same time as me." Yolanda sat up and leaned over to touch the bed next to hers. "It's cold."

"It is?" A cold certainty crept over him. "Why would she leave without us?"

"We don't know that. She might be downstairs. Maybe… maybe she got up and… and…"

"And, what? Made herself a cup of tea? No, she's gone, and the Mags I know wouldn't do that." The cold slithered from Paul's belly and up into his chest. "No. Something has happened. We need to find her. Find her and get out of here."

Urgency blasted away the last of his lingering sleepiness. He couldn't quite put his finger on it, but he knew something was wrong. Everything felt skewed, like he was in one of those crooked houses they sometimes set up at fairgrounds, off kilter and twisted. By the way Yolanda screwed up her face, she felt it too. By unspoken agreement, they didn't even pack; he grabbed the tiny camera with their only hard-evidence as she stuffed her feet into her walking boots and they both all but ran out of the room.

Regretting his former carelessness, Paul signalled for Yolanda to be quiet as they crept down the stairs. The clatter of cutlery against plates told them someone was up – probably Mrs Kelly at this hour (whatever that hour was) – and they held their breath as they tried to sneak across the lobby. Paul was almost to the entrance before the door leading to the kitchen opened and Mrs Kelly stepped through. Behind her, Paul glimpsed the hulking figure of someone else. Judging by the way they stood, he guessed it was one of the police constables.

"Oh!" she said. "It's you. I wasn't expecting you up yet."

"Um, yeah, hi," Paul said, desperately trying to marshal his mind to come up with a half-decent reply.

"Just going out for a jog," Yolanda said. It took all of Paul's self-control not to stare at her. She really was a little too good at this lying thing sometimes. "We'll be back in half an hour."

"A jog? At this hour? In walking boots?"

*Damn!*

"Uh," Paul started.

"Didn't pack a spare pair of trainers. They got wet yesterday and haven't quite dried yet. Still, no excuse – if you miss a day, you'll never get back to it." She offered Mrs Kelly a bright smile and stuck a knuckle in Paul's back. The message was clear. Get out, now.

Paul flashed Mrs Kelly a grin of his own and opened the front door. Outside, the night continued with not even the faintest trace of dawn, but he didn't let that stop him. He charged out like a racehorse straight out of the gate and sprinted up the road, Yolanda hot on his heels. He thought he heard a door bang in the direction of the guest house and visions of the burly constable charging after them filled his mind. He knew he couldn't out run him, not in this town, and so ducked behind a crumbling dry stone wall, dragging Yolanda with him.

"What are you-" she spluttered.

"Shhh." Paul held a finger to his lips. Even though he could see the question in her eyes, she didn't say anything. Together they crouched, occasionally daring to peek over lichen-stained flint, and waited.

No one came.

Still, they waited.

And still, no one came.

"What are they playing at?" Yolanda breathed.

"I don't know," Paul said. "Either they think we've gone the other way, or they're confident we can't escape."

"Or maybe there's nothing to escape?" Yolanda sounded hesitant. "Yes, things seem weird around here, but it is still a possibility."

"You can't be serious. They arrested us, ransacked our rooms. Took our gear. Drugged us. Mags is missing, and God knows what's going on with Decker... do I need to go on?"

Yolanda paused and he heard her blow out a long sigh. "No. I suppose not. Look, I don't think anyone is coming. Let's just... let's just find the road out of here and find help."

Paul rubbed both his hands over his face. He wanted to ask her to wait, to help him find Mags, to make sure she was okay, but something told him she was now as lost a cause as Decker was. He didn't really want to admit to it, but now was the time to forget Mags. She was beyond their help.

"I know it's hard, Paul... but I figure the best thing we can do now is get out of here. Come on."

She took his hand. Together, they peered through the mist, trying to catch sight of any potential pursuers.

"This is ridiculous," Yolanda whispered. "Why is it still so dark?"

Paul shook his head. "I think the clocks were wrong." He glance up and shivered. No stars were visible against the pitch black sky. "I don't know how, but they all said different things. I don't know if you noticed, but the one in your room was ticking backwards."

"Backwards?"

"Yeah. I don't know what it means, but maybe those legends about this town are correct. Maybe there is something truly evil going on here. But whatever it is, I'm not about to hang around and wait for it to play out."

Yolanda gave him a long look, then nodded. She didn't have to say anything for him to know she agreed with him.

They spilled out onto the pavement and sprinted to the end of the road. No one stopped them. No one passed by. In fact, if it wasn't for Mrs Kelly this morning, they'd have said the whole town was deserted. It had that curiously flat feeling a house gets when left empty for too long, devoid of all personality and life.

Halfway down the next street they found a parked car. They rushed up to it, but slowed when they realised just how old and beaten up it was. Yolanda frowned and traced her fingers over the bonnet. A thin veil of rust coated their tips.

"This isn't right," she said.

Paul hunkered down next to it. The lock was rusted over, the tyres flat and degraded. Cracks filigreed the windows, and inside, mouldy stuffing spilled from holes in the worn seats.

In the distance what sounded like a fog-horn sounded, so deep it made the ground vibrate.

"It looks like it's been here for years – decades, even," he said. "So much for nicking it and getting out... of... here..."

He trailed off as he stood up. For the first time, he saw the town for what it truly was. Grass grew unchecked through the cracked paving stones, and the verges were veritable jungles. The houses, once so neat, were dilapidated jumbles of broken stone and glass. Yolanda straightened up, her mouth agape.

"What the *fuck*?" she breathed.

Above them, the sky split open, filling it with dark, blue-tinged clouds. They boiled out, churning around them despite there being no breeze. Little arcs of electricity crackled between them, and the air tasted of metal and smelled of salt.

"I told them."

Paul whipped his head around. What he had thought was a mound of rubbish uncurled to reveal a man – or what approximated a man. He wore tattered clothes and an old plastic sack was tied around his shoulders like a cloak. His face was lined, his teeth crooked and blackened, but his eyes were two bright pools, gleaming with an unholy intelligence. Paul's first instinct was to run, but curiosity stayed his flight.

"You told who?" he said.

The man chuckled and ambled over to them. Yolanda stood behind Paul, gripping his arm, her fingernails drilling into his flesh. "Let's get out of here..." she whispered.

Paul didn't listen to her. Although he shared her fear, her desire to flee, he had to know what the old man meant.

"I told them," he repeated. "Both of them. Your friends. The dead one and the woman. They didn't listen. They didn't tell you, did they? I told them about the dark and the sacrifices, and the beast in the loch... but they didn't listen," the man shook his head, sadly. "They never do. And then they get trapped."

"Trapped? Who? The townspeople?"

"Oh, no. No, no. Not them. They couldn't leave, even if they wanted to, but you and your friends... you had a chance. A small one, but still a chance. I told them. I said they should leave. But now it's too late. It's the dark. The dark does it. The townspeople try to stop it. They do. But it's like trying to hold back the sea. You can only do it for so long before it breaks through your defences and continues to consume all. They have one last chance now to hold it back; not stop it, no, never stop it, but maybe buy some more time before the inevitable comes to pass." He sighed. "Sometimes I wonder why they bother, but humans are such optimists, such fighters. Even when times are bleak, they think they can change the outcome."

Despite everything, Paul had to ask. "Well... can they? Change it? The outcome, I mean."

"No, they can't." The man sounded sad now. "But they'll try. One life for many. That's how it has always worked. Old Nine

Eyes grows hungry. It's time is nigh, or so it thinks. It called and called... and then the one they lost heard it. And he came back. The Prodigal Son. Back, just in time,"

"The Prodigal... You mean Decker, right?" Paul suddenly felt very queasy. "What do you mean? What do they want with him?"

"No. Won't answer that. Not to outsiders. You shouldn't have come with him. I told your friends to leave. Outsiders complicate things. If it'd been up to me, I'd have slit all your throats the moment I saw you. Easier that way."

Paul took an uneasy stop backward. Whilst it was obvious from his mutterings that the man was stark raving mad, it didn't stop him from being dangerous. Quite the opposite, in fact.

"But no... they kept you alive. Couldn't send you back once the sacrifice had been accepted, oh no, that wouldn't work. So they had to keep you safe. Well... safer. Not safe for her. They didn't factor her into it all."

"Her?" Paul drew himself up to his full height in an attempt at seeming more fearless than he felt. "What do you mean, her?"

"Her. The woman, the one I warned. They had to take her. She must be purged."

"P... purged?" Yolanda said.

"Aye. Purged of the evil growing within her."

"Paul," Yolanda pulled as his arm. "I think he means Mags."

"Yeah, I know. When I say so..."

Yolanda's grip tightened and Paul knew she understood. The decrepit man cocked his head to one side and flicked his tongue out, running it quickly over his cracked lips.

"You two don't matter now. Redundant, both of you. They won't miss you. Won't miss you at all."

He lurched forward, but Paul and Yolanda were ready for it. They both jumped back and ran. Behind them, they heard the man curse and the lollop of his footsteps as he tried to follow them, but years of neglect meant his body wasn't up to matching theirs. That didn't stop them, though. How many more of his ilk were here? They ran on, up the street and past rows of now-derelict buildings until they could see the shadowy form of the sign that had welcomed them to Dùisg a' Pheacaich. Even then, they did not stop; lungs burning, they staggered past it and on to the road outside.

Paul slowed and dared to glance back. The village leered drunkenly back at him. He heard a retching sound. Yolanda throwing up. He took in huge lungfuls of flat air and willed his heart to slow.

They were out. Just.

"We need to keep going," he said. Yolanda wiped her mouth with the back of her hand and nodded, an exhausted determination haunting her eyes.

"The further the better," she said.

She didn't need to say any more.

# chapter Twenty Five

He awoke to his mother gently shaking him.

"Brandon… darling… time to get up."

He uncurled himself and looked up into her bleary eyes. It didn't look like she'd had any sleep at all. She smiled weakly at him. "Come have your porridge, then get ready."

Outside, it was still dark. Brandon frowned. His mother shook her head, but said nothing. He clambered out of bed and followed her downstairs where his father was already sat at the breakfast table, stirring his bowl.

"Morning, son," he said. He tried to be bright, but could not hide the strain in his voice.

"Morning, Dad." He sat down and his mother poured a whole dessert spoon of sugar over his porridge. Now he knew something was wrong; his mother never allowed that much sugar, no matter how much he might beg.

"Why are we up so early?" Brandon said.

"We aren't." His dad shovelled a spoonful of his own breakfast into his mouth so he didn't have to explain further.

"But it's still dark outside."

"Aye. It is. It will be, today. Dark, that is."

"Why?"

He heard his mother's breath catch. His father smiled wanly and reached over to cover Brandon's hand with his own.

"It just is."

It wasn't an answer. It was a long way from an answer. But it would have to do.

They ate in silence. His mother joined them soon after, but she didn't eat anything. Instead she sat there, as still as stone, letting a cup of tea grow cold in front of her.

After breakfast, Brandon was sent upstairs to get washed and dressed. His mother had picked out his Sunday best, all freshly laundered and starched to within an inch of its life. She helped him put on his tie, then brushed his hair flat. Newly shined shoes followed. She then put on her best dress, a blue one that complimented the colour of her eyes. She pulled her auburn hair back into a tight bun and she, too, pushed her feet into shiny shoes.

"Mammy… what's happening?"

She paused, a hat pin gripped between her teeth. With a soft sigh, she sat down on the bed she shared with his father and took the pin out.

"Oh, Brandon, my bonny boy… I don't know how to tell you. I want to, but I simply don't know how. Today is important – important for everyone in Dùisg a' Pheacaich. But most of all, it is important for us. For, today, your father has been chosen. He is our saviour – not just yours and mine, but the whole village's. He will be revered, and his name will be spoken with nothing but pride."

"Is that why Grandma Sadie is so happy?"

Her eyes hardened for a moment and Brandon caught a glimmer of icy hatred in their sky-blue depths.

"Yes."

"Then why aren't you happy?"

The hatred shattered as if struck, replaced by a pool of sorrow so deep he thought he might drown in it.

"Because he is no longer ours," she whispered. "Oh, Branny, my baby, my life… I wish I could tell you, explain why all this has to happen, but I can't. Because no matter what happens, no matter how much I've tried to deny it, or hope it would never come to pass, today has to happen. It has to. Or…"

"Or… what?"

"Or…" she tried to smile, but failed. "It doesn't matter. It truly doesn't." She stood up, placed her hat on her head and jabbed the pin into place. "It doesn't matter because it won't change anything. The best we can do is just face it. Come on. Let's go and find your father."

# chapter Twenty six

They decided to follow the road so they wouldn't get lost. The moorland stretched seemingly forever either side of them, forcing their fear of being seen to battle with their fear of getting lost. In the end, they struck a compromise and hiked beside it, hoping the overgrown heather would be enough to hide them from prying eyes.

They hardly spoke, and when they did, they didn't finish their sentences. Neither of them knew the answers to the questions that swarmed their minds, so why bother asking? Paul wrapped an arm around his stomach in an attempt to soothe the constant pangs of sickening guilt at leaving Decker and Mags behind, but it did nothing but make the already difficult terrain impossible to traverse. More than once, pools of stagnant water pushed them closer to the road than they felt comfortable with, forcing them to scuttle out onto the cracked tarmac, their hearts in their mouths. Ducking back, Yolanda tripped, pitching her forwards into the mud.

"Jesus, are you okay?" Paul helped her up whilst she swore under her breath.

"Yeah," she said. "I think so- hey. Look at this."

She picked up the rock she had fallen over, wiped it clean with her hand and then immediately dropped it as if it had bitten her.

Paul could see why.

It was another one of those little stone heads, identical to the ones that bordered the loch.

"They're everywhere," Yolanda whispered. "Look – there's another one up ahead. We've probably walked past loads more."

The little head's sightless eyes stared up at them, it's mouth drawn in a perpetual scream. A shudder crawled over Paul's skin. What were they doing here? He thought Decker had said they only protected the loch. At the time, he'd thought it nothing more than a quaint rural superstition. A giggle bubbled up within him. Well, that just went to show what he knew.

163

They pressed on for what seemed like hours, carefully dodging round anything that might be another stone head, but no hint of dawn broke through the swirling clouds. The place felt flat; dead, as if everything had fled, leaving them them only living things for miles. More than once, Paul wished they had thought to bring water with them, but it was too late now. Every now and again he eyed one of the pools, but every time he thought about risking a drink from one, some instinct that went beyond mere hygiene made him stop.

Finally, they spied the dark oblong shape of a road sign. Relief broke over Paul, washing away the blackness of the day. Next to him, Yolanda grinned. Feeling buoyed, they picked up their pace, daring now to leave the relative safety of the wild verges and walk on the road itself, but as they drew nearer, their grins faltered.

"Fàilte a Dùisg a' Pheacaich," Yolanda said. "No... that can't be right..."

The tentative flower of hope budding within Paul's chest shrivelled and died. Somehow, they'd managed to circle back to the town. But how? They'd been following the road – the road *out* of town. How could they have circled back? How? A fierce heat seized his throat and he tilted his face up towards the sky. How had this happened? How? How could they have done this?

Yolanda placed a tentative hand on his shoulder. "Shh... it's okay... don't shout..."

Paul lowered his hands – hands he hadn't realised he'd balled into fists and was using to punch the air. Had he been shouting? He hadn't realised.

"We must have turned around in the mist somehow," she said.

"We didn't get turned around," Paul said. "It's this place."

"Come on; let's try again," Yolanda said. "This time we'll stay on the road."

Paul went to tell her no, there was no point, but decided it was useless. If she needed to do this to understand, then so be it. So be it.

They turned back and started walking. Every now and again, Yolanda would turn around and walk backwards, just to make sure the sign was still behind them. The mist crept back and thickened to a blueish fog that flowed around them until everything was invisible. In the distance it stirred as shadowy figures flitted through it, or so Paul thought. Still Yolanda kept looking back, checking until she couldn't see any trace of the sign at all.

They continued on.

With this new influx of fog came the smell of mud, salt and something else, something less definable, like burning metal and fish guts. Yolanda crinkled her nose.

"Is that the loch?"

"I guess so."

"Probably where the fog is coming from."

"Yeah."

It was as good an explanation as any.

The fog closed in further, wrapping them in a coldness unlike anything Paul had ever experienced before. Despite his warm clothes, he shivered as if naked. Every step took him closer to exhaustion, as if it was sapping away his energy, siphoning away any will he had to continue on. Judging by the way Yolanda stumbled, he guessed it was having the same effect on her. She stifled a yawn, but didn't stop walking,

The road stretched forever onwards. They followed it blindly, wrapped in silence save for the constant drip, drip, drip of moisture from the stunted trees.

In the distance, a black shape formed. It was oblong and looked like a sign.

Yolanda let out a sob.

Fàilte a Dùisg a' Pheacaich.

# chapter Twenty seven

There was nothing left to do. No point in turning back. They'd only end up back here. So they made for the sign, the only landmark in this lost place. As they drew closer, another, less distinct shape formed, no more than a dark splodge on the edge of their vision. Paul stopped. His tired heart juddered as it found its second wind.

The shape moved. Due to the strange distortions of the fog it took him a little while to work out that it was coming towards them. Yolanda took a step backwards, ready to flee. Paul grabbed her hand, steadying her. What was the point? There was nowhere to run now, nowhere to hide. They'd only end up here again and whoever this was would still be waiting for them.

The mists parted, revealing a woman. She was tall with a regal bearing, helped by the sombre clothes she wore. Her face was lined, but not unattractive, and her greying hair was scraped back into a plait that was then coiled around her head like a snake. She stopped a few feet in front of them, her arms folded, her lips thin. Paul recognised the gesture. He'd seen it before, so many times. Decker did that when Paul did something stupid or disappointing.

"Well, now. What do we have here?" the woman said. "You don't have to be afraid of me, you know. I'm not here to harm you."

"Yeah, right," Paul said. "Just like you wouldn't harm Decker, or Mags. We know you've got them. We know what you're doing."

"You do?" The woman arched an eyebrow at them. "Pray, do tell."

"Paul…" Yolanda whispered. Paul ignored her.

"You're going to do something with the… *thing* in the loch. I know it's there. I… I saw it. Part of it, at least. You want to keep it a secret, keep what you're doing here a secret, so you can carry on."

The woman chuckled and shook her head. He'd expected angry denial, not amusement, and that made a fury he'd never felt before erupt inside him. His face flushed red and he balled his fists, ready to strike this old woman down. Decker's Grandmother or not, he wasn't going to be laughed at-

"No. You think you have worked it out, but as with all of your ilk, you've added two and two and come up with the square root of evil. Yes, we do want to keep it a secret – and we largely succeed. But not for the reasons you think. We do it to protect, to ensure your safety-"

"Safety!" Paul exploded. The dead air made him sound petulant, which angered him even further. "Piers is dead! Mags has disappeared, and Decker... Decker... I don't know. But he's lost to us, of that I am sure. He's one of you now. How is that protecting us? How is that ensuring our safety?"

"Typical. Always thinking of yourselves as individuals who matter more than the collective." The woman sighed and suddenly looked smaller and older, making Paul feel ashamed for shouting at her. "You were all lost the moment you stepped foot in the town. No, I was referring to humanity in general. We are the last keepers of the gates to Hell, Mr Ryan. We alone keep them closed, as best we can. We satisfy the beast just enough to keep it asleep... but then you came." Sadie Decker drew herself up and all hints of any frailty fled her. She was now made of steel; her voice, of iron. "You fed the beast. We told you not to, but you ignored us. You came with your pitiful curiosity and your desire to make money, thinking yourselves better, more important, more *worthy* than us. We asked you not to, told you to desist, but still you continued. Even now, you insist on making all of this about you. It has never been about you. It never will be. It is about us, and the beast, and keeping this world safe."

Despite the fog, her words rang out, echoing around them. Yolanda snivelled and Paul cringed back involuntarily, as if her proclamations were physical blows he must protect himself from. But he still asked. He still had to know.

"What about Decker? What about your grandson? He fears this place, yet you have taken him! Where is he? *Where is he?*"

Sadie Decker shrank back, once again an old woman. "Oh, my precious Brandon," she said, more to herself than to Paul. "His mother sought to protect him. And why shouldn't she? A mother's instinct is such a strong thing. It could move mountains if need be. I wanted to do the same for my sons, but the weight of this all lies on my shoulders... I did not have the luxury of choice. Not like her." To Paul's alarm, tears gathered in Sadie Decker's eyes. "We had hoped this period of slumber would last longer, that distance would not stir the blood... that Brandon's mother was right. But, alas, no... distance is but an illusion when you can hold the world in the palm of your hand. As the God slept, it dreamed... and Brandon heard those dreams. I did too, though I prayed they wouldn't be answered. But they were."

Paul's mouth ran dry. He'd mocked Decker's nightmares at first, thinking him childish for being so afraid of them... but he now understood. Shame knifed him once again, right in his gut.

"He wasn't supposed to bring others with him," Sadie continued. "He was supposed to come alone. That would have made things much easier and much, much safer. That is where his mother failed. She took him from here before we sealed ourselves in again and she allowed him to live, to love, in the outside world. I should have seen this, seen that he would bring those who loved him with him. I should have turned you away that first night, but pacifying the beast... it takes so much from me. I couldn't keep the gate closed. Brandon's blood is too strong, too potent... he tore through as if nothing was there at all." She gave him a pleading look. "Please understand. We tried to stop you. We tried to warn you. We tried to satiate your curiosity, hoping that would sustain you long enough for us to convince you to leave. May the Lord forgive us, we even tried to make you sleep through all of this to spare you. But it was all for naught. You went to the loch and offered yourselves so willingly. There was nothing we could do. Now the beast is awake and everything we have done to keep humanity safe is at risk. There is only one thing left to do."

"And that is?" Paul whispered.

"Not for discussion here," Sadie said. "Worlds are colliding, and time is short. What you see here is the Beast's world – the world we inhabit – coming into alignment with your reality. I've managed to keep the doors closed for now, but the Beast is abroad and is seeking entrance. All we can do now is lure it back to its prison and reseal the gates."

"And if that doesn't work?"

"Then may the Lord forgive us all."

# chapter Twenty eight

Unlike his son's finery, Brandon's father wore a simple robe. Beside him stood Grandma Sadie. She wore something similar, although infinitely more ornate, its coarse brown cloth shot through with threads of silver and gold, forming swirling designs that shimmered in the lamplight. Another memory tickled at Brandon's mind; he'd seen these robes before, a long time ago, when he was no more than a baby, but the memory refused to be coaxed clear and remained indistinct and nebulous.

His mother did not cry now. She stood, as straight as an arrow, her eyes flat and emotionless. Grandma Sadie nodded, allowing Brandon's father to embrace his wife just once. He whispered something to her and for a split second her armour slipped and her eyes crumpled, but as soon as his father pulled away from her it was back, as strong as ever.

He turned his attention to Brandon next. He knelt down in front of him and pulled him into the roughest, tightest hug Brandon had ever experienced, and he knew beyond a shadow of a doubt that this was the last time he'd ever see his father. Together, they clung on to one another, father and son, each wishing this moment would never end, but it did, as all moments must. His father released him and straightened up. Grandma Sadie nodded, a beatific smile playing around her hard mouth, and without a word of goodbye, she led his father out of their lives.

# chapter twenty nine

Paul and Yolanda followed Sadie through Dùisg a' Pheacaich in silence. The buildings had deteriorated even further to the point where they were now mere ghosts of their former glory, their roofs lost, their brickwork crumbled and windows broken. Thick ropes of bramble covered everything and once accessible streets were crowded with vast swathes of stinging nettles and gorse. Above them, there was a dull boom and the clouds rippled, like someone tapping the side of a pail of water. Sadie glanced up and muttered something under her breath, picking up the pace so Paul and Yolanda were forced to jog to keep up.

The fog grew thicker until it became a physical barrier, obscuring everything. Dewdrops formed on their skin, in their hair, trickling down the backs of their necks, the aroma of mud and salt all-pervading. They hustled after Sadie, aware that if they lost sight of her, they would never be found again. Occasionally, there would be another boom, so deep it was felt rather than heard, followed by a stirring of whispers that danced on the edge of their hearing.

Still, Sadie plunged onwards, her head held high. Was this really the reality of her world? Was this how they truly lived? In a world of shadows and decay, forever holding back the dark? Or was this how the town now looked in the real world, in his own reality? If that was the case, how many people had stumbled over it without realising they were walking a thin line where two realities converged? Whichever one it was, Paul couldn't puzzle it out. Not that it mattered. The only thing that mattered was finding Decker. Paul's heart ached for him. If only he could take it all back, all the fights, the accusations, the coercion... but it was too late now. Whatever had been started had to be finished, one way or the other. Whether he liked it or not, he had no choice. He wasn't even a pawn in this game – just a mere speck of dust to be wiped from the board after it had been played.

The dark devoured what remained of the town. Still Sadie kept going, taking them down a winding path through a thick stand of fir trees. More than once, Paul had to duck under their branches, loathe to let their spidery limbs brush up against him. On the edge of his vision, he caught glimpses of forms flitting in between the damp trunks, matching their pace. Snapping his head this way and that, he tried to make out what they were, but they remained stubbornly indistinct. A stray root tripped him and he sprawled forwards only to be caught by one of the trees. He let out disgusted bark as he scrabbled back, his skin crawling. Drawn by the sound of his distress, the forms scurried over to them, not so close as to reveal their true natures, but enough for him to glimpse as a bristled, skittery leg here and a bloated, glistening sac that may or may not have been a body there.

Sadie whipped around, her face like thunder.

"Keep quiet!" she hissed. "Drawing attention to yourself here is not a good idea." Then she muttered something under her breath and made a complicated gesture in the air with her hands. The forms squealed and slunk away.

The fog thinned a little and Paul spied a flicker of light up ahead. Sadie headed towards it. Having no other option, they followed her. The light grew with every step until it formed a sizeable bonfire that would have sat by the edge of the loch, had it still been there. Now, a never ending vortex of water funnelled down into a deep chasm, deeper than the loch, deeper maybe than the Earth itself. Occasionally, a flash of blue light would ignite in the heart of the vortex and a rolling boom would cause the clouds above them to shudder. At its centre, standing on a pinnacle of rock hundreds of feet tall, was the drowned Church, its windows gleaming with myriad rainbows each time the lightning within the vortex flashed.

The inhabitants of Dùisg a' Pheacaich stood around the edge of the abyss. Paul whipped his head around, trying to spy Decker amongst their ranks, but if he was there, he couldn't spot him, even though there had to be no more than three hundred of them. They ranged from the decrepit to babes in arms and despite everything, he couldn't help but marvel at this. Here they lived, on the edge of Hell in a broken town with no hope of escape… and yet they lived and loved, bringing children into their miserable lives. He didn't know whether to be in awe of their indomitable spirit, or disdain them for their unimaginable cruelty. Instead, he stood in silence, not daring to draw attention to himself.

The air was thick with expectation. Every eye was on the vortex; even the infants were still and staring, as if they knew what was at stake. Paul felt movement beside him and two huge figures, easily seven feet tall, stepped up beside himself and Yolanda, flanking them. He risked a glance up, but he couldn't work out who they might be. Their faces were obscured by the hoods they wore, but judging by the way they bulged in unnatural places, they were not entirely human. It was only when he lowered his gaze that he realised they were wearing those nondescript, shiny dress shoes police officers wore to official engagements. These were the two constables, those near-silent sentinels that did everything the Sergeant said. A cacophony of shivers played along his spine. They had looked so... so *human* before. One shifted its weight, and something rippled under its uniform, bulging out the back like a balloon being pumped up. Paul snapped his attention back to Sadie, his curiosity over the constables' true nature completely smothered by a revolted terror.

Now she had her guardians watching them, Sadie took her place beside the bonfire. A villager  passed her a book, a thick, ancient tome bound in black leather. She bowed her head as she accepted it, placed it open on a rock beside herself and threw her hands in the air. The lightning deep within the chasm answered her. She cried out something in a guttural language that Paul did not understand, and the villagers intoned a reply back as one, drowning out the thunderous peals. Static built, making the hairs on Paul's arms raise and he felt the urge to scratch as his skin crawled with electricity. Sadie shouted again. This time, the groan of tortured rock filled the valley and in front of her, huge slabs of stone sprung up and floating in mid-air, forming a precarious path down to St Machan's. Sadie turned back to the vortex, her arms still high, her face alight with an unholy air of excitement. As one, the crowd bowed their heads and muttered something under their collective breath. Then she scooped up the book and stepped out on to the floating bridge. Without question, her congregation arranged itself into a single line and followed her. The constable guarding Paul seized his upper arm and gave him a rough shove forwards. He tried to dig his heels in, but it was useless; the constable jerked his arm with such force it was clear it could have ripped it from its socket if it wanted to. Much to his surprise, the guardian dragged him towards the front of the procession, and he found himself only a few people behind Sadie. A struggling Yolanda and her matching guardian followed. His stomach lurched as the bridge loomed closer; everything within him said no, it was impossible, there was no way it could hold his weight, but he had no choice as the guardian simply pushed him on to it. It took all of his self control not to stumble over the side. Beneath him, the waters of the loch span and crashed down into an interminable void that Paul at last recognised only too well; this was the beast's lair, the place he and Piers had unwittingly swam into. He baulked and tried to back away, his pulse building up behind his eyes until he felt his head might explode. The desire to get off the bridge and run as far away from this cursed place as he could filled every part of his being, but his guardian simply dug its knuckle – or what he hoped was its knuckle – into his spine and forced him onwards.

Now revealed, the church loomed over them, sinister yet beautiful, its slick walls pulsating with every lighting flash. As they drew closer, the roar of the water receded away to nothing more than a whisper. The spire of rock which the church perched upon was wide enough to accommodate most of the congregation, who now pooled behind Paul with an air of dreadful anticipation about them. Everything was still when Sadie raised a fist and struck the door of the church once, twice, three times, each knock echoing throughout the vortex as if someone had rung a great bell. After the echoes died, she took a step back. After a pause, it groaned open and the stench of age-old mud and decay wafted out over them.

Paul knew there was now no turning back.

# chapter thirty

The sun still had not shown its face and a thick fog that smelled of mud and rot rolled in over the moors. Its searching fingers crept into the village and wrapped themselves around everything, metamorphosing the village into something forbidding and sinister. Brandon edged closer to his mother, his heart beating so fast he thought he might faint.

Everyone was there, but no one spoke. The silence was eerie. As one, the people of Dùisg a' Pheacaich filed out of their houses and down the main road, a road that was now pockmarked and cracked, with battalions of weeds poking their heads up from the ancient streets where only yesterday they had been smooth and well-tended. The buildings around them fared no better; once tidy houses were now tumble-down wrecks, and in the distance, just about visible through the mist, the Town Hall stood as a shell, its roof gone, its windows broken. It was as if time itself had abandoned them and it frightened Brandon out of his wits.

Judging by the wide eyed glances the other children of the village were giving their parents, he wasn't the only one who felt this way. He couldn't help but notice that all their fathers – those who had them, anyway – were with them. Today, only his father was missing. And, oh, how Brandon missed him.

They all marched on, out of the village and down the winding path that led towards the loch. All around them, the trees leered and Brandon was sure he saw things moving in the fog, just far enough away so he couldn't make out their nature. Sometimes, one would scuttle a little closer and he would hear its skittering passage over the pine needles that carpeted the ground, but they were always too quick for him to get a good look, so his imagination filled in the gaps. He cringed against his mother's skirt as his mind conjured up bloated bodies, full of poison and bile that sat atop long, spindly legs that would allow them to pounce with ease upon any of the unwary. His mother's hand tightened around his.

"Don't look," she said. "Don't attract their attention."

He glanced up at her, at her calm mask-like face, and shuddered.

Onward, forever onward, the procession marched. Above them, the clouds tumbled, and as the villagers drew closer to the loch, little flickers of electricity danced around their edges.

Then the trees opened out and the loch spread out before them, its surface as smooth as glass. Silently, the villagers formed a loose semi-circle at its edge, leaving a sizeable gap by the water's edge. Sticks had been piled up to form a sizeable bonfire, which was now lit. It sizzled as the damp wood caught, sending up great clouds of smoke heavenwards. The surface of the water shivered and Brandon's mother gripped his hand so tightly her nails dug into his skin. He bit back a small cry of pain, but he didn't let go, not now, not ever.

The silence built to an almost physical force, making his eardrums ache. One huge bolt of lightning coruscated down from the boiling sky and struck the surface of the loch. Everyone held their breath.

The calling had begun.

Grandma Sadie stood in the centre of the space in front of the villagers. No one saw her arrive: one minute the gap was empty; the next, she was there. She looked taller than Brandon remembered, and there was fire in her eyes. She raised her hands, and as one, every member of Dùisg a' Pheacaich began to chant. The children watched as the adults intoned words they didn't understand, but still knew on a soul-deep level and tried to join in, their mouths working around the complicated sounds as if hypnotised. Brandon did not. He was too dismayed that his mother had joined in; that whatever was going to happen, she was as much a part of it as everyone else.

Another bolt of electricity shot down and this time the loch answered. Its waters began to churn, and then swirl, forming a whirlpool, revealing a deep, black chasm. Suspended at its heart on a thin pinnacle of rock was the church, whole and resplendent, its windows gleaming, its walls like new.

The villagers sang on.

A ball of light erupted from the church, exploding outwards, sending sparks streaking out to infect the waters of the vortex. Every few seconds they would flash, and the sky would answer. The pressure built further until Brandon's ears popped and his nose bled. He wanted to scream, to run, to get away from this awful scene, but he knew to do so was forbidden; to do so would doom them all. Those nebulous memories, the ones that had worried at him all night, suddenly opened up and he knew with crystal clarity that he'd been here before, in this very spot, as an infant. Only then, his father was with them. Now he wasn't.

And Brandon knew why.

# chapter thirty one

It took everything Paul had to stop himself from turning tail and running, screaming, from that church. He now knew why everything had been ripped out of it, why it was just one big room. It was the only way to fit the whole village in. The constables dragged him and Yolanda to the centre of the congregation, near to where Sadie stood behind the black altar that had so intrigued Piers. Upon it, a black stone pulsed with a malevolent light as threads of dull silver slid over its surface. Every now and again it would subtly change shape, bulging out almost imperceptibly, as if something caged within was seeking to break free. A horrified sense of realisation crawled up from Paul's gut and surged upwards: that was it. That was the gate, the creature's way of entering their world. As if answering him, a volley of cackles echoed round the room from the galley above. His head snapped up, and he saw shambling figures leaning over the balustrade, watching the people below with pale, hungry eyes. One figure in particular held his gaze; a feeling of horrified disgust seized Paul's heart and squeezed hard when it gave him a familiar grin.

It was Piers.

But it wasn't Piers. The naked malevolence in its eyes, the sludgy quality of its complexion, the cruel point of its teeth – all this told Paul that whatever animated his body was not Piers. He looked away and discovered many of the villagers were staring at the floor, each one avoiding the taunts of the demons that inhabited the bodies of their long-departed loved ones.

Sadie held up a hand and said something in that strange language, silencing villager and demon alike. Then, slowly, the congregation peeled back to form a corridor and a litter carried by six villagers was paraded through the gap. Whatever they bore was covered with a tattered blanket. As they lowered it to the ground, it twitched. Paul craned his head forward and watched as they helped whatever it was up from the floor. His breath twisted and caught in his throat when they straightened up to reveal a heavily pregnant woman, her arms slung awkwardly around the shoulders of two of them. Yolanda whispered something under her breath and let out a low, primal moan as the woman limped towards the altar, but there was nothing Paul could do to comfort her. With the clarity of pure horror, he knew what was going to happen next, but was helpless to stop it and could only watch when Sadie Decker stepped up with a black stone knife in her hand.

The woman shuddered and her belly rippled. Now she was closer, Paul could see why she limped; her left leg was swollen and a mass of writhing tubes snaked from her calf. They twisted around themselves wetly before plunging back into her thigh. A thought tickled the back of his mind, nagging at him, willing him to make the connection, but the pure, visceral nature of what he witnessed made him stupid. It wasn't until the woman threw her head back in a silent scream that he realised it was Mags.

The world pulled away, leaving Paul floating in a black void. Nothing existed but himself and Mags. He heard nothing of what Sadie Decker said; did not register the harsh hand that grasped his upper arm as he stumbled towards her; did not feel the damp stone beneath his knees when he was thrown to it. Mags' head lolled forwards again, strings of her hair spiralling down to obscure her features. What had they done to her? He struggled to his feet again, but before he could take a step, his guardian pulled him back and held him still, one thick arm wrapped around his neck to stop him from interrupting the ritual. He didn't go quietly; he fought against his captor with all his strength, clawing at the arm and lashing out with his legs hoping to catch a knee, or even better, whatever passed for its crotch, but the constable was as iron, hard and unyielding. All the while, Sadie Decker ignored their tussle and continued beseeching the heavens until the entire church was lit up by a blue light. Electricity strobed around the walls until every hair upon Paul's body stood on end. Sadie then raised the ancient knife above her head, eyes staring madly at the woman held in front of her.

Exhausted, Paul tried one last time to wriggle free, but he knew it was hopeless. Even if he could fight free, he would be too late to stop this. Unable to look away, he watched as Sadie bent down beside Mags and held the knife to the underside of her swollen belly. For a split second, Paul wondered if he saw pity flash across her face, but if it had been there, it was soon replaced by the stony purpose of concentration. With one swift movement, she drove the point of the knife into Mags abdomen and yanked it back, opening a bloody smile that stretched between her hip bones. Mags' whole body convulsed as a congealed mass of squirming grey worms spilled from the wound and splattered onto the ground at her feet. They slithered over one another, flopping feebly upon the stone, raising their eyeless, blunt heads in search of their host who had so crudely birthed them, but she was no longer there.

At last, Paul found his voice.

"Mags! MAGS!" he screamed as a new source of adrenaline surged through him. Again, he took up kicking and biting, but as before, it was no use.

She was gone. All that remained was the grey mass of abominations that wriggled on the ground where she once had been.

Another figure stood forward. This one was taller, their face obscured by a hood. Now everyone fell silent, including Sadie, who bowed and stepped back, away from Mags' diseased brood and closer to where Paul was being held. Outside, the vortex continued to spin, faster now, but the crashing waters sounded muted, distant, even, and the flickering arcs of electricity paused as if in anticipation.

The figure stood tall and dropped its hood.

Decker.

# chapter thirty two

Paul had been half expecting it, but it didn't stop his body from slumping as all strength fled him. The only thing that stopped him from crumpling to the ground was his guardian's arm wrapped around his neck.

After all the weeks of anxiety, of doubting, of fear, Decker now looked steady; peaceful, even. It was as if he now knew exactly what was expected of him and exactly how to do it, and that had driven out all the doubts and fear that had haunted him these past weeks. And in a way, he was right. Whatever this was, this was his purpose. This is what he had come to Dùisg a' Pheacaich to do.

He could only watch as Decker drew two stones from his robes. He held them above his head, one in each hand, and spoke one short sentence of a gibberish Paul didn't have a hope in understanding. But the crowd did. The weight of their expectation was suffocating as each one leaned forwards, their eyes staring, their mouths open. Decker then looked over at Paul, found his eyes and mouthed one word: *Sorry.*

He smashed the stones together. Outside, the sky split open with a deafening crack and a sheet of blue sparks rained down on the seething mass at his feet. They combusted immediately, a ferocious fire that ate the flesh from their soft, cartilaginous bones as they writhed on the damp stone floor, seeking something, anything, to quell the agony.

From the loch outside, there came a guttural roar. Paul's head snapped round to the source, yelping when his neck cricked against the muscle of his captor's arm. Above them, the roof of the church shuddered and peeled open. Its tiles flew up into the churning sky and its windows blasted out, showering the congregation in shards of brightly coloured glass. The vortex still swirled around them, but it was now dark; no electricity danced in its walls. Another grunt shook the church to its foundations. The demonic choir on the now-floating gallery yammered and heckled as the clouds parted and a stinking, black fog streamed down, making everyone cough.

Everyone apart from Decker, that is. He continued to stand still and proud, the stones still in his hands, the fire at his feet still raging.

The air pressure dropped. Paul's ears popped painfully. The fog still billowed down, past the church and into the heart of the vortex. A rush of foetid wind followed and the pressure built again. Paul felt something warm trickle from his nose. A deep clunk from below made the crowd take a purposeful step backwards, leaving Decker the only one left standing by the altar.

A gigantic thump made the ground shake. Everyone jumped. A ripple ran through the fog, splitting it open to reveal the universe. Huge pulsating nebulae of green and red billowed out and a billion tiny pinpricks of light glittered within the swirls of ancient galaxies. More ominous still was the gaping black void at the centre of it all, drawing all light to it, crushing it to nothingness.

Paul now knew. Now he understood. And, judging by the determined expressions on everyone else's faces, so did they.

That was what lay in wait for them if this failed.

As if answering the black void's call, the stone on the altar pulsed. It floated up and began to spin, slowly at first, but gained speed as it expanded. Its surface shuddered and stretched as whatever it held within its heart fought its way free. Finally, the tip of a claw broke through and shredded its surface, and a jumbled mass of flesh and oil spilled out upon the floor, smothering the funeral pyre of its kin. Great clouds of sulphurous smoke billowed out, making Paul's throat seize, choking him. Within the heart of the smoke, the mass stretched itself out and it began to take shape before their eyes: a huge, vaguely crocodilian head formed with a mouth full of oversized, broken teeth. Nine red eyes blinked balefully at them, and a powerful, serpentine body followed as it leaned down to stare at its congregation. Its arms were elongated and misshapen, with long cancerous-looking tumours dangling from them. It had no legs, but a long, sinuous tail which it wrapped around itself as it hauled itself upright until it loomed over them all. It stared at Decker, who looked so tiny next to this behemoth, but he did not look away. Instead, he raised the stones again.

The beast sniggered, an unpleasant bubbling sound.

"Tiny human. You think you can immolate me, as you have done my young? All you have done is return them to me. Now stand tall and fulfil your destiny. My hunger grows, and you know of our pact."

As it to prove a point, the beast leaned down and plucked a handful of villagers from the crowd. They screeched as it tossed them into the air, the way a cat might play with a mouse, and caught them easily in its cruel jaws. But it did not bite down; instead, it held them there, trapped within a cage of its teeth. Tiny arms reached out beseechingly to their loved ones, who screamed back with tears streaming down their cheeks, begging Sadie to stop the monster and save them, that this wasn't what was supposed to happen, that they were innocent. As this, the monster snorted in amusement and bit down, turning the people held there to mulch.

Sadie Decker, her face pained yet calm, nodded towards Decker. He said nothing in reply and gave her a sad smile before raising the stones above his own head. Sadie stared at the God of Nine Eyes.

The God of Nine Eyes stared back.

Decker smashed them together again. This time, the sparks cascaded down upon himself.

# chapter thirty three

Sadie threw up her arms again, and the chanting stopped. She shouted something, and a terrible groan emanated from the vortex.

It was coming.

Another figure joined Sadie, a hooded figure that stood straight and tall in drab robes made of brown sack cloth. He did not need to remove his hood for Brandon to know that it was his father.

He stood, mesmerised, as his father took two stones drew two stones from his robe. He held them aloft and spoke a few, unintelligible words. Before he could smash them together, Brandon's paralysis broke. He ripped his hand from his mother's grasp and darted forwards, crying, "No! Daddy! No, no, no!"

The whole village gasped, but no one broke ranks. That was forbidden.

Sadie Decker, incandescent with fury, tried to intercept him, but Brandon was a fraction of a second quicker. Before she could grab him, Brandon leapt at his father and wrapped his small body around his legs, begging and pleading for him to stop, to not do this, to not leave them.

John Decker, bereft at the sign of his anguished son's face, allowed the rocks to tumble from his hands. They struck the ground with a dull thud.

"Son... no... son... go back to your mother," he pleaded, wrapping his arms around Brandon. "This has to be done. It has to be. Otherwise all is lost. You must understand. You will understand."

"No... Daddy... no," Brandon panted.

Another pair of hands, these ones hard and cruel, grasped Brandon's shoulders and tried to wrench him away. He held on tighter. He would stop this. He would make them stop.

A guttural roar shook the ground. Instinctively, Brandon looked up, and for the first time in his life, he saw true fear in Sadie Decker's face.

"It comes," she whispered. "We must be ready." Using that moment of confusion, she pulled Brandon back, away from his father, and flung him to the ground.

"Daddy!" Brandon sobbed, trying to scrabble forwards, to reach his father once again, but another pair of hands, these ones softer and more familiar, pulled him back.

"No, son – we must not interrupt," his mother said.

"Mammy," he whimpered.

"I know," she said. She bent her head towards his and whispered. "When I say run, run."

Together, they filed back towards the edge of the semi-circle and watched as his father picked up the rocks once again. He raised them above his head and looked directly at Brandon before smashing them together. Sparks rained down, igniting the very stones at his feet, and the resulting crash rolled through the valley like thunder.

All the lights in the vortex went out, and the black stone that sat upon the church's altar began to pulsate and grow. All eyes were on it. No one moved.

"Run!" his mother whispered.

# chapter thirty four

The fire ran hungrily over Decker's head, down his arms, along his torso, until his entire body was aflame. Beside him, his grandmother was swaying and chanting. He screamed out one final word before stepping into the smouldering remains of Old Nine Eye's bastard offspring. The fire rekindled and leapt higher, transforming into a pillar of blinding flame that stretched up towards the heavens. The beast hesitated, its nine eyes widened in what Paul could only think of as shock as it recoiled from the blistering heat.

"No," it said, its voice louder than thunder. "No! This is not the way!" The God of Nine Eyes swooped down to confront the matriarch of Sinner's Wake. "You have broken the pact. I was promised blood – blood from your line, and the line of your beloved. He is mine! Mine!"

"No." Sadie said, triumphantly. "You always forget. Every time this happens we go through this charade. In your greed you called him back – and now he fulfils his purpose."

Obeying his grandmother's instruction, the pillar of flame that was once Brandon Decker floated forwards. The God sneered and coiled its serpentine tail underneath it, ready to strike. Sadie looked back and gave her congregation a self-satisfied smile as her grandson stretched out out his blazing hand to touch the beast, confident that this was it. But before Decker could touch it, the God lashed out, ripping through the blistering heat of his fire to seize his throat.

The villagers staggered back, aghast. Paul, having no idea how the ritual was supposed to go, turned to Sadie for guidance. She offered him no comfort; her eyes stood staring from their sockets, one hand clutching at her horrified mouth.

"No!" she gasped.

The God of Nine Eyes laughed and squeezed. The fire guttered and died, leaving Decker dangling from its malformed hand. He scrabbled at his neck in a futile bid to break its grip, but the beast simply smiled, lifted him aloft and dropped him into its open jaws.

"Brandon!" Both Paul and Yolanda shrieked. Sadie sank to her knees, dumbstruck, but Paul ran forwards, shouting expletives as if that might convince the beast to stop, to release him, to return what was rightfully his. The God ignored him.

"You were too late," it said to Sadie. "In your arrogance, you grew complacent. This fragment might forget, but the whole does not."

It lifted its eyes heavenwards. The universe shivered as if in recognition and the void at its centre blinked, just once, and Paul was filled with a terrible certainty.

This was it. The God of Nine Eyes was but an emissary, a small part of something so huge it defied all human understanding. The veil was now gone; their reality, broken. Now there was nothing to hide them from its gaze, no defence against its unfeeling indifference to their tiny existence. It would devour them, not because it was evil, or even hungry, but simply because that is what it did. That is what it had always done, and what it would always do.

The floor cracked beneath their feet. The vortex froze and began to fragment as time snapped. Matter itself began to dissolve. People screamed as pinpricks of darkness punched through their bodies, pulling them apart at the seams. Some ran for the floating bridge, scrambling over each other, clawing at each other's skin in their desperation, not caring if those they knocked into the ever-growing abyss were friend or foe, young or old.

Through all of it, Sadie Decker did not move. Curled in a ball, she wailed, beseeching the beast to listen to her, to obey, to honour their pact. At this, the God laughed.

Paul staggered over to Yolanda. "Come on!"

She didn't follow. Instead, she raised a hand and pointed at the beast.

"Look," she breathed.

"Yolanda, come on! We have to get out!" Paul tugged at her arm, but she refused to budge.

"No... seriously... look!" She reached out and grasped his chin, forcing him to look back.

The God of Nine Eyes had stopped laughing and was now staring down at its chest. If he didn't know better, Paul would have said it looked confused. Light shone through the cracks in its scaled armour, building in intensity until it hurt his eyes. Its abdomen swelled and the tumescent growths that hung from its twisted arms smouldered and blackened. It let out a roar and flailed backwards, ripping at its own form in an attempt at quelling the flames that now burst forth from the gaps in its hide.

Sadie stopped her wailing and looked up, her eyes full of a manic glee as the beast began to disintegrate. As the fire ravaged it, it too shrank, down, down, down until it was the size of a man. It trembled so violently that it stumbled forwards. Sadie staggered to her feet and snatched up her knife. She slashed it down with such force that she cleaved what remained of its head from its shoulders, which bounced once before shattering into a thousand pieces. A triumphant smile curled her lips as Decker exploded from the remains of the God of Nine Eyes and smothered them with his righteous fire. As he did so, a low rumble ripped through the night, making what was left of the ground tremble. Its conduit destroyed, the void retreated, clouds swarming in again as the veil was remade, turning the sky from black to blood-red, to orange and then to grey. Another crash, and the altar crumbled to a fine black dust. The vortex span again and what remained of the villagers, bloodied and broken, lifted their heads in disbelief. Finally the pillar of flame that surrounded Decker diminished until it winked out of existence completely.

Everything fell silent. No one moved. Above them, stars winked in existence again and the night sky reasserted itself.

Sadie Decker, her eyes wet with tears, stumbled forwards and threw herself to the floor. By her knees, a crumpled form lay, naked and shivering. It reached up and grabbed her hand, which she dragged up to her lips and kissed fervently. The other hand snaked up and caressed her cheek. The God of Nine Eyes was no more; instead, there was a man, thin and scarred.

"Sadie," he croaked. "Sadie, my love, my life… this must end. It was so close this time. We cannot risk this again. You must let me go."

Sadie shook her head furiously and gulped back a sob. "No. Never-"

"You must," the man interrupted. "You must. What we did was wrong. You know that. And yet you still play this game, sacrificing generation after generation of our own blood to trick the beast and keep me alive-"

"They don't matter!" Sadie keened. "All that matters is us. I can't survive without you. You can't leave me."

"No. Sadie, my love... we can't go on like this. If you let me go, let me die, the demon has no vessel to inhabit. Keep me here and it will keep coming back. Next time, it might succeed. It pushed me to my limits tonight. I cannot hold it back again. One day, there will be no blood left, and then what will you do? Nothing will stir me and it *will* break free."

Callum Decker, Brandon Decker's distant Grandfather, lay back against the cold stone and sighed.

"I'm ready to go. Do it,"

Sadie shook her head again. "No. I can't. I can't. If you die, I die too and we will forever be separated by death. We will never be together again. Even these fleeting moments are better than that."

"How do you know?" Callum said. "How do you know we will never be together again? My love, I am exhausted – and I know you are, too. We've both been alive, after a fashion, for too damn long… we've condemned an entire town, sacrificed our own children's blood, risked bringing great evil to the world… and for what? So we can spend a few moments together again?"

"But these moments are everything to me. We should have had more. The demon lied – it said it would show us everything and that we would be together forever-"

"Yes, I know, my love, I know. It lied. That's what demons do. They lie. But, let's be fair – I lied. You did, too. What we did was selfish. What you continue to do, even more. I am so tired, so weary of this half-life, this poor excuse of existence. It needs to end, Sadie my dear, and it needs to end now. This time. Please.

Just do it. Before it comes back and I do not have the strength to ask again."

Sadie stroked her husband's head, tears now streaming down her face. In a way, Paul couldn't help but feel sorry for her. She'd lost her husband to the demon and the only way to see him was to summon it and destroy it, albeit temporarily... but at what cost? He looked at what remained of the villagers; each one wore a conflicted expression of both pity and hatred. They knew no other life, true... but to keep doing this, to keep sacrificing their children, just so she could see her husband? That was wrong, and they knew it. He wondered how many other times they had clustered around this spot, waiting, willing for Sadie Decker to do the right thing, knowing that no one could stop her from making her selfish choice over and over, putting her happiness ahead of their needs time and time again... knowing that no matter how much they wanted to plunge a dagger into her blackened heart, they couldn't as she was the only one who could lead the ritual and prevent the beast from escaping and devouring the world.

She bent forwards, the weight of their judgement too much to bear, and pulled Callum in her arms. Jealousy, treacle thick and dripping with resentment, rose within Paul. Even now, he could tell she was hesitating, putting herself before those whose lives she had wrecked. She might not see her husband often, but at least she still had that chance, that hope. Every single other person here didn't. They'd all lost someone they cared about, never to be seen again. Today, he joined their ranks. Whilst Sadie crooned and stroked Callum's wispy hair, Paul balled his fists up at the injustice of it all. There she was, alive and whole, and just in front of her was a pile of ashes that had once been Brandon-

He paused. His heart gave one, huge thud.

Did he just see movement?

The ashes stirred and a hand reached up, blackened and scorched, followed by a head. Paul staggered over to it, not caring that the villagers gasped and murmured at such a break in etiquette. He scrabbled at the mound of ashes, uncovering Brandon's withered body. His breath came out in hitched sobs as he pulled him clear and cradled him close like a child. He had no idea how he lived – every part of his body was burned to a crisp, his skin cracking and weeping, but he didn't care. Sadie and her husband stopped and watched as Paul murmured words of love and understanding to Brandon. His breathing degenerated into nothing more than a rasp, Paul knew the end was near. Sheer will alone had kept Brandon alive long enough to say goodbye, to feel the touch of his love's skin against his own before he could die. He smiled.

"I love you. I'm sorry."

He fell back, limp. With his final breath, Brandon's body crumbled to dust.

# chapter Thirty Fiue

Brandon didn't hesitate. All attention was fixed on the monstrous shape forcing its way out of the stone and into their world, and so no one was in the right frame of mind to stop them.

There were a few shouts when his mother barged past the slack-jawed villagers, but she plunged on, one hand gripping Brandon's like her life depended on it. In many ways, it probably did. He tried to match her stride, but his legs were too short and he stumbled more than once. Each time, she yanked him up and continued on. This made his arm ache, but he never once complained.

They raced up the floating stone bridge, never once looking down or up, just straight ahead, towards their goal. The black hole leered down over them as a growing roar shook the church, followed by a strident shout. Brandon couldn't make it out, but he knew it was Grandma Sadie. A flash of light illuminated the trees that bordered the loch, and for a split second, Brandon saw the horrors that accompanied the demon; evil, misshapen byblows of its foul design. Some had more eyes than legs; others had more mouths filled with needle-sharp teeth that erupted from random parts of their bodies. The only thing they had in common was that all bore no resemblance to anything natural. One leapt at them, its long legs scrabbling at his mother's head. She let out a shriek and batted it away with her free hand, snapping one of its limbs as she did so. It hit the ground with a squelch, its body bursting like ripe fruit. Other things swooped down and fell upon it, devouring its stinking innards; others, emboldened by its kin's attempts at waylaying them, flung themselves at Brandon and his mother, trying to bring them down so they might feast.

Brandon's mother shrieked again, but this time it had nothing to do with fear. Pure rage, the primal fury only a mother knows, surged out of her as she ripped the creatures away from her and her son. She threw them to the floor, stamping down on the ones who still moved, grinding their flabby bodies under her heel. Spurred on by his mother's bravery, Brandon grasped one that had become entangled in his hair; it felt both soft and slimy in his hand, and a shudder of disgust coursed through him as he threw it away from him as hard as he could.

Wary now, the monsters hesitated; some skittered up to their fallen brood and started to feed; others hung back and watched Brandon and his mother once again run through the trees and towards the road. Another flash of light illuminated the night, accompanied by another foul roar. Brandon dared to glance back; a pillar of pure white light now reached the heavens, piercing the sky, banishing the shadows back to whence they came. The God of Nine Eyes roared again, but it now sounded in pain, almost mournful. The light pulsed, and the shadows that made up its infernal body caught alight, sending a shower of sparks heavenwards. The clouds rolled back and the void disappeared from view.

And Brandon knew that his father was gone.

His mother let out a great sob, but continued running. The road was in sight now. The demon temporarily banished, Grandma Sadie would have her way, but then it would seep back into the world, for the vessel was still alive in its own diminished way.

Brandon, only seven years old didn't know how he knew this, but he did. He also knew no matter how far they ran, no matter how hard he tried to fight, the day would come when the demon would call to him and he would take his father's place, like his father before him, and his father before him. Like every member of his family eventually did.

Everyone apart from Grandma Sadie, of course.

# chapter thirty six

Paul gathered the dust that had once been Brandon Decker and let out one, last, furious sob. He looked up at Sadie, his eyes filled with hatred.

"He did this because of you. I have lost my love because you cannot let go of yours. Brandon lost his father – his mother lost her husband. I wonder, how many people here can tell the same tale?" He flung his arm out and gestured to the crowds. A murmur of agreement rippled through it. He said what they all had thought, but never dared voice.

Sadie's countenance grew stony. "How dare you. Our love stretches over centuries, born of blood and sacrifice, a mighty oak compared to the damselfly of your life. How *dare* you!"

"How dare I?" Paul wrenched himself to his feet and towered over Sadie Decker, his eyes blazing. "How dare *I*? Your selfishness knows no bounds! You damned this entire town due to your own petty desires. You both should have lived your lives, raised your families, then died, together. Instead, you condemned everyone here to this living hell so you could continue on. I can't even begin to think what was going through your head when you thought this was a desirable alternative to natural death."

"No! I won't hear it... I won't listen... It wasn't natural – he was ill... we wanted to find a cure, a way to avoid it..."

Callum Decker reached up with a shaky hand to stroke his wife's hair. She was no longer the iron-willed harridan that ruled Dùisg a' Pheacaich with a fist of stone, but a grieving old woman with nothing left to live for. Still, Paul could find no pity within himself to spare her. She had used the town's folk as commodities to bargain with, her own flesh and blood as the means to an end. For this, there could be no forgiveness.

"Sadie... Oh Sadie, my girl... you still believe that? That is not true. I wanted to know the secrets of the universe, and I paid the price. Even my illness was self inflicted. Listen to him. He speaks the truth. You know it. I know it. I am tired. End this curse.

We should have known nothing in this life is free. He has shown courage to cut through the demon's lies. Please. End it. End it now."

Sadie sat back on her heels and lifted her face to the sky. Her whole body shook with grief. The villagers stared, as silent as the grave and Paul couldn't help but wonder: how many times had they done this? How many times had they stood here whilst Sadie Decker wrestled with her conscience?

"Please."

The amount of pain in Callum Decker's last entreaty brought fresh tears to Paul's eyes.

"Don't let Brandon's sacrifice be in vain," Paul whispered.

Sadie let out a shuddering sigh. From her robes she drew out the black stone knife and laid it on the ground. Then she reached over and gathered the stones Decker had used to start the cleansing blaze. With a stone in each hand, she held them up high and whispered the same words Brandon had screamed out at the demon and slammed the rocks together. Sparks flew, engulfing both her and Callum. The inferno caught quickly, the ferocity of its heat forcing Paul back, away from them, but he was still close enough to see Sadie pick up the knife again and plunge it deep into Callum's chest.

There was a shriek, followed by a rush of blistering air that swept over the congregation. It whipped up the flames, twisting them into unholy forms, sending them spiralling upwards. Beneath their feet, the ground trembled. No one spoke as the remaining inhabitants of Dùisg a' Pheacaich turned tail and fled the church, up the precarious stone bridge and out onto the safety of the shore. Paul was the last to leave. He turned to watch as the fire burned out, leaving no trace of Sadie or Callum. The waters forming the vortex slackened and Paul knew it was time to leave or be drowned. Slabs of stone fell away under his feet as he raced up the bridge, crashing into the waters below and more than once, he feared he would not make it. But he did, the last stone falling away as he raced onto the bank.

With a rush, the loch settled back to its former self, its surface once again calm. Except now, no steeple pierce its surface.

Like its keeper, the Church had gone.

# chapter thirty seven

Like lost children waking from a nightmare, the villagers regarded their surroundings in bewilderment. Gone was the carefully maintained illusion of the town, replaced by the derelict reality. Buildings they had dwelt in, raised families in, safe from the ravages of time, now stood as wrecks, their walls crumbled, their roofs lost.

What happened to them after that fateful night, no one knows. Once again the name of Dùisg a' Pheacaich was lost to the mists of time, consigned to nothing more than folk legend and an uneasy sense of forbidden things made flesh.

oOo

Almost fluorescent streaks of pink and orange slashed the night sky, heralding the birth of a new day. Tomorrow had finally arrived.

Paul and Yolanda sat by the water's edge, both lost in their own little worlds of loss and shock. Nothing remained of St Machan's; it was as if it had never existed. But that didn't mean it was gone. It had burned an indelible mark on both of them, and for that reason alone they both knew it would never truly die.

It took them until the sun was comfortably up to find the energy to move. They trudged back up to the skeleton of Dùisg a' Pheacaich and tried to find their vehicles, but they too had been caught up with time reasserting itself, rusting them to useless lumps of metal. A hollow sense of impotence filled Paul. That just about topped everything off. Well, it would be something people might puzzle over in years to come, if nothing else

It also meant they were reduced to hitch-hiking, which was hard given the remoteness of the now dead town. They saw no-one as they plodded down the broken road; maybe they too had faded away to nothing, ghosts of another place, another time, unsuited to this world, doomed to wander the Highlands forever. Neither of them could even begin to speculate. All they knew is that both of them had sprouted a few grey hairs, and a few new wrinkles had been added to their foreheads and around their eyes. Not that they talked about it. Neither of them spoke at all. What could they say? Talking about it meant admitting it, and admitting it meant it had to be real, and neither of them were quite ready to broach that obstacle right now.

A solid drizzle settled over the moors, misting the ground and soaking their clothes, They still walked on. Finally, after what felt like hours, they reached a proper road, one that was maintained and smelled of oil and bitumen, a living road with living smells. It was only then they could finally breathe more easily. They'd escaped. Sadie Decker's curse no longer held sway over them.

There were still no signs of traffic, though. It dawned on them that even though the road was maintained, the area was still remote. It might be hours – days, even – before they might come across anyone, and even then they weren't guaranteed a lift. In a way, it would be a fittingly ignoble end, to escape the horrors of Dùisg a' Pheacaich only to die of exposure on a Scottish hillside.

The light around them dimmed and the damp turned cold. Even though they wore thick fleeces, they still felt it. Night would come soon, and they both muttered private prayers that someone – anyone – would pass them by and offer them a lift before that happened.

Just as dusk turned over to let the night in, a pair of headlights twinkled in the distance. For the first time in what felt like months, they allowed themselves to smile and chatter as they stuck their thumbs out and hoped. The Land Rover sped past, and for a heart-stopping moment they feared it would just pass them by, but it slowed and stopped a few yards ahead of them. Despite their exhaustion, they found strength to jog up to it. The driver's door opened, revealing an older man clad in scruffy overalls and Wellington boots.

"You need a lift?" he said.

"Oh, God, yes – thank you. Thank you so much," Paul said.

"Stupid question, I suppose. It's a long way from anywhere, here. What the hell are you out here for?"

"You wouldn't believe it if we told you," Paul said. "You know Dùisg a' Pheacaich-"

"Dùisg a' Pheacaich?" the man frowned. "Och, why in all that's holy were you out there? That town's been nothing but ruins for decades. And out there dressed like that?" He rolled his eyes and muttered "bloody tourists" under his breath.

Paul made to say something, but stopped before the words could form. What was the point? Judging by the way Yolanda's shoulder's slumped, she pretty much felt the same way. There was no point.

They clambered into the Land Rover, luxuriating in its warmth. The man introduced himself as Sean and that he was a local crofter on his way to Wick. He chatted to them about nothing much until their eyes felt hot and heavy and it became a struggle to stay awake. Slowly, Sean's chatter became a soft buzz and they both gave into their exhaustion. It did cross their minds that sleeping could be a dangerous thing to do, but considering everything they'd gone through, they simply didn't care.

Their doze was broken by Sean asking them if they wanted him to take them to the train station. True to his word, he had driven them to Wick. Paul felt a rush of gratitude and said he'd rather he took them to the bank so he could pay him, but Sean shook his head, saying he wouldn't accept a penny from them; it looked as though they'd been through enough and it was the least he could do as a good Christian. At that, Paul had to bite back a snort of amusement. The people of Dùisg a' Pheacaich had thought themselves good Christians, too.

The trains from Wick were sporadic and the guard surly, but eventually Paul managed to buy two tickets to London with his credit card; his wallet was mercifully still in his pocket. He sat opposite Yolanda, who refused to meet his eyes. Instead, she stared blankly out of the window, watching the countryside flash by in a blur of green and grey. He stared at his hands. They were filthy. To the outside world, it might look like mud, but Paul knew the truth. The gritty residue that collected in the creases of his palms and under his nails was all that was left of Decker. Furious tears scalded the back of his eyes. He blinked, trying to force them back, but their onslaught was merciless. He sobbed like a newborn babe into his hands, the tears washing away the ash, cleansing them. Yolanda offered no comfort, but continued to stare out of the window, her expression glassy.

The train stopped and started again many times before Paul managed to wrestle himself under control. He glanced out of the window, catching sight of his reflection. A ghost glanced back, pale and gaunt with red, staring eyes. No wonder no one sat near them. He would have avoided him, too.

Outside, the world had changed from one of heather and hills to a more familiar vista of concrete and brick. A tea trolley, dragged by a bored-looking youth, rattled past, but neither he nor Yolanda took any notice of it.

At Edinburgh they changed, lost in a sea of suits as people went about their daily business, chattering and laughing, treating the day just like any other until Paul screamed at them to stop, to have some respect, that they were ignorant fools living on borrowed time, didn't they know he was dead, that he died for them? People shrank away from him as he ranted until a steady hand was laid upon his shoulder and Yolanda guided him away, just in time to avoid the security guards who were making a beeline for them. Luckily the crowds masked their retreat and they managed to duck on a train heading south before they could be detained. Again, they sat opposite each other, avoiding each other's eyes, lost in their own personal world of torment.

Stations came and went. They presented their tickets when prompted, ignoring the looks of revulsion from the guards, and changed trains when told. At Peterborough, Yolanda wandered away, melting into the crowds before Paul could follow her.

He never saw her again.

He continued on to London alone. The carriages became fuller and noisier as they drew closer, but no one sat with him. It was if he exuded a physical barrier that no one dared cross; his wild eyes and dishevelled appearance frightening them. He could tell by the looks they shot him, by the way they scuttled past him, choosing to stand rather than sit with him. All of this was just fine by him. Let them scuttle. Let them judge. He didn't care. Not any more.

The train pulled into King's Cross. Paul hauled himself from his seat and sleep-walked to the tube. The journey was now so familiar he didn't have to think; he just had to trudge, down the stairs, down the escalator, cramming himself into a clanking metal tube that smelled of stale sweat and dust. Change. More stairs. More escalators. Dodging commuters, then outside. After the open moorland of the Highlands, London smelled of smoke and tasted of metal, a testament to the lives that thrived there. Usually, he would have relished it. Now, it meant nothing to him.

Finally, the journey ended and he found himself standing in front of the scarred front door that led to his flat. Their flat. He paused, his hand half way to his pocket. He still had his keys – his habit of putting everything he might ever need in his pockets had never left him, even in his fear and panic – but now he was here, he was reluctant to enter. Everything about home would remind him of Decker, of the life they shared, of the life they lived, and he wasn't sure he was ready to confront it quite yet. He let out an exhausted sigh and rested his head against the frosted glass. But what else could he do? Where else could he go? Sure, he had friends, but that would lead to questions, questions he had no hope of answering.

He dug out his keys. The lock was stiff, warning him not to enter. The hallway, stuffy and carpeted with junk mail, greeted him. That used to annoy Decker, that no one would take responsibility for it and tidy it away. At the end of the hallway, a set of stairs reared. They led to number 3. His home. Their home. He placed one foot on the bottom step, but he may as well have been climbing Everest. He ascended, his breath came in juddering sobs and his heart hammered, making him feel dizzy. He fumbled with his keys, dropping them once, twice, three times before he managed to guide the right one into the keyhole.

He pushed the door open.

The scent that emanated from the flat overwhelmed him and he almost fled. It wasn't strong and it carried a stale element, but still he drowned in it. Across the hall he could see the door to their living room was open, and beyond that, the mantelpiece upon which a large, framed photo stood: Decker and him, laughing, their arms around one another as they stood at the edge of the Grand Canyon. The memory surged up: the swooping sensation in his stomach as he looked down; the dry, dusty quality to the air, the sense of security he gained from Decker's arms about his waist.

He groped for the wall, his throat tight. Those arms were gone and there was nothing he could do about it. He slid to the floor, his face buried in his hands. He felt something crumple beneath him. He pulled it out and examined it through tear-stung eyes.

A letter.

It was addressed to Decker in handwriting he recognised. Only one person added such ridiculous loops to the B and D in his name.

Decker's mother.

He tore the letter open, his hands shaking. Inside was a sheaf of papers, all handwritten. He tried to read, but the words blurred together in a sea of blue, forcing him to blink.

*"My Dearest Brandon,*

*I know things have not been right between us in a while and this pains me more than you will ever know. I'm writing to you in the hope that you might listen. I would phone, but I'm afraid you would refuse to take my call. I'm sorry for everything that has happened, for all the secrecy, for the lies, for my behaviour... I know you don't believe me, but in truth, it had nothing to do with you or your life choices. My darling son, please believe me when I say I don't care who you love, who you live with, as long as you love and you live. What drove my outburst was fear, pure and simple.*

*When you were a boy, I could keep you safe. I could soothe away the nightmares and protect you from harm. But now you're grown, you're beyond me. Yes, I know this is normal and should be encouraged, but I couldn't help it. I held on too tightly, I can see that now, and that is my biggest regret. I should have let you go, let you fly... and told you the truth. But I didn't, and now I fear you are in more danger than you've ever been in before.*

*I know you're angry, Brandon, but please, please listen to me. I don't want anything from you, not even a phone call – I only want you to take care and read this. After that, you can make your own mind up. Over the last few weeks, you've been having dreams. Nightmares, I would guess. I know, because I've been having them too. If yours are anything like mine, then they will be stirring all* manner of memories that should have remained forgotten – memories of your father and of the village of your birth.

I will be honest, I am struggling to put all of this in words that make sense. It isn't just the memories, but the desire to go back there, to Dùisg a' Pheacaich. I can't say this enough – don't give in. Don't go there. Please, Brandon, resist it. There are things there that you don't understand, things you won't ever understand. To put it bluntly, I believe if you go back, you'll die. I know this sounds crazy, but I can't put it any other way.

I know I told you Sadie Decker was your grandmother, but that isn't strictly true. She's your ancestor, your many-greats grandmother, born in the 1800s. She is also mad. Nearly two hundred years ago, she and her husband, your I don't know how many greats Grandfather, Callum, made a bargain with a demon. Yes, I know how that sounds, but there is no other way to describe it. I don't know what drove them – greed, curiosity, insanity – but together they sought every avenue they could find to discover the secrets of the universe. I don't know where they went or what they experienced, but it all ended in that village. They are the reason for its name – it means Sinner's Wake. They learned too late that demons are not to be trusted, and only Sadie's devious mind stopped them all from being devoured and the evil they courted from being unleashed to roam free in our world.

That place is cursed, just as your blood is cursed, cursed by Sadie Decker and doomed to repeat forever. Every few years, blood must be offered to appease the beast. Every twenty five, that blood must come from our line. This allows Sadie to summon it so she can trick it again and keep it from escaping. I suspect she could offer her own blood and stop it for good, but she won't entertain the notion, preferring to sacrifice her own kin to keep the cycle going. The demon holds Callum, you see and this is the only way they can be together, for while the beast lies defeated, her husband returns to her – until it gathers strength and he is once again doomed to his fate. What that fate is, I don't know. All I do know is that this time, it's your blood she will want, just as she wanted your father's all those years ago. That is the reason I am writing to you, Brandon – it will call you, but you must not answer. No matter how enticing it may be, you must resist it. You must stay *away, or you will be next. I know it sounds callous, but they'll find another victim, another sacrifice amongst those who live there and you, my boy, my life, will be safe. That is why I took you from that accursed place. To keep you safe and to stop history from repeating itself.*

*I am sorry I didn't tell you this before. I'm sorry I kept secrets. I am hoping that now the truth is out, it might go some way to rebuilding the relationship we once had. I miss you, Brandon – I miss you every day and I just want to know you're safe. Again, I know this all sounds like insanity, but look deep within yourself and you will know that I am telling the truth. The nightmares... the memories... that incessant call that pulls you back to that accursed village... it's all there, all buried within you.*

*You don't have to visit me or call me or even acknowledge that you have received this letter... I don't mind. Just, please, do not go there. I have already lost so much to that town. Please don't let it take my only son from me.*

*Love you, forever and always,*
*Mam.*
*Xxxx*


Paul stared at the letter. Reread it again. An anger like none other welled up within him.

She'd known. She'd known, but she hadn't told him.

He looked at the top of the page. It was dated three days before they left.

She'd known. None of this needed to happen.

Would he have listened to her? Paul didn't know. Decker's relationship with his mother had always been complicated, but then again, whose wasn't? Would he have believed her, or just put it down to her obvious mental health problems? The anger shrank back, smothered by a black fog of despair. Decker wouldn't have listened. Paul wouldn't have let him. He would have encouraged him to ignore her – look, demons? Really? I know you've been having nightmares and everything recently, but that happens to us all, come on, let's go, it's a chance of a lifetime... Guilt joined the despair. Oh, they still would have gone, because he would have made sure of it. Because he was that selfish.

He closed his eyes, the back of his head resting against the wall. The letter dropped from his hand, fluttering to the floor.

It was his fault.

And that was all there was to it.

# chapter thirty eight

Imagine a scene. The camera pans across an open plan flat; once tidy, but now littered with filth. Bottles are strewn across the floor, half eaten meals left to fester on discarded plates. The focus zooms in on a sofa, once a pristine white, now stained. On it, lies a man. His clothes are crumpled and filthy. His hair is unkempt and a good growth of stubble had been allowed to grow, framing a mouth paralysed by grief.

One arm is thrown up over his face, hiding his eyes. The other dangles uselessly to the floor. From it, a bottle has fallen, empty except for a couple of pills that spill out on to carpet.

Here lies Paul Ryan.

It was his fault.

# EPILOGUE.

The clouds raced above them, chasing down the ever-present drizzle that shrouded the hills. The walker shielded his eyes with one hand and gazed across the water whilst his friend checked their map.

"Is this it?"

"I don't know. I think so." He frowned and studied the map further.

The walker sighed. Despite the weather, it was beautiful out here. Unlike other lochs in the area, the water was crystal clear. He drank in the vista, an enormous sense of well-being swelling within him. This was how it should be, away from the hustle and bustle of modern life. Peaceful and... wait.

What was that?

He leaned forwards, as if that would help him focus before bringing his binoculars to his eyes. Yes. He was right. There was something there. Something sticking out of the loch.

"Would you look at that..."

His friend looked up from his map reading. "What?"

The walker handed him his binoculars. "Over there. What's all that about, I wonder?"

The walker's friend adjusted the focus to clear the fuzz of blue and grey. He gasped.

"My God. Is that a church?"

"I think it is."

"Wow. A drowned church. You'd think we would have heard of that, wouldn't you?"

"I know." The walker took the binoculars back and took another look. Now he had his eye in, he could see every detail of the spire that stuck out of the water. It just went to show, even in this hyper-connected world, there were still things to discover if you just went out and looked for them.

"I wonder what the history of this place is?" His friend tore off one glove and fumbled in his pocket for his smartphone. "Damn. No reception."

"Must be connected to that derelict village we passed," the walker said. "I wonder how old it is?" He glanced at his friend. "Shall we go and take a closer look?"

"What – go down there?"

"Why not? There might be more ruins near the water's edge."

They grinned. Why not indeed.

oOo

*In this merciless universe, life is but a blip, a mistake, a fleeting moment that will be soon usurped by rock and fire, something the void barely acknowledges and will all too soon forget, dooming it to repeat these mistakes time and time again.*

*From deep within its lair, it felt their arrival, small specks of red in a never-ending vacuum of black.*

*It stirred.*

*They thought it dead. But how can something beyond time, beyond life, die? All it could do was wait.*

*Wait for the cycle to begin again.*

# THE END

# CHECK OUT OTHER GREAT
# DEEP SEA THRILLERS

## MEGA
## by Jake Bible

There is something in the deep. Something large. Something hungry. Something prehistoric.
And Team Grendel must find it, fight it, and kill it.
Kinsey Thorne, the first female US Navy SEAL candidate has hit rock bottom. Having washed out of the Navy, she turned to every drink and drug she could get her hands on. Until her father and cousins, all ex-Navy SEALS themselves, offer her a way back into the life: as part of a private, elite combat Team being put together to find and hunt down an impossible monster in the Indian Ocean. Kinsey has a second chance, but can she live through it?

## THE BLACK
## by Paul E Cooley

Under 30,000 feet of water, the exploration rig Leaguer has discovered an oil field larger than Saudi Arabia, with oil so sweet and pure, nations would go to war for the rights to it. But as the team starts drilling exploration well after exploration well in their race to claim the sweet crude, a deep rumbling beneath the ocean floor shakes them all to their core. Something has been living in the oil and it's about to give birth to the greatest threat humanity has ever seen.

"The Black" is a techno/horror-thriller that puts the horror and action of movies such as Leviathan and The Thing right into readers' hands. Ocean exploration will never be the same."

# CHECK OUT OTHER GREAT DEEP SEA THRILLERS

## PREDATOR X
## by C.J Waller

When deep level oil fracking uncovers a vast subterranean sea, a crack team of cavers and scientists are sent down to investigate. Upon their arrival, they disappear without a trace. A second team, including sedimentologist Dr Megan Stoker, are ordered to seek out Alpha Team and report back their findings. But Alpha team are nowhere to be found – instead, they are faced with something unexpected in the depths. Something ancient. Something huge. Something dangerous. Predator X

## DEAD BAIT
## by Tim Curran

A husband hell-bent on revenge hunts a Wereshark...A Russian mail order bride with a fishy secret...Crabs with a collective consciousness...A vampire who transforms into a Candiru...Zombie piranha...Bait that will have you crawling out of your skin and more. Drawing on horror, humor with a helping of dark fantasy and a touch of deviance, these 19 contemporary stories pay homage to the monsters that lurk in the murky waters of our imaginations. If you thought it was safe to go back in the water...Think Again!

# CHECK OUT OTHER GREAT DEEP SEA THRILLERS

## LAMPREYS
by Alan Spencer

A secret government tactical team is sent to perform a clean sweep of a private research installation. Horrible atrocities lurk within the abandoned corridors. Mutated sea creatures with insane killing abilities are waiting to suck the blood and meat from their prey.

Unemployed college professor Conrad Garfield is forced to assist and is soon separated from the team. Alone and afraid, Conrad must use his wits to battle mutated lampreys, infected scientists and go head-to-head with the biggest monstrosity of all.

Can Conrad survive, or will the deadly monsters suck the very life from his body?

## DEEP DEVOTION
by M.C. Norris

Rising from the depths, a mind-bending monster unleashes a wave of terror across the American heartland. Kate Browning, a Kansas City EMT confronts her paralyzing fear of water when she traces the source of a deadly parasitic affliction to the Gulf of Mexico. Cooperating with a marine biologist, she travels to Florida in an effort to save the life of one very special patient, but the source of the epidemic happens to be the nest of a terrifying monster, one that last rose from the depths to annihilate the lost continent of Atlantis.

Leviathan, destroyer, devoted lifemate and parent, the abomination is not going to take the extermination of its brood well.

www.ingramcontent.com/pod-product-compliance
Lightning Source LLC
Chambersburg PA
CBHW031955170626
46807CB00006B/2501